His Last Wife

Also by Grace Octavia

Southern Scandal series
His Third Wife
His First Wife

Take Her Man
Something She Can Feel
Playing Hard to Get
Should Have Known Better
What He's Been Missing

Reckless (with Cydney Rax and Niobia Bryant)

Published by Dafina Books

His Last Wife

GRACE OCTAVIA

KENSINGTON PUBLISHING CORP.
www.kensingtonbooks.com

DAFINA BOOKS are published by

Kensington Publishing Corp.
119 West 40th Street
New York, NY 10018

All Kensington titles, imprints, and distributed lines are available at special quantity discounts for bulk purchases for sales promotion, premiums, fund-raising, and educational or institutional use.

Special book excerpts or customized printings can also be created to fit specific needs. For details, write or phone the office of the Kensington Special Sales Manager: Kensington Publishing Corp., 119 West 40th Street, New York, NY 10018. Attn. Special Sales Department. Phone: 1-800-221-2647.

Dafina and the Dafina logo Reg. U.S. Pat. & TM Off.

ISBN-13: 978-0-7582-8884-4
ISBN-10: 0-7582-8884-0
First Kensington Trade Paperback Printing: November 2014

eISBN-13: 978-0-7582-8886-8
eISBN-10: 0-7582-8886-7
First Kensington Electronic Edition: November 2014

10 9 8 7 6 5 4 3 2 1

Printed in the United States of America

To all of my old friends with whom I embark upon new adventures that spark new ideas for discovery and change: Thank you for contributing.

Part 1

Chapter 1

"Put more of that cheese on my plate." This directive murmur that edged on the possibility of a growl came from the cigarette-blackened lips of a woman in an orange jail jumpsuit, whose stereotypical back-braided cornrows and decidedly mean mug announced that not only had she been incarcerated for a very long time, but that this was likely not her first incarceration and it wouldn't be her last.

Six feet tall with a wide back and muscular arms, she was standing toward the middle of a rowdy line at a metal food-service counter in the gray-walled cafeteria at the Fulton County Jail. All around was a mess of loud, trash-talking female inmates in various stages of eating dinner and wide-eyed guards with their hands on their guns.

"I can't do that!" This uneasy response that was dipped in fear came from the Vaseline-coated lips of a woman whose orange jumpsuit was hidden beneath a white apron. However, this inmate's stylish two-strand twists that only had three inches of gray at the roots made it clear that not only had she just gotten to jail, but also that she didn't plan on staying and still wasn't clear about how life had led her to that place. Indeed, like half of the women in the jail, Kerry Ann Jackson had maintained that she was no criminal. But that didn't stop officers from putting her in handcuffs and placing her behind bars for allegedly tossing her ex-husband off the roof of a downtown Atlanta skyscraper.

"You better put more of that cheese on my plate, bitch!" The murmur coming from the black lips was definitely now a growl.

"But I already gave you the serving. One scoop. That's it," Kerry tried to rationalize, pointing to the soggy pasta shells on the growler's plate. Kerry was standing behind the service counter, holding a one-cup serving spoon over the pan of pasta shells and processed cheese that was supposed to be macaroni and cheese. The kitchen manager had given her one instruction: "One serving spoon per inmate. You fuck that up and you're back on the toilets."

"You think I'm simple, bitch? I know what the fucking serving is, but ain't no cheese on mine." She slammed the tray on the counter in a way that made the soggy noodles shake in the soupy yellow cheese sauce on her plate, and all eyes to the front and back of the line looked over at the spectacle. Guards chatting nearby craned their necks to get a look.

Kerry was ready to disappear. If the pan of artificial macaroni-and-cheese surprise were big enough, she would've jumped right in and swam to the bottom to escape. Drowned herself in the yellow paste just to avoid what could happen next. And it could be anything. Anything. She'd been in holding at the jail for three months and in that time she'd seen women spat on for less. One woman got stabbed in her right tit for chatting up one of the female guards who'd been sleeping with another inmate.

"Problem, Ms. Thompson?" a youngish white male guard

with tattoos up both arms posed, approaching the confrontation from the back of the line.

Cornrows looked at him through the corner of her eye and spat, "Nah—none at all."

The guard looked at Kerry. "You okay?" he asked rather politely. He'd been working at the jail for over five years and in that time he'd seen Thompson and her cornrows come and go and stir up trouble in the jail each time. Kerry was new to him.

"I'm fine," Kerry lied nervously.

"Move it along then, Thompson." The guard nudged Thompson in the back with his index finger.

After taking two steps, she looked back at Kerry and mouthed, "*You mine.*"

Fear shot through Kerry's veins like electricity and she would've tried to run right out of that cafeteria had it not been for a whisper in her ear from the inmate serving green beans beside her.

"Girl, don't mind Thompson. She all talk. She'll set shit off, but if you buck up at her, she'll back off," she said, dumping green beans onto another inmate's plate. She was Angelina Garcia-Bell, a Latina with a short black buzz cut and beautiful long eyelashes that looked out of place on her mannish face. She was one of the two friends Kerry had made since she'd been locked up—the other was the inmate who'd gotten stabbed in the tit. "I told you that you can't let these chicks see you all scared. Bitches feed on that shit in here."

"How am I supposed to seem like I'm not scared when I *am* scared?" Kerry whispered, watching Thompson continue to peek back at her as the guard forced her down the line. "I'll just be glad when this is all over and I can get away from these people. When I can go home. See my family—my little boy."

"Won't we all be glad when that day comes?" Garcia-Bell

agreed, scooping out another serving of green beans. "Won't we all?"

Most evenings after dinner, Kerry didn't go into the recreational common area to watch soap opera reruns on the outdated projection television with the other inmates. Instead, she'd head to the library, pick up a book, and sit at one of the tables in the back of the room where volunteers taught GED prep classes. There, she could read and think and pretend none of this was happening to her.

But Kerry didn't do that after the incident in the cafeteria with the macaroni and cheese. To avoid a confrontation with Thompson, she went straight to her cell and climbed into her bunk, vowing to stay there until the lights went out and later the sun came up. Maybe tomorrow would be different. Maybe Thompson would've forgotten their spat in the cafeteria. Maybe Kerry would wake up and be away from this place altogether. Tomorrow, she'd be sitting on the back deck of the Tudor off Cascade drinking margaritas with Marcy. Tomorrow, she'd be driving up I-85 in the old Range Rover with the windows down and the air-conditioning on. Music blasting, open road in front of her. Going to wherever she wanted. Tomorrow, she'd see Tyrian. Jamison. Home.

Kerry laid back in her bottom bunk and looked up at the picture she'd tucked into the spring beneath the top mattress. Two faces smiled down at her. A man and a boy with the same brown skin, dark eyes, and pug noses. They were standing beside a large wooden sign that read CHARLIE YATES GOLF COURSE AT EAST LAKE. The boy, who was a little taller than the man's waist, held a golf club in his hand. The man's right arm was draped around the boy. Both looked proud.

A tear left Kerry's eye and rolled back toward the pillow beneath her head. She closed her eyes tightly and tried to go back to the day she'd taken that photo. It was Tyrian's first golf demonstration, about nine months earlier. She and Jamison were already divorced by then, but that day was peaceful. Agreeable. Tyrian woke up that morning so nervous, anxious, and excited that he wouldn't stop asking his mother questions.

"What if I lose? What if it rains? What if it snows? What if I faint? What if my coach faints? What if no one comes? What if too many people come?" he listed so intensely Kerry wondered how a six-year-old could come up with so many worries. But he'd always been very smart. Advanced. Precocious. Like his father.

"And what if everything is perfect? Just perfect?" she'd said, placing his clothes on his bed. "Have you thought about that, my little worrywart? What if everything is wonderful and everyone has a great time?"

Climbing from beneath his bedsheets, Tyrian looked off to consider this like he was much older and wiser. "Okay," he said after a long pause. "It could be perfect. You're right, Mama."

Kerry winked at Tyrian, kissed his cheek, and said, "I'm always right."

And she was right. While her ex-husband was usually late to Tyrian's practices at the golf course and had gotten into the habit of using his recent victory in a tight race for mayor of Atlanta as an excuse to be absent to most of Tyrian's scheduled events, he was waiting outside the golf course, right by the sign, when Kerry and Tyrian arrived. Sitting in the backseat of his mother's truck, Tyrian squealed with the delight of a six-year-old son when he saw his father standing beside the sign.

"Daddy's here! Daddy's here already! He really came!" Tyrian cheered, tearing off his booster-seat seat belt before his mother could pull into her parking space and turn off the engine.

She was about to tell him to wait for her before he hopped out of the truck and bolted right to the person who'd become his favorite as of late—but she decided to let it slide that morning. All of the other little golfers unloading from their parents' cars had both mother and father in tow. She knew Tyrian wanted that too—for his parents to be together like everyone else's. And at that moment, he was just ecstatic that his life would look like all of the other kids' lives that day.

"My big boy!" Jamison said, gathering his son into his arms. "Man, you're getting heavy. I'm not going to be able to pick you up much longer!" Jamison laughed. The phone in his pocket was already vibrating with other things he needed to do, but he didn't reach for it. He promised himself he wouldn't. Today was about Tyrian.

"Hi." Kerry's greeting was flat and uninspired when she walked up carrying the golf bag Tyrian had left behind for her to caddy.

Jamison looked over at his first wife. "Good morning," he offered, smiling civilly.

"Good morning," she added to her greeting.

A few parents walked past with their little golfers straggling behind, waving at Tyrian. The whole time, just seconds really—but to the exes it felt much longer—Jamison and Kerry eyed each other for signs of anything new. Kerry had recently cut off her long, black permed hair and was wearing a short, natural do that Jamison thought made her look younger and thinner. Maybe she'd lost weight too. Jamison was wearing a new, expensive watch. He had the collar on his old gold fraternity golf shirt popped up to hide a hickey on his neck, but even with the carefully planned disguise and brown skin, and two feet of distance, his first wife could see it.

"Think we need to get to the clubhouse. I'm sure they're starting the demonstration on time," Kerry said drily.

"Of course. Of course," Jamison agreed and then added, "Hey, can you take a picture of Tyrian and me?" He pulled his phone from his pocket and stretched to hand it to Kerry.

"Guess so," she said, taking the phone.

"Cool!" Tyrian cheered, standing beside his dad.

The three organized the perfect photo shot in front of the club sign and just before Kerry was about to take the picture, Jamison added one of Tyrian's golf clubs from his bag.

Kerry held up the phone and took a few shots. In the background, a new spring had the grass emerald green.

Once all were satisfied that the moment had been captured, Kerry was about to hand Jamison the phone when it rang and a familiar name came up on the screen Val—Jamison's sultry assistant, who was making it pretty clear she was sleeping with her boss.

"Here," Kerry said, rushing to return the phone to Jamison.

"Wait, Mama! You get in the picture!" Tyrian posed with a big smile. He was becoming quite the diplomat. "We can take one with all of us."

Kerry and Jamison looked at each other like they were heads of nations always on the brink of war. The phone was still ringing with Val's name on the screen.

"Oh, we can't do that," Kerry said, handing the phone to Jamison. "There's no one to take the picture."

"I'll take it!" A fourth voice cut into the negotiations suddenly.

Behind Kerry was a young man in a Morehouse College golf shirt, holding what was clearly an expensive camera in his hand. An overstuffed camera bag with *Fox Five News* stitched into the top flap was hanging over his shoulder.

"It would be an honor to take a picture of our new mayor and his family," the man remarked.

"Thanks, brother," Jamison said, flashing his practiced public smile. "We'd appreciate that. Hey, what's your name? I love meeting my Morehouse brothers, you know?" he continued, reaching out to shake the young man's hand.

"I'm Dax Thomas—a reporter with Fox Five News Atlanta," he said. "Good to meet you, Mayor Taylor. You're doing us Morehouse men proud."

"At your service," Jamison said and the men chuckled at some inside joke.

Kerry reluctantly got into the picture, standing behind Tyrian's shoulder opposite Jamison.

In minutes, the image would be featured on Fox News's main Web site. The caption: *An awkward moment at East Lake Golf Course this morning, when Mayor Taylor takes a picture with his ex-wife, Atlanta socialite Kerry Ann Jackson, and six-year-old son, Tyrian.*

The bottom bunk where Kerry lay remembering her past rattled with a thud. She quickly opened her eyes, ready to react and jumped up, hitting the top of her head on the bottom of the upper bunk.

"Owww!" she let out, looking at a boot on the floor beside her bed that was no doubt the source of the rattling. Her eyes left the boot and nervously forged a path up the orange jumpsuit to the face of the kicker she was certain had come to pummel her.

"Damn! Calm down, boo! It's just me!" Garcia-Bell held out her hands innocently as she laughed at Kerry's head bump and fearful eyes. "What? You thought I was Thompson coming to kick your ass?"

Kerry rolled her eyes and looked out of the cell past Garcia-Bell. "Where is she?" She sat up, rubbing her head.

"Probably somewhere starting more shit with someone else. You in here hiding out?"

"Basically."

"Well, what was you gonna do if I was her? This ain't some dorm room. She can see your skinny ass right through them bars," Garcia-Bell said, pointing to the open cell door as she took a seat beside Kerry on the bottom bunk.

The mattress above them was bare. Kerry's first cell mate, a white woman who'd stabbed her boyfriend five times in the head, had bonded out.

"Guess I don't care," Kerry said. "If I'm going to get beat up, what does it matter if she does it in here or out there? I'm still getting beat up."

"It would be worse in here. No one around. It'll take a while for the guards to get here," Garcia-Bell explained. "Plus, Thompson got a lot of enemies. You never know if someone might want to sneak some licks in if she starts something with you on the yard."

Kerry looked off and laughed a little to herself.

"What? What's so funny?" Garcia-Bell asked.

Kerry's mind switched from inside the walls of the prison to outside, where her world was so different. A simple word like *yard* could mean so many other things; however, none of them included a tiny outside space with nothing but dry, depleted dirt and female prisoners fighting fiercely over turns to use deflated basketballs and rusting gym equipment.

"That word—*yard*—it reminds me of where I went to college," Kerry replied, not knowing if she should mention her alma mater, Spelman College, if Garcia-Bell would've heard of the historically black college or knew what the term meant there. In 1998, Kerry's time on the yard included watching her best friend Marcy step with her sorority sisters, sitting on the steps in front of Manley Hall, chatting with her Spelman sisters and professors about images of black women in the media, the future of the black woman in politics and, of course, black love. There she was a third-generation Spelman girl, was called "Black Barbie," and had dozens of Morehouse brothers from the college across the street chasing after her. There she met Jamison.

"You gonna have to let that shit go—all that shit from out-side—who you were, who you thought you were—if you gonna make it in here," Garcia-Bell cautioned. "Ain't no tea and crumpets behind these here bars. In order to survive, you gonna have to knuckle up."

"Knuckle up?"

"Fight, Kerry. You gonna have to fight. Ain't nobody ever taught you how to fight?"

"You mean, like actual fisticuffs?" Kerry said, watching a group of prisoners who always stuck together walk by her cell.

"Don't ever say that word again, but, yes, that's what I mean," Garcia-Bell confirmed, laughing.

"No—no one taught me how to fight. Who would? Who taught you?"

"*Mi madre*," Garcia-Bell said, as if it should've been obvious.

"Your mother? Please. The closest Thirjane Jackson came to teaching me to fight was how to keep the mean girls in Jack and Jill from talking about me behind my back," Kerry said.

"Jack and Jill? Like that nursery rhyme?"

"Yes. It was a social club my mother made me join when I was young," Kerry explained. "Had to be her perfect little girl in Jack and Jill."

"Well, you far from that now. And thinking about that out there ain't gonna do nothing but get you caught up in here."

"That's the thing: I don't plan on getting caught up in here. I'm not staying here." Kerry had convinced herself of this. After days and weeks and months of not seeing the sun rise and set, and missing the joy of witnessing the summer season shift to a muggy Georgia fall while enjoying a walk through Piedmont Park, she promised herself she'd be home by the holiday season. She'd be with her family. Dress Tyrian as a pirate for Halloween. Help make Thanksgiving dinner. Trim the tree for Christmas without complaining. Dreams of those simple things kept her hopeful.

"Hmm. You keep saying you're getting out by this and that time, but then I keep seeing you here in the morning."

Kerry had already told Garcia-Bell all about her case—about how when she ran up to the rooftop of the Westin to find her ex-husband that gray morning, she knew something was wrong, knew something was going to happen. There was a woman up there. The woman was the one who threw Jamison over the edge to his death. Not Kerry. Kerry still loved Jamison. In the hotel room where they'd been cuddling just hours before, they'd talked about getting remarried. Kerry would be his third wife—after he divorced his second wife, Val.

Garcia-Bell already knew the whole story. Like everyone else in Atlanta, rich and poor, young and old, black and white, criminals and noncriminals, she wanted to know how in the world the city's fourth black mayor—who'd come from nothing and promised the people everything—ended up split wide open with his heart and everything hanging out and his face crushed beyond recognition in the middle of Peachtree Street during morning rush-hour traffic. She'd even heard this very version of events from Kerry's mother when Thirjane Jackson had been interviewed by a reporter with Fox Five News. But she let Kerry retell it all a few times anyway. She felt Kerry needed to.

"Well, one day you're going to come looking for me and I'm not going to be here. I've got people in my corner rooting for me. It's going to work out. I believe that," Kerry said.

"People?" Garcia-Bell struggled not to sound cynical, but it was too hard. "By that you mean your ex-husband's widow? The one who's supposedly going to bust you out of here and help you find the killer?"

"Yes. I do," Kerry replied resolutely. "I told you, she knows I didn't do this and she has proof. It's taking her a little time, but she's helping my lawyer build my case and soon, everyone will know the truth. I'm innocent."

"Sure's taking her a long time."

"These things take time. You know that yourself."

Garcia-Bell had shared the particulars of her case with Kerry too.

"Well, there's long and then there's *looooonnnng*," Garcia-Bell pointed out.

"What's that mean?"

"Nothing." Garcia-Bell stood up, ready to leave. She didn't want to hurt her friend's feelings. Since she was a teenager, she'd been locked up for some reason or another and she knew the worst thing in the world was knowing the one person on the outside who could do anything about her case was doing absolutely nothing. She didn't want to put that on Kerry.

"Come on, spit it out," Kerry pushed.

"It's nothing. It's like I said—it's taking a long fucking time."

"But you know the situation. You know Val can't just bust me out of here," Kerry pleaded in a way that sounded like she was actually coaching herself.

Garcia-Bell pointed to the top bunk. "White girl stabbed her old man in the fucking head five times and she bonded out. Ain't got no kids. Ain't have no job. They got a fucking confession out of her. She home." She pointed to Kerry. "Ain't nobody see you throw your husband from the roof. You got a child. A career and you say you innocent. And you rich. You mean to tell me that woman and that lawyer she hired to get you out of jail can't even get you out on bond? Come on, girl. You ain't stupid. I know that."

"It's not that simple," Kerry tried.

"To me it is. You said it yourself: Y'all hated each other. Then your ex-husband threw her ass out on the street after she had a miscarriage and you and the broad got all chummy just because you gave her a couple of dollars so she could get a hotel room. Then your ex-husband ends up dead while she's still married to him and she's got all his money and is living up in his house and running the business you partially own. But you think she rushing to get you out of jail? You believe that?" Garcia-Bell paused and looked at Kerry with a friend's concern in her eyes. "Please say you don't. I mean, maybe you want to believe it because she the only card you got to play, but *wanting* to believe it and *actually* believing it—that's got to be different things."

Tears returned to Kerry's eyes. A lump in her throat obstructed any response to Garcia-Bell's damning assessment.

Garcia-Bell sighed and cursed herself inside for opening her mouth. "I'm sorry," she said, bending down to look at Kerry. "Look, don't stay in this cell. Get out until lights-out and if you need anything, you holler for me." She looked into Kerry's eyes and kissed her on the lips quickly before walking out.

Save the guards and guns and jumpsuits and poorly selected paint, visiting day at the women's jail in Fulton County might look like it was a family reunion or big birthday party. Children and grandparents were everywhere. Babies being burped over the shoulders of mothers who were strangers, husbands sneaking in kisses. Aging parents begging their daughters to do it right the next time she got out. Sons and daughters, silent but hopeful, some still young enough to think Mommy was away studying at college and led to believe this place with cinderblock walls and bars was a dormitory and not a jail. And it could look like that. It was a women's jail, so the guards kind of pushed back when the families came to visit. With too many limitations the women could become bothered and act up later unnecessarily, so the warden—whose mother had been locked up for writing bad checks when she was just seven years old— told the guards to keep a close eye, but not pry. The women were prisoners. Not their families.

The day after the incident in the cafeteria, Kerry was actually surprised when one of the guards showed up at her cell to announce that she had visitors waiting. She hadn't seen anyone in three weeks. She kept calling Val, but there was no answer. Even her lawyer seemed extra busy whenever Kerry got through. After her divorce, her best friend Marcy had been in Haiti working with Nurses Without Borders for months. While she promised to be at her Spelman sister's side as soon as her contract was up and she was stateside, the village where Marcy was assigned had few working phones and the mail system was spotty at best. And Kerry's mother? Well, Thirjane was no jailhouse regular—even with her daughter there. That's why Kerry was surprised a second time when she got to the visitation room and found Thirjane sitting in there on a bench. Tyrian was beside her, looking down at his feet. Thirjane placed her hand on his knee when she saw Kerry walking toward them with her hand over her mouth, like she was already holding back a cry.

Tyrian looked up and bolted for his mother like she was running in the other direction and he needed to catch up.

While this wasn't an uncommon scene in the visitation room, where over fifty inmates were sitting with their families, most everyone paused to get a look at the reunion. This wasn't just any seven-year-old son greeting his mother. It was the dead mayor's fatherless child wrapping his arms around the murderous ex-wife, who half of them believed was a woman scorned—and . . . well . . . *hell hath no fury* . . .

Kerry got down on her knees and let her only baby smash right into her with his arms open. He nearly knocked her over and certainly knocked the wind out of her, but she was grateful for the intensity of the greeting. She'd need to hold on to that feeling for as long as she could.

"I love you," she whispered into Tyrian's ear once she wrapped her arms around him. "I love you so much." Saying she missed him always sounded like a given when she was coming up with something to say to Tyrian, during the few times her mother had brought the boy to the jail. She decided she'd go with the one thing she wanted him to think of when he was away from her: that she loved him.

She backed up and looked him over. Saw how much he'd grown. Those front teeth were almost back in place now and he was so much taller, had long arms and legs. Kerry touched them like maybe they were fake. She thought of Jamison. How he'd feel seeing Tyrian looking like this, becoming a little man-child. The tears she'd promised she wouldn't let loose were rolling down her cheeks.

"What's wrong, Mama?" Tyrian asked like he'd done something wrong.

"Nothing, baby. You're just all grown up. Getting so big and tall," Kerry said as they walked to the bench and table where Thirjane was waiting.

"You always say that, Mama. But I ain't taller. I'm the same," Tyrian said.

"No, you're growing. You just can't tell because you see yourself all the time. It's perspective," Kerry said.

"Perspective?" he asked.

"It means point of view—like how you see something or someone is based on your point of view," Kerry replied, stopping in front of her mother.

Thirjane stayed seated in her red St. John's suit. Her quilted Chanel purse was on her lap, her hands clasped over the top. She snapped, "It's not *ain't*, Tyrian. That's not proper English. I told you to stop using that slang."

"Sorry, Nana," Tyrian mumbled, sitting down beside her.

"Hello to you too, Mama," Kerry said, bending down to kiss her mother. Through thirty-five years of trial and error, she knew better than to be upset that Thirjane didn't run toward her with open arms, saying how much she'd missed her daughter in the month since she'd been to see her. This was Thirjane Jackson. All old black money, blue-vein Atlanta. She was the kind of Southern belle who likely had a silk handkerchief with her initials stitched into it in her purse. She was the kind of Southern belle who took pride in openly revealing that she had no idea on God's green Earth where a motel, crackhouse, or jailhouse might be located. Now, here she was, visiting her only child in a jailhouse, and everybody knew it.

Kerry kissed her on the cheek and she pretended to do the same, but really only kissed the air. She'd begged her daughter not to marry that Jamison Taylor boy. He wasn't even a real Morehouse man like Kerry's father had been—not with having only gone to the school because he lucked up on a full scholarship. That wasn't good breeding. That was a handout—a hand down. Who were his people? She never forgave Kerry for marrying him and the current situation seemed like punishment for both of them for that one betrayal.

Kerry sat down and went through all of her motherly questions with Tyrian. She asked about his schoolwork and his golf game. Listened to more stories about his new teeth and new friends. The girl in his class who was so pretty none of the other boys would speak to her. But he always did. He always sat right next to her and said something nice.

Nana Thirjane was on hand to correct each of his poorly selected words—both those with bad grammar and weak diction. Kerry smiled and listened intently, but as the judging went on, she couldn't help but to remember when her mother would carry on like that whenever she tried to get a sentence out.

"Sounds like you have a crush," Kerry joked with Tyrian.

"I like her," Tyrian admitted, poking out his chest a little, "but I'm keeping my options open."

"Options?" Kerry repeated, looking over at her mother and laughing at how adult he sounded. "Boy, what do you know about options?"

"My daddy told me it's not enough for a woman to be beautiful. She has to be smarter than she is beautiful. And nice. Be really nice to me, always. Nice to everyone." Tyrian looked proud to remember his father's advice, but also sad. As could be expected, he'd taken the sudden death very hard.

Kerry reached over the table to touch Tyrian's hand. "Your daddy gave you some good advice," she said softly. "Very good."

After a while, Thirjane sent Tyrian off to play with some other children who were putting a massive puzzle together on the floor in the center of the room as the adults took time to chat.

"So how are you doing?" Thirjane asked.

"How do I look like I'm doing?"

"Well, your hair is growing out. Maybe you could perm it again. It's so nappy." Thirjane reached over the table to finger Kerry's gray roots. "Could definitely use some hair dye."

"I'm in jail and you're worried about my naps and grays?" Kerry snapped. "There's no one in here to impress, Mama. Not your sorors or their stuffy sons." She flicked her mother's hand away like she was thirteen again and being forced to wear her hair up in a bun to attend one of those Jack and Jill balls she so hated.

"That has nothing to do with anything. What did you go bringing that up for?"

"Why haven't you been here to visit me in a month?"

"I was just here three weeks ago."

"You promised you'd bring Tyrian every week. You said you'd do it."

"So you want me to bring my grandson to a jailhouse every week to see his mother?" Thirjane leaned toward Kerry and whispered through her coffee-stained dentures, "You know that boy is urinating in the bed almost every night? And that's on the nights when I can actually get him to sleep without crying his eyes out about missing you and his father. How's seeing you in jail going to help him?"

"His therapist said—" Kerry tried, but Thirjane cut her off.

"That therapist doesn't know a thing about raising a black boy!" Thirjane said so directly Kerry knew to leave the matter alone. "Got me bringing my grandbaby to a jail to see his mama. Then when he's sixteen and ends up here on his own, everybody's going to wonder why. The less he's here, the better."

"Fine. Just once a month then, Mama. Please." Kerry sounded like a teenager negotiating curfew.

Thirjane cut her eyes hard on Kerry. "I know. It's only been three weeks. And have you thought about me? About me coming here? What people are saying?"

"Yes. I have. Because this is all about *you*. Right?" Kerry pointed out sarcastically. Every time her mother visited, it went this way—it would somehow go from being all about Tyrian to all about Thirjane; Kerry was always last. And it was interesting too, because as ashamed as Thirjane claimed she was, aside from her onetime interview on the news, she was hardly involved in Kerry's case. She cried and promised to avenge her child when Kerry had gotten arrested, but as soon as the cameras turned on her and one detective suggested that maybe she'd had something to do with the murder too, Thirjane quickly disappeared. She wouldn't even talk to Kerry's lawyer. She'd hired her own and said she needed to protect herself and her "interests."

"Don't be flip with me, Kerry Ann. You're not the only one suffering here. That's all I was saying," Thirjane said. "And what's going on with your case, anyway? I thought that Memphis girl and that Jewish lawyer you two hired were getting you out on bail, at least until the trial starts, anyway."

"Under the direction of District Attorney Brown, the judge agreed that due to the nature of the crime, I'm a threat to society." Kerry waved at Tyrian, who'd held up two pieces of the puzzle he'd fit together.

"A threat? That imposter of a DA, Chuck Brown, is the real threat to this city—sleeping with any woman who'll open her legs. And to think, he's a Morehouse man." Thirjane put her nose in the air after that comment.

"Well, Chuck Brown also cited your connections and my money and Jamison's money—adding that I'm a flight risk."

"That's a sack of manure—pardon my choice of words. But I don't believe that for one minute. Seems that lawyer and Val could do something about it. Listen to me, girl: that whore means to keep you in here. Meanwhile, she's out in the world living it up like her kind never knew how. You know she moved her mama into Jamison's house? In Cascade? Driving his cars. Using his club memberships." Thirjane clutched her purse and whispered, "I saw her at the country club."

Kerry looked down.

"Hmm . . . She's living high on the hog and you're living here." Thirjane looked around at the prisoners and guards, the walls and discreetly placed bars.

"Well, if you really feel bad about it, you can always help with my case. It's not like I have a whole lot of people in my corner right now. I just know Val has my back and she was the only one who stood up when I needed her" Kerry said, looking into her mother's eyes.

"What am I supposed to do? Put my house up to bust you out of here?" Thirjane whispered angrily.

"You know I have money. It's not about that."

"I'm an old woman. I'm not cut out for this. I have Tyrian and he's already a handful. Between his grades and acting up in school, I'm just holding on here." Thirjane's voice weakened like she was about to cry.

"Right. Sure." Kerry was getting tired and she refused to placate her mother.

The buzzer sounded over the loudspeaker in the room, letting the inmates and visitors know visiting time was over.

As the guards started walking through the room to facilitate the proper good-bye procedures, Thirjane reached out and held Kerry's hand.

"I'm really sorry about this," she said with her wrinkled, diamond ring–clad fingers shaking a little under early symptoms of palsy. "More sorry than you'll ever know."

Tyrian appeared and hugged his mother with his arms around

her neck. He was already crying. He knew what the buzzer meant.

"I want to stay here with you," Tyrian mumbled in his mother's ear. "I promise I won't pee in the bed."

Kerry kissed him on the cheek. "It's not about that, baby. You just can't stay here. That's not how it works."

"But you didn't kill my daddy. You shouldn't have to stay here," Tyrian said a little louder.

"What?" Kerry backed up and looked at him hard. "Where did you hear that?" She looked at her mother, who shrugged.

"In school. Matthew Warrenstein said you did it—said you killed my father, but I know it's not true, Mama. I know you didn't do that."

"No. I didn't." Kerry's hand was wet from wiping away both her and Tyrian's tears. "And you don't believe that. You don't listen to those boys at that school. You understand?"

"Yes."

The room was clearing out and a guard walked past to give Kerry a sharp stare before she came back to inform her that it was absolutely time for her guests to depart.

"I'll see you next time." Kerry tried to loosen Tyrian's arms from around her neck, but he wouldn't let go.

"No! Mama! No!"

"Don't do this," she said, feeling his heartbeat quickening against hers. "Please."

"No!"

Thirjane stood and put her purse over her shoulder before reaching for Tyrian. Once she touched him, the boy started hollering and tightening his hold around his mother's neck.

"No, Mama! No! Don't make me go! I can stay. I'll be good. I won't pee in the bed!"

His tears were coming too quickly for Kerry to wipe them,

so she started the heartbreaking task of peeling her son's powerless, pencil-thin arms from around her neck.

"No, Mama! Don't!"

She closed her eyes to escape the scene.

The boy's hollering turned to something like funeral wailing. It went deep down to his gut and sprang out with so much register the guards knew there was no way his grandmother would be able to get him out of that room by herself.

"No! No! No!" Kerry cried when two guards stepped in to pull Tyrian away. "Please don't. Please!"

"Mama! No!" Tyrian hollered furiously with the guards, who were nice enough, calling him "son" and such, physically lifting him off of the ground and carrying him away from his mother, kicking and screaming.

Kerry left the catastrophic farewell a wreck. She was crying so hard, the other inmates just moved out of her way as she headed back to her cell. They'd heard Tyrian's screams. It was a mother's pain too many of them knew. They made a little pathway for Kerry to walk along, undisturbed. Some showed support by patting her shoulder knowingly as she passed. Others called out, "It'll be okay" and "Be strong." It was one of those moments when being a woman or being a mother superseded all other circumstances and surroundings for these inmates in a jailhouse.

But Kerry couldn't really see or hear or feel any of this. Though she was moving along, every part of her being was with her child, hurting and aching, mourning the reality of separation. The only thing that kept her putting one foot in front of the other to get to her cell was knowing his little face was waiting there in the picture above her bed. She could lie down there. Let her pain fall back into the mattress. Close her eyes and be with him again that morning in his bedroom before they took the picture. She would tell him everything was going to be okay. It would be perfect. He would say, "It could be perfect. You're right, Mama." She'd wink at him and kiss his cheek.

But all of that would have to wait. Because only a few steps from the cell, someone blocked Kerry's pathway.

"What? You thought I forgot about your ass-whipping?"

Thompson was standing there, cracking the knuckles on her fat fingers.

"I'm not in the mood for this," Kerry said, sounding more tired than fearful. "I just saw my little boy and—"

Thompson cut her off. "I don't give a fuck about that."

"Thompson, I just said I'm not in the mood for this," Kerry said solemnly. "I can't deal with you and whatever pathology you're demonstrating right now. I just want to—"

"Path—what? What you call me?" Thompson poked Kerry's shoulder enough to push her back a few steps.

Some of the women gathering in a tight fight circle started telling Thompson to back off and leave Kerry alone, but all still stayed to see what would happen.

"I didn't call you anything," Kerry said. "I'm just letting you know I'm not trying to fight you. I'm upset about my son—"

"Fuck your son!" Thompson spat, stepping in so closely to Kerry's face a spray of saliva dotted the bridge of Kerry's nose.

"What did you say?" Kerry asked, feeling some switch of anger flicked on within the mix of sadness, loneliness, and now humiliation. "What did you say about my son?" Kerry didn't know it, but she was stepping up higher, up on her toes a little bit, so she could be eye to eye with Thompson. She was also balling up her fists and tightening her jaw.

"I said: fuck your—"

This time Kerry cut Thompson off—but not with words, with a tight fist to the mouth. Kerry flung her closed hand up high and came down on Thompson's mouth so hard it sounded like a bag of sand hitting the earth.

Every mouth in the spectators' circle was hanging wide open with surprise. Even Thompson seemed unprepared for the blow to her face.

"What the fuck?" she shouted loud enough to get some of the guards' attention. "You hit me!"

Before Thompson could cock her fist back to get a lick in, some rush of blood to Kerry's already heavy heart pushed her into a hysterical rage.

She just attacked.

Started clawing at Thompson's face with her arms flying in an uncontrollable pinwheel that made everyone around her back up and left Thompson taking hits and trying to figure out where and when she could get some in.

Kerry pounded and pounded as tears shook loose from her eyes. She was crying like she was the one being beat on.

With all of the fists landing on her, Thompson found herself backing up to a wall. And Kerry followed. Swinging and kicking. Cursing, even. "Fuck my son? Fuck my son? No! Fuck you! Fuck you!"

Thompson cowered into something that looked like a ball or a porcupine trying to hide herself away. But Kerry kept coming for her.

By the time security pushed through the circle (and it was only just minutes into the battle), they had to pull Kerry off Thompson the same way they'd peeled Tyrian from Kerry less than an hour ago.

Even when they got her loose and Thompson jumped up from her cocoon like she was ready to do something, Kerry looked like she'd been possessed, with her extremities flailing and obscenities of every language she could remember coming from her mouth—Latin in junior high, Spanish in high school, French in college—she cursed Thompson out in every language.

As guards dragged her away, the other inmates looked at Thompson with serious scrutiny.

"Guess you showed her," someone shouted from the back of the crowd and they all laughed.

"Bougie bitch beat your ass!" someone else added, giggling.

"She snuck me!" Thompson defended herself. "Y'all saw that! The fight wasn't fair!"

As the other guards started yelling for the inmates to clear the floor, some replied, "Bet you won't be looking for a rematch!"

She wouldn't.

Chapter 2

*W*idow.

Val was sitting on the edge of her brand-new queen-sized bed, naked. Fresh out of the shower, her skin was still supple from the steam of the hot water she'd stood under just long enough to get the smell of some sweet French cologne she'd encountered on her companion the night before off her neck and nipples. She dabbed a bit of lemongrass-scented shea butter out of the glass tub resting beside her on the tousled silk bedsheets beneath her and rubbed the golden moisturizer into her knees.

The shower water was still running. Along with clouds of steam, the sounds of joyous, comfortable singing slipped underneath the closed bathroom door and into the bedroom with her.

Val slid her left foot onto the bed and massaged the shea butter into her ankle. Between eye rolls at the steam and caroling coming from the lingering visitor in the bathroom, she caught glimpses of herself on the behemoth of a flat screen mounted before the bed.

It wasn't her reflection cast on the high-definition television. It was actually a recording of an interview she'd done with

CNN two weeks prior. On the screen, she was sitting on a couch in a respectable black-and-white tweed Carolina Herrera sheath dress, smiling at the reporter and answering questions her publicist had received and reviewed with her a week before the interview. Beneath her name was a word that kept catching her eye: *widow.*

Val hated everything that word meant to the world: Someone who'd lost something. Someone broken. Helpless. Hopeless. Cut in half. She was none of those things—felt none of those things. Yes, her husband was dead and in the ground, but any loss she could've known—any brokenness, helplessness, hopelessness, dissection—occurred before she'd gotten the call that Mayor Jamison Taylor had been tossed from the top of the downtown Westin. In fact, in life, he'd been the one who'd made her feel those ways. So much so that she was actually surprised when she'd gotten the call to come to the morgue. They needed her to claim the body. To make arrangements. To make decisions. She was his wife. Wasn't she? *Was she?*

Val rolled her eyes at the steam and singing coming from the bathroom and again looked back up at the screen.

"So, you were estranged from your husband when his first wife murdered him?" the reporter asked.

As instructed in numerous media trainings, Val nodded as the reporter posed his question, she smiled, sat up straight, kept her freshly manicured hands clasped over her right knee. She paused for a second before answering the question. Her response should appear new, natural, honest, direct.

"Actually, AJ, I wouldn't use those words," she said to the reporter. "Yes, Jamison and I had problems. The miscarriage, which was very public—it was hard on both of us, but I believe that if Jamison was alive, we would've been together again. We would've found our way back to one another," Val lied softly. "And let me also make it clear to your viewers"—she turned from the reporter and looked directly into the camera "—there is no evidence that Kerry Jackson murdered Jamison Taylor."

"Actually, there's lots of evidence." The reporter looked down at his notes and counted off on his hand: "The couple who heard Jamison and Kerry arguing in the hotel room downstairs. The worker at the Sundial Restaurant on top of the Westin, who said he saw Kerry Jackson on the roof just before the mayor was tossed over. And then there's Ms. Jackson herself. She was actually there—standing on the roof when police got there. I believe they call that 'caught red-handed.' " He chuckled inappropriately.

"None of that's conclusive evidence," Val replied with a clause from her note cards.

"Well, then there's motive," the reporter added. "Jackson had motive to kill Taylor."

"What motive?"

"You." He looked at Val like a mouse caught in the corner of a snake's cage. None of this banter had been included on her prep sheet before the interview. They were off the script. This was where things should get interesting. He looked down at his notes again. "Isn't it true that Kerry Ann Jackson went into a jealous rage after she found out that he'd married you?"

Val took the words hard, like a fist to the face, but it was nothing she hadn't suffered through before. She used another line from one of those note cards to avoid encouraging the reporter with his interrogation: "I am not here to discuss my dead husband's private life." Still, her voice was nervous. Shaken.

"But it is that private life that led to Jackson hating Taylor. Wouldn't you say? He cheated when they were married. Slept around after the divorce—and we have proof of his attendance at numerous swingers' parties and fraternity clubhouse romps.

And then he moved on to his secretary, a former stripper, whom he impregnated and married. That's you—isn't it?"

The camera zoomed in on Val's fake smile. Not one muscle in her face moved under the condemnation of the reporter's words and tone.

"I have a quote here," he went on, reading from his own note card. "When a reporter asked Jackson how she felt about her ex-husband marrying you, she said, and I quote, 'I've moved on. I had to. If I hadn't, I'd be insulted right now.' " He looked at Val again. "What do you have to say about that?"

"About what?"

"She called you an 'insult.' Surely you have thoughts on that."

"No. I don't. No comment." Val grinned and looked down at fingernails, clearly done with the conversation.

"Okay. Well, I'll conclude with what everyone wants to know. What all of America wants to know: Why do you care? Why are you involved in this case at all? Trying to get Kerry Jackson out of jail for murdering a man in cold blood—a man you were married to. A man you loved. After everything she said about you. After what she did to your husband. Why are you in this fight?"

"Because she's innocent," Val said. "She didn't do this."

"Well, all right. I guess that's all we'll get right now. Thank you for stopping by."

The reporter sat and stared at Val as the cameras stopped rolling.

Looking at the television from her bed, Val could see herself looking like a mouse in the reporter's eyes and hated herself for it.

The bathroom door flung open and a masculine brown body came dancing out behind a dramatic dissipating cloud of steam.

"*Girl you know it's true-ue-ue-ue, I love you!*" he sang into an invisible microphone in his hand. "*Girl you know it's true-ue-ue-ue, I love you-u-u-u.*"

Val watched, rolling her eyes as he pretended to throw the microphone to the floor and broke into a high impact running-man dance routine that sent the only bit of fabric covering his manhood—a cream towel—to the floor. This man was big and brown and had muscles everywhere. He either was an athlete at the moment or had been in the past. He had a name. Val didn't know it.

Val sighed, but neither her clear displeasure nor his exposed, flopping genitals stopped her male companion's entertainment. He kept jerking about all around the bedroom with his flaccid penis slapping against his legs and then hitting his stomach as he went along singing and dancing.

Just when Val was about to tell him to stop, he sang the chorus again: "*Girl you know it's true-ue-ue-ue, I love you!*" then raised his hands over his head and took a bow.

"Thank you, ladies and gentleman! I'm Ernest Hinds. I'm here every weekend! Come back and see me!" he said to his audience of one, who was not clapping or smiling.

"It's time for you to leave," Val snapped, standing and snatching the towel from the floor. "I put your clothes and shit beside the door." She nodded toward the pile of wrinkled male clothing beside the bedroom door, before trying to head to the bathroom to put the towel into the dirty-clothes bin, but her guest interrupted her path.

"Leave? Why do you want me to leave?" He tried to reach for Val, but she pushed him away and went into the bathroom. "I thought we'd go get some breakfast. You know? Maybe talk."

There was wicked laughter coming from the bathroom.

When Val returned in her robe, she looked at the naked dancer. Those athletic muscles really were everywhere, but Val wasn't fazed. "Talk about what? Are you kidding?" She giggled.

"No. Why would I be kidding?"

"Because there's nothing for us to talk about—not unless you're referring to directions to the interstate." Val headed to the pile of clothes.

"Damn, you're cold. Ice cold."

"You have no idea," she said, tossing pieces of the clothing at her visitor one at a time.

The man caught his jeans and tossed them over his shoulder before sitting on the bed to put on his socks.

"I thought I did have an idea, but I guess I had the wrong idea," he said dejectedly.

"Look . . . um . . . Ernest," Val said vaguely. "I think we both had the same idea last night. And you were good—great—but now the sun is up and it's time to go home. Right?" She smiled pleasantly but with an air of annoyance.

"Right." He shook his head, bewildered, and continued to put on his clothing as Val watched and waited. "Guess you're not a huge Milli Vanilli fan," he joked to cut the ice from Val's stare. "Most chicks really dig that dance routine too—especially when the towel falls off." He stood to button his pants and looked into Val's eyes. This was actually his second time sleeping with her. When he'd approached her at the bar last night, he hadn't brought up the first time. He knew she'd hardly remember. Really, it was odd that he did. It had been more than ten years ago, when a summer night out in Atlanta meant flashing lights, white lines, stripper poles, and random sex. Back then, Val was just a club girl. A pretty face with a tight body in a crowd of so many others. He was still playing for the Falcons football team. Nothing big—just a benchwarmer. But he had a penthouse and a little red sports car. His cousin was in town visiting from North Carolina and Ernest figured he'd show him around. They went to Club Vision, a mega–hot spot on Peachtree, and met two girls in short spandex dresses and tall neon heels at the chic white bar in VIP. Between drinks, his cousin purposely let it slip that Ernest played for the NFL and the girls responded accordingly. With no prodding, they followed Ernest's little red sports car back to the penthouse, jumped out of their clothes and into the rooftop hot tub, where Ernest had sex with one of the girls as his cousin kissed and fondled the other. Still, Ernest could feel the other girl's eyes on him the entire time. Feeling weak and dizzy from the mixture of alcohol, cocaine, hot water, and sex, Ernest got out of the tub and went inside to cool off in the shower. While he'd left the hot tub party alone, after being in the shower for a few minutes, Ernest felt slender arms around his waist and soft lips kissing his spine. He assumed it was the girl he'd had sex with in the hot tub. "I'm good right now. I'll catch you for round two in a minute," he'd said flatly. He wasn't really into the girl. She was cute but Ernest had always been pretty introspective, even about sleeping with groupies, and had decided that he'd only had sex with the girl in the hot tub to impress his cousin. "Round two?" he heard. He turned around and there was the other girl, the one who'd been watching him. "I'm waiting for round one." Ernest laughed and looked out of the shower for his girl. "Are you crazy?" he asked. "What's your friend going to say?" The girl rolled her eyes. "I ain't worried about her. She knows how I roll—whatever Val wants, Val gets." Then Ernest asked, "And who's Val?" She responded in a way he'd never forget. She dropped to her knees and looked up at him ambitiously and sort of emptily. "I'm Val," she said. "You'll remember me."

Ten years later, standing in Val's bedroom, Ernest thought of how interesting it was that Val had been right back then. He didn't forget her. But she'd forgotten him.

Val was about to respond to the comment about Milli Vanilli when the bedroom door suddenly opened.

"Sorry, I thought you were in the shower," Lorna, the maid, said to Val. She was holding a fresh set of silk sheets in her hands. "I didn't know you still had company." She looked past Val and the nearly naked chocolate Ernest to the clock on the wall. This was routine.

"Actually, he was just leaving," Val said, walking toward the bathroom. "Why don't you show him out—the back way." She stopped and looked over her shoulder in a way that let on that maybe she had remembered Ernest and that maybe this was just payback for the way things had ended after the scene in the shower. Ernest's ego had led him back to the hot tub to have sex with the other girl again.

Lorna led Ernest out of the house and to his car in silence before returning to the master bedroom once again to change the sheets.

"Cutting it close now, huh?" she said to Val, who'd changed into the black-and-white tweed suit.

"What?" Val looked at Lorna with her normal disdain.

"You usually have them out of here before sunrise. Before she gets up," Lorna replied, referring to Val's mother, a new resident in the guest room down the hall.

"I couldn't care less what she thinks about what I do," Val said. "Not you, not her, not the people in this fucking neighborhood. No one." She looked at the bed where Lorna was changing the red sheets. "I stopped caring about shit like that a long time ago."

When Val had decided to move into the house three months ago—a week after Jamison's funeral—she insisted on removing two things: the mattress in the master bedroom and any pictures of Jamison's mother anywhere in the house.

The mattress had to go because that was where her baby

died inside of her. The pictures of Mrs. Dorothy Taylor had to go because that was who had caused it all.

"Fine," Lorna said, replacing a pillowcase. "No law saying you have to care about what people think. I just thought you wouldn't want your mother knowing what all goes on in here, every night." Lorna's tone was meant to reveal a mere observation, but there was clear judgment involved.

Val ignored it. Lorna had been Jamison's maid. The two women hardly liked each other even then. "Is Mama Fee awake?" she asked.

"Out in the garden by now, I'd guess," Lorna replied. "Don't worry—she didn't see your visitor. I made sure of it. Even if you don't care."

Val slid on her shoes and went to stand at the east-facing window in the bedroom, where her mother's herb garden had just been installed behind a row of overgrown, flowering bushes that bloomed blood-red the day Mama Fee had arrived in Georgia to help her daughter bury the dead.

Val locked eyes on her mother's bare knees in the cool, fall dirt. Everything she'd planted was just sprouting out now and Val knew Mama Fee was out there, singing to the baby leaves that would never make it into a pot of anything they'd eat. These weren't those kinds of herbs. These herbs would be plucked and stashed in cloudy glass jars in Mama Fee's room. They'd come out again, bunched together in ribbon and rope to be burned or drenched in oil with instructions to be tucked behind something or buried beneath it, hung over it. Possibly for tea.

"You're gonna have everybody calling you a witch if they see you out here singing," Val said to her mother's back once she'd made it outside to the garden.

"Maybe I am a witch," Mama Fee said soberly into the dirt.

She turned and squinted up at Val, looking all aglow between the sun and the bloody bushes. "And maybe you're a witch too."

"Maybe," Val confirmed flatly. "Perhaps if you can change that *w* to a *b*, then you probably have me."

Mama Fee didn't laugh at the joke with Val. It was too true to be funny. This was her third and last baby girl. The one who thought she never needed her mother, but who always did. Seemed Val had been hell-bent on being a bitch since she came kicking out of the womb. She wanted everything on her own terms and obviously thought that being a bitch was the best way to go about it.

Mama Fee snatched off the face of a new, blooming lavender Morning Glory and held it up to her daughter. "Put this in your pocket."

Val sighed and waved off the gesture. She knew Mama Fee had already started drying the roots of that flower and had been grinding it into a fine powder and stashing it in corners all around the house.

"I won't be needing John the Conqueror's luck where I'm going," Val said, sliding on her Chanel frames.

"It ain't just for luck, girl. It's for protection too."

"I won't be needing that, neither." Val turned to head to the front of the house, where the car Jamison had bought her was waiting in the circular drive. A too-thin stray cat nearly knocked her over trying to get to Mama Fee's side. Val hissed and kicked at the cat. She knew Mama Fee had been feeding the thing but Val refused to let it into the house. "And get out of the dirt. You're not in Tennessee anymore, Mama Fee. We have people who can tend to our gardens here."

It might have been wise for Val to have accepted that blooming head from her mother in the garden. While she was correct that they were far from the voodoo conjuring women and their tricks practiced at St. Peter's Spiritual Temple in Memphis, protection and a little luck were certainly needed to navigate the new political landscape in Atlanta, where politics as usual now meant scandal, murder, and a quick cover-up.

Driving into Atlanta that morning after refusing the aid of John the Conqueror's bloom, Val was preparing to cover up a murdered politician's scandal. Ironically, she'd once been in the same shoes as the woman who was waiting for her in a back booth at the Buckhead Diner. But that was when she was trying to get everything she had. Now she just wanted to protect it.

"So, you're Coreen," she said, sliding into a booth across from a petite, light-skinned woman with a fiery red bob that swooped over her right eye.

Coreen hardly smiled as a response.

Neither woman held out her hand for salutations. They'd slept with the same man years apart, but still there was envy simmering between them. One had the baby. The other had the ring. Neither had the man.

"Do you have my money?" Coreen asked tightly.

"Well, let's order some drinks, a little food, before we get down to business," Val said, beckoning the waiter over to the table with a dubious smile Coreen could easily read.

Coreen had seen so many pictures of Val on the Internet. At first, she was standing beside Jamison at the podium after he'd won the election. Val was smiling in her red business suit with the high split, trying hard to look like she was just there supporting her boss, but Coreen could tell there was something there. Something Jamison had to see in her. Her complexion was a milky tawny, just a few shades darker than Coreen's, and she had a hard body wired into the perfect figure of an *S*. She looked like the kind of woman a man would brag about sleeping with. The kind a man couldn't resist. Her assumptions proved correct just months later, when she learned on a gossip Web site that Jamison had married his assistant and was expecting a child. His second child. But Coreen knew better right then. It would be his third.

Coreen sat silent, eyeing Val's real diamond earrings and Oyster Collection Rolex watch as she ordered a cotton-candy martini and fruit salad. It wasn't even noon yet.

"So . . ." Val batted her eyes at Coreen, like she was a man who'd asked her out on a date, and grinned. "Remind me of why we're here. You know, my schedule is so crazy these days."

"Please stop. You know exactly why we're here and what I want," Coreen snapped. "I'm here for my money. The ten thousand dollars Jamison would owe me for this month, the fifty K for the last few months, plus the two he missed before he died. You said you'd have my money."

"No. I said I'd look into having your money," Val snapped back, correcting Coreen as the waiter dropped off the drink and fruit tray. "Besides, I can't possibly have money ready for a child my dead husband never claimed. How do I know how much he was giving you? What you all agreed on?"

Actually, Val was lying. Before he'd died, Jamison told Val all about Coreen and the little boy. Well, she figured it out the old-fashioned way—snooping—and then he'd told her. Jamison admitted that he'd produced a little boy with the mistress he'd run off to California to be with after Kerry found out about their affair. After he'd left Coreen high and dry on the West Coast when Kerry decided to take him back, Coreen kept the child a secret, planned to raise the boy on her own. But then Jamison's name ended up in the news and . . . well . . . Coreen couldn't resist coming for what she felt was rightfully hers—or her son's. A part of Jamison's growing fortune.

"Jamison loved his son," Coreen said. "He wasn't the best father, but he knew Jamison Jr. was his. He accepted him." Coreen's voice faded thin as her statement was clearly meant for her own ears and Val had long blocked her out. But Coreen really needed to hear herself say that to someone other than herself. She hadn't expected her relationship with Jamison to produce anything. She learned early on after his mother introduced them that Jamison had a pregnant wife at home. She tried to push away from him, to move on, but when he'd come into her life she was splintered wide open from an old thorn in her heart. Her husband had died. She wanted a new start, a new love, and while she knew inside Jamison couldn't be it, one answered e-mail led to another answered e-mail, and then so went the story. His hands were big enough to hold her. His words were healing. His promises were just endless. And then he left. And then she realized she was pregnant.

"What was he like with him?" Val let out after her third sip of cotton candy–flavored vodka. She was still trying to sound detached and tough, but she had her own needs lingering in her voice.

"Patient. Funny." Coreen looked away distantly and spoke with detachment. "They were always in their own little world when Jamison came to L.A. to see him. He'd just take Jamison Jr. and they'd go into their space."

Val felt a little flutter in her stomach and pushed the fruit tray away from her. She took another sip of the martini, though.

"Look, if you're not going to give me the money—if you're not going to give *us* the money—I'll just move forward with my original plan. Just like I told Jamison before he—" Coreen stopped. "I know every news station in this country will be happy to hear—"

"No, no, no," Val said with her full attention on Coreen then.

This was Coreen's ongoing threat: How she'd gotten money from Jamison and now was working on Val—taking her story of a love child to the media. As dated as this kind of dirt was, it was the sort of information that could start a domino effect that could dismantle the carefully built house of cards Jamison had tendered to the public, his friends, and business associates. All of whom supported Rake it Up, the corporate landscaping and preservation service Jamison opened in lieu of going to medical school after college. Since then, the company had amassed a list of loyal corporate clients whose businesses dotted the entire southeast. Corporate clients who still maintained old-world values that could mean they would have to disconnect from an evildoer. Though a love child produced in an affair wasn't nearly a new concept, it was mucky. And in the South, mucky was supposed to stay behind closed doors. Moreover, all those contacts and connections that had made Jamison a rich man wouldn't think twice about taking their business elsewhere if they had any reason to disconnect from him. And he was black. And he was dead. Or, as Val's lawyer had put it, "First, the big clients would leave, then the small, then the money would dry up, and then you'll be broke." Val had to stop this.

"I need some time to get you the money," Val said abruptly. "I don't have it right now, but I can get it. I just need time."

Coreen sat back and observed Val suspiciously.

"You're lying," Coreen stated.

"No. I'm not. I don't even know how Jamison was getting you that much cash."

"He owns a multimillion-dollar company. Don't play me. I know exactly how much he has, how much Rake it Up made last year alone," Coreen said.

"Kerry took fifty percent of the business after the divorce and then Jamison sold her another ten percent when he ran for mayor."

"That means when Jamison died he still had forty percent of that company and my son will get his share," Coreen asserted wickedly. "You think I don't know what you're doing—what both of you think you're going to do?"

"Who?"

"You and Kerry—you think you can get rid of me. Cut me out of the money. But I'm not going anywhere." Coreen rolled her eyes and looked at the waiter who was standing nearby and clearly struggling to listen in on the gossip. "I don't know what I was thinking—meeting you. Like you would really be looking out for me. Like you'd understand." After uttering that last sentiment, Coreen gave Val a long, hard stare and then picked up her purse. "Jamison was right about you." Coreen got out of the booth and leered down at Val. "You're a fucking mess."

Val had to grab the ends of the table in front of her chest to stop herself from going after Coreen. To let her walk away without causing an incident that would shut down all of the Buckhead Diner and end up all over the Internet, like all of the other public battles she'd endured since becoming the lady on Jamison's arm. Back then, she was a different person. A country girl with a quick temper and a mean left hook. Back home in Tennessee, Val wasn't ever afraid of a tough fight; in fact, most times she was the cause of it. It just always seemed like someone or something was trying to steal something away from her.

Val gulped down the last of the cotton-candy martini and reminded herself that she wasn't that person anymore. Everything she'd been. Everything that had happened. She'd come out on top. Maybe Jamison never loved her. He'd just married her because she was pregnant and would add an ugly blemish to his political portfolio. But he was dead now and she was left with the best part of him. All that money. And she was willing to do anything to keep it. Even if it meant shutting her mouth. *Sometimes.*

"You know, I don't give a shit what Jamison said about me!"

Val had run out of the booth and surprised Coreen in the parking lot from behind by pulling her arm and spinning the red head around.

"He wants to call me a fucking mess? No, he's the fucking mess. He's the one who was fucking his assistant with no condom and had a child in another state and wasn't even man enough to claim him publicly. He was the fucking mess! Not me! Not me!" Val was pointing a sharp finger at herself and tears were coming from her eyes. "After everything I gave that nigga? Everything? And when my baby—our baby—died in a goddamn toilet, he couldn't wait to leave me in a hospital-room bed. That's fucked up. That's a fucking mess."

"Val, if he did all those things to you, then why are you protecting him? Why are you still out here protecting him?"

"Money. Isn't that why you're here? You keep talking about me, but what about you?" Val asked suspiciously.

"I already said why I'm here."

"A little more to the story, isn't there?" Val said accusingly. "I know about that phone call the morning Jamison died. He was going up to that roof to meet you." Val stepped in close to Coreen and crossed her arms over her chest.

"Look, I'm telling you, just like I told the police Kerry sent looking for me: I had nothing to do with Jamison's death. I was not on the phone with him that morning," Coreen said very confidently.

"That's really interesting, because Kerry was there with him in the hotel room and she's sure it was you on the phone."

"Kerry is in jail for a murder she committed and she'll say anything to try to peg this on someone else," Coreen said. "She's desperate and she hates me. But just like I told her long before you were even a thought, *her* husband slept with *me*. He wasn't my problem; he was hers. When my son was born, I just wanted my money. How was killing him going to get me any more? I loved Jamison, but I didn't hate him enough to kill him. And you want to know who loved him, but hated him enough to kill him because of those times he lied to her and cheated on her and made her look like a fool? Kerry. She's looking for the killer? Tell her to look in the mirror. I heard about Jamison's death just like everyone else—on television."

Chapter 3

"Leaf—I mean, Detective Johns—this is Val Long calling again. I called you last week. I'm calling this week. I know we haven't seen each other since . . . everything happened . . . but I wanted to talk to you. I just . . . you know a lot of things just don't add up. And you were there. You know. Some of these things they're saying . . . that are happening . . . they just don't add up. I don't know. Give me a call. You know my number."

Certain things were supposed to make other things okay. For children, an ice cream cone can make a recent slip and fall a painless memory. For a teenager, a new love erases the once-shattering tumult of the last lost love. And adults—well, by then it's a "pick your pleasure" game: Alcohol. Sex. Money. Drugs. God. Guns. Grown folks have a treasure chest of little psychological titillations designed to help the human move on, let go, forgive and forget. And there's only one rule involved in the deal of replacement: One must never look back.

Basically, that's how Detective Leaf Johns was supposed to feel two weeks after his last undercover assignment with the Georgia Bureau of Investigation ended with an unearned, unsolicited and—to his knowledge, unwarranted—monumental raise and epic promotion up the ranks at the GBI.

Leaf had been sitting at the bare desk he hadn't sat at in a month at the Bureau, thinking through his last year on assignment. He'd been handpicked by the chief to infiltrate the new mayor's staff. His pale, alabaster skin, those emerald eyes, the strawberry-blond hair atop a svelte male frame, made him look like a brainy overachiever, a political wannabe who'd sacrifice all as Mayor Jamison Taylor's new assistant. The governor, who'd been under suspicion of corruption for years, had strategically placed some of his key players on Taylor's sponsor list. That meant his dirty politics would turn into the mayor's politics and the Bureau's director wanted to take them both down. The only problem was that Leaf had been there alongside Taylor, working most days elbow-to-elbow, and though he'd been suspicious at times, he never found a thing that could spell out corruption for Taylor. In fact, following a fraternity house melee that sent Governor Cade and all of his cronies to jail, Jamison appeared to be the lone political survivor. But then, the very next morning, Jamison was dead. The police pegged his ex-wife for the murder, but for Leaf that was too fast, too cut-and-dry. Too clean of a solution in such a dirty equation. And the one thing that Leaf couldn't get off his mind even after he left that barren desk and was elevated to a swanky corner office in the newly minted international-residents division of the Georgia Crime Information Center, was that every single person Jamison had helped Leaf put away just hours before he died was now free, out on the street, and back in business. Even Cade managed to run for office again. He lost, but was getting ready for a national run for office. Word was that he'd probably win.

Still, none of that could be any of Leaf's concern. Conveniently enough, his ascension took him far away from politics. He'd been removed from investigations altogether and placed in an administrative executive role in IRGCIC. Nothing in his past was any of his business anymore. This new thing, this new work, which required far less time and stress, but also paid far more money, was supposed to make that old thing, that old work, okay . . . and he tried so hard to follow suit, but the one thing inside of him that made him a great detective just wouldn't let it go. And then there were those calls, the many calls from Val.

When Leaf listened to that last message Val left on his voice mail at work, he did something he hadn't done to the other messages: He didn't delete it. He didn't save it, either. He just hung up the phone and pushed away from his new mahogany desk in the swanky office. He stood and surveyed all of Atlanta outside his window. It was just before noon and from his floor-to-ceiling window that gold dome that marked Atlanta's City Hall in the city's ever-changing skyline looked like it was just six inches away from him. He remembered how Jamison would look when he'd walk into his office each morning. His new eyes. Both nervous and excited at the same time. Leaf spent weeks trying to understand if this was an act. If it was real, there could be no way Jamison would ever make it in politics. If it was fake, he'd climb all the way to the top.

"Dude, don't cry. She'll come back someday!"

Leaf turned away from the window to find one of his old teammates from Investigations standing behind him in his office, grinning.

"Delgado!"

" 'Sup, sentimental motherfucker!"

Delgado walked over to the window and the two gave each other an informal hug that noted the years they'd known each other and worked out in the field together.

"Glad the glass is here. You look like you would've jumped," Delgado added. He was just as skinny and young-looking as Leaf, but he was actually in his mid-thirties and had a wife and two children at home.

"Never that. If I killed myself, I wouldn't be able to see your wife again. That would be terrible," Leaf joked and they both laughed. "No, really, I'm just in here thinking about old stuff. Wondering if I made all the right decisions. You know? Agent shit."

"Of course I do, brother. I've been out here just as long as you, but you know the rule: You have to let that shit go. Whatever it is, you have to let it go."

"That's what they tell us. Right?"

"And for good reason. I've been out there with you. I know. If we held on to all of the shit we've seen—half of the shit we've done, we'd never be any good to anyone. We have our orders. We follow them," Delgado said mechanically. "When that case is closed, there's nothing else to do or say."

Leaf nodded along and bit at his upper lip. After a pause, he asked, "And who says when the case is closed?"

"The motherfucker who cuts your check," Delgado replied, tapping Leaf on the chest. He laughed. "Listen, don't get caught up. Whatever it is, saying something—doing something, that isn't going to make a difference." He lowered his voice to a near whisper. "I've seen some of the best guys go down thinking otherwise. And not all of them left the Bureau on their feet." He looked Leaf in the eye soberly and stepped back from him before completely changing his demeanor to something more decidedly chipper. "So, what's up? I stopped by to see if you wanted to head over to lunch at Daddy O's with me to get some ribs."

"Ribs? What are you doing eating ribs? What's up with your high blood pressure?"

"Got it down, now I'm trying to get it back up," Delgado joked. "Seriously, though, don't worry about me. I'll get the rib salad. That's collard greens and ribs."

"God, I don't miss you lame joke-telling motherfuckers in Investigations," Leaf said.

"Well, we miss you—king of the lame jokes," Delgado snickered. "So, what's up? You down for some Daddy O's? Or are you going to stand in here and weep for the rest of the afternoon?"

His hands in his pockets, Leaf grinned at his old comrade and bounced his eyes from Delgado back to the skyline. "Yes. Daddy O's is probably a good idea." He turned away from the city and pulled his hands from his pockets. "Ribs on you," he said, grabbing his suit jacket and cell phone from his desk and following Delgado out the door.

Chapter 4

This was about money. Everything was about money. But the truth was, there wasn't enough money. Not *enough* money. Now, there was a lot of money. Maybe more than a lot. But not *enough*. No. Not enough money for someone who had no money to keep money after everybody else got all their money. And while Val didn't know a lot about money, she knew that. If she played nice and she played fair with this money, she was going to come out on the bottom. And that wasn't going to happen . . . not again.

When Jamison kicked Val out of his house in Cascade and promised to divorce her, leaving her broke without a dime to her name, she just knew her everything was about to crumble. Everything she'd worked for. Everything she had promised herself so many times would materialize in her life was about to dissipate into a memory. Now, maybe finding a rich man and living the rich life as his rich wife wasn't everyone's plan, but it was hers. Some women went to law school. Some to medical school. Some to hair school. Val wanted a rich man, so she had to endure her own course of study. For some time she was a straight-A student in the curriculum, and at one point it seemed that she was about to graduate with a ring and get that terminal degree and title before her name: Mrs.

She'd set her eyes on the mayor of the fastest growing little city in the entire world. And somewhere between letting him remove her fishnets with his tongue and doing lines of cocaine off her ass and watching him lead press conferences from the front row with nothing but white people behind her, and seeing a picture of herself on his arm on the cover of a national newspaper, she'd fallen in love. She'd gotten pregnant by him and then—dear God above—Val had gotten that ring—the ring—and the promise that she was going to be his second wife.

And then it happened. Just like that. She became Mrs. Jamison Taylor. The mayor's wife. Not just a lady, but a first lady. Her face was everywhere and everyone knew her name, and more importantly, how powerful and very rich she was. Everyone from her past—her sisters, those men she'd met in the night, the fake friends, Jamison's first wife and his mama—they could all see what Val had done. And everything she'd ever talked about. Everything she ever wanted was hers for the taking.

But she knew Jamison was never really along for the ride. Yeah, she really did truly love that man. His back. His voice. His smell. How he loved. How he gave love. But none of that ever seemed to rightfully trickle down to her. She was quite clear on that. Still, she thought a baby and ring would somehow change that major impropriety. However, like most broken-hearted little girls with such dreams, she'd soon learn that there could never be anything but fool's gold at the end of that rainbow.

The baby died in her belly one night in their bed after Val had eaten Jamison's mother's mysterious summer soup, the man sent her packing, and somehow poor Val ended up crying salty tears on the shoulders of Jamison's first wife. Here was ground zero. Here was luck run out. Here was, "What the fuck do I do now?" She'd be a grown woman playing a young girl's game if she went back out there to find someone new. Even the old—the oldest men—wanted the youngest women. Their taut tummies and high-sitting tits. What next? A job at Macy's? Waitressing? Home to Mama? Down on her knees to beg a no-body man with a 401(k) and health insurance to take her ass in? Hell, no. And then . . . hell no, again!

And then she got the call about the man's unfortunate flight from the hotel rooftop. Though Jamison and Val had called it quits by then, that wasn't how it was seen in the eyes of the law. There had been no divorce, so she was called to play the weeping widow. And the Tennessee beauty queen learned four things that would save her life. One: While she'd signed an agreement stating what would happen to Jamison's money upon divorce, as no such divorce occurred before his death, the prenuptial agreement was null and void. Two: When Jamison found out she was pregnant, he dutifully went to see his lawyer to change his will. He'd removed Kerry as his sole bene-factor and entrusted his funds to the mother of his unborn child—Mrs. Jamison Taylor—who was to do one thing: *split his belongings among his children as and where fitting.*

Whatever all that meant . . . Val didn't care. All she heard was that she was about to cash in and move up. Between the money in Jamison's insurance policies, dividends from Rake it Up, and investments, she'd be more rich with him dead than she ever could have been with him alive. Her mouth started watering and her head started swelling. But that was all too soon. There were still the matters of lessons three and four: In addition to making moves to change his will behind Val's back after they got married, Jamison changed the benefactor on his private insurance policy, which was worth five million dollars.

And four—that same benefactor was awarded 20 percent of his dividends from Rake it Up.

Whatever all that meant . . . Val *had* to care. That's what had led her to Jamison's lawyer's office so many times. What led her there that day she'd met with Coreen.

"So there's no more money?" Val asked.

"No. Not until the end of this quarter when the next dividend check is cut." David Bozeman was sitting in his high-back leather chair in his office in Decatur. His arms resting over his lap, he tried not to look as annoyed by another one of Val's random visits as he actually was. It was common for widows and widowers and just anyone feeling like they needed to seek some kind of justice after such a tragedy as the one Val had encountered at the beginning of their grieving process. Bozeman was an Atlanta lawyer. His father had been one too. And so that had been the only thing he ever really wanted to be. He'd gone to Morehouse and pledged Alpha with Jamison and after he graduated from law school, his Morehouse and frat brother became his first major client. When he'd heard about Jamison's death, so many things about their last encounters suddenly made sense. But then again, maybe none of this made sense at all.

"But that's two more months. I can't survive two more months. I don't have any more money," Val said, looking at David like most of his clients did when they were down on their luck—like he was supposed to do something efficient and magical. Make it better than all right. Make it go away.

"You paid off the house. The cars. And that last dividend check was for sixty-eight thousand dollars," David said, looking down at the sheet on his desk, though he knew the number very well.

Val hardly blinked at this retelling of her history. She knew it all. Val was no top-ranking collegiate scholar, but she wasn't stupid, either. When she realized the only insurance money she was getting from Jamison's death was a paltry six-figure payoff from the state after his short term in the mayor's office, she immediately used his savings and any red dime she could find to pay off that big, beautiful house, those brand-new, drop-top Jaguars, and any other bill she could find that might pop up and put her out. But then Mama Fee came calling. Big Mama's old property was in foreclosure. And then Mama Fee couldn't pay her own mortgage anymore. Val bought both properties with the rest of the money and enjoyed looking like she'd done something right in her mother's eyes for the first time ever.

"So, you have no money?" David pushed.

"I'm eating. The power isn't about to be turned off, but . . . ," Val paused and looked off. "There are other things."

"Look, Val, I'm no financial adviser. I was only responsible for giving you—"

"Coreen wants money," Val said, cutting David off. She waited and watched him struggle to swallow the spit in his mouth and loosen his tie. "And don't pretend that you don't know who she is. No way Jamison didn't tell you."

"I don't want to get involv—"

Val cut in again. "You already are. Jamison got you involved when he put you in charge of his will. She wants fifty thousand dollars or she's going to the media. She's going to tell everyone about . . . you know."

"Let her. What's the big deal?" David said nonchalantly, shuffling around more paper.

"The big deal is the bottom line. The money. You know Jamison's major clients are nothing but a bunch of Southern good old boys, who are only a generation from the Klan and probably only gave Jamison a contract because of his low prices.

The first thing they'll do after hearing about Coreen is switch services."

"So? Rake it Up will lose some clients. And gain some more."

After hearing David say this, Val crossed her legs and sucked her teeth at him.

"What?" he said. "That's not enough to keep you in Chanel? Keep you in Hermès? You're in business now and you can't worry about that. You're going to have to take some blows. What does Kerry say?"

"I haven't told her."

David exhaled and shook his head worriedly. He remembered the first time he saw Val. It was at a dinner party where one of his and Jamison's frat brothers planned to celebrate the mayoral victory. The brother, who was much older and had over fifty years in the fraternity, was one of Jamison's biggest donors, so the party was guaranteed to be well attended and highly publicized in their social circle. David's own wife begged to come with him so she could get a "posterity" picture with Jamison. When Jamison walked in the door with the woman he was calling his "assistant" on his arm, all the talk shifted from being about the magnificent affair to everything from Val's red dress to her twenty-inch curly weave, red lips, thick hips, and boldly displayed breasts. Of course, the brothers gave Jamison winks and hand grips of support for the vision on his arm. But they also knew how dangerous the whole thing could be, could get. Just by looking at Val in those six-inch stilettos and fake eyelashes, they knew what it was. She didn't look anything like anyone's assistant. David's wife leaned into him in the car on the way home, hollering, "How is she going to type anything with those long-ass fake nails? Yeah, right, that's his *assistant*. Yeah, fucking right. And I'll tell you right now, if you ever get an assistant that looks like that, I'll kick your black ass and then her ass and then I'll kill us all." David rolled his eyes at his wife's jealous rant, but she was right, as usual. Even if Jamison wasn't sexing the girl in the tight dress, he would soon. And then, what next? Well, all men knew what was next with a woman who looked like Val. She'd bleed him dry.

"I can't believe there's no money," Val wondered aloud in David's office. She'd leaned into the desk and he could see straight down the path between her breasts to her belly button. "Well . . . what about the other money? That twenty percent from Jamison's will? You know."

"No. I told you I can't talk about that. We already had that conversation." David struggled not to look down Val's dress. He felt some electricity roll through his body to his groin. He slid his cell phone off the desk and sent a text to his assistant to come in and save him with a list of things he had to do.

"No, we didn't. Look, I want to know where that money is going, David. I have a right to know," Val pleaded.

"I already told you. When Jamison came in to update his will, he said he wanted to donate his money to charity. His entire life insurance policy and half of his dividends from Rake it Up."

"That policy was worth five million dollars and half of what I get each quarter. All to some charity?" Val said. "And what is the Fihankra Organization, anyway?" she added referring to the group where Jamison's monies had been wired. "I looked it up and I can't find it anywhere. No organization operates with that name here in Atlanta or anywhere else where I could find it. That doesn't sound odd to you?"

"It's really not my business to know. I simply follow my clients' wishes. And, if you really want to know: No, actually, it doesn't sound odd to me that someone like Jamison would want to donate money to charity," David answered as his assistant walked in, holding the stack of files she kept beside her desk for such occasions. "Many of my wealthy clients donate their money to charity. Especially when they have so much money to go around." He looked at Val as the assistant came and stood by his side with the files. "Now, if you'll excuse me, I do need to get back to work." He pointed to the folders and his assistant worked to look especially annoyed with him. "I have all of these contracts to look through. A tough afternoon of litigating ahead of me." He smiled graciously at Val, as if he'd been so generous with his time and was sad to indirectly send her away.

Val sucked her teeth loudly again to demonstrate her displeasure. The assistant had come trudging in with that same salty face and pile of papers during her last visit. "Something ain't right about that twenty percent and either you know it or you're hiding what you know. It don't matter to me which one." She stood and slung her Céline purse over her arm with marked attitude. "I'm going to find out either way."

"Don't go making trouble, Val. Come on," David said. "Stop while you're ahead. Just do what you were supposed to do with that money in the first place. You know what Jamison intended. It was for the child—"

Val's coldest stare stopped David's lips from uttering another word. He knew not to go any further with anything he was going to say.

Val turned from the desk and started to walk out.

"I'll be back," she said without looking back at David and his assistant watching her walk away with their mouths open. "And don't try to play me with that stack-of-files routine again. I ain't stupid."

Val had never been a club girl. Not really. She'd partied a lot. Partied hard and all night long. Did splits and all kinds of tricks on speaker tops and bar tops and tabletops and even on a few poles here and there, but she'd never gone for a "good time." For her it was work. From the right shoes to the right hair and scent of Tom Ford's Black Orchid sprayed here and there and between this and that, going to the club was about finding the right man or the man next to the man to get to that man to get whatever she wanted at that moment. Now, that could range from attention to rent money, so the stakes were too high for any night out at the club to be considered a good time.

While Jamison's publicist made Val swear off any of her old haunts when they'd gotten married and Val was supposed to be learning how to be a "respectable" first lady of Atlanta—a plan that included new wigs, less makeup, and more fabric above her nipples and below her knees—she'd found herself a returning customer during her newfound widowhood.

But like the bright lights and nightlife had changed, Val's reasons for being there had changed too. It would be rather zealous to say she was no longer on a search for a suitable suitor—that could never be far from Val's imagination, even with Jamison's money in her hands. Still, her participation was less easy to define. It started with a drink. A reason to get out of the house. Out of *that* house. Away from her mother. Away from everything in her head. She'd follow her old routine. A long, hot shower. Hot shea butter on her skin. Black Orchid between her thighs and behind her ears. A dress so tight she couldn't wear a bra or a thong. Legs out. Arms out. Hair down her back. Eyelashes batting. Lips puckered and glossy. A ride into the city with the windows down. A big tip for the valet. Saunter in with her vacant eyes straight ahead. No line outside to wait on. The bouncers know her. Sit at the bar in VIP with a drink that came in a small glass with no ice cubes.

"Hey, I'm Monty."

It never took long after she was seated and had ordered a drink for someone to show up and take the seat beside her. That night after the meeting in David's office about Coreen and the money, it was Monty.

Val just smiled over her shoulder at him. It was never a good idea to show any kind of attention that quickly.

Then the bartender came over and asked Monty what he wanted to drink and he requested something like a Gentleman Jack and Coke.

When the drink came, Monty reached out for the glass and Val, who'd been silent and only nodding along to the loud music, got a peek at his dated but respectable Rolex.

"You come here often?" he asked, noting to himself that Val had peeped the watch.

"No. Not really," Val lied. She'd been there two times that week and to most of the clubs on that row in Midtown on the other nights. There was always a reason. Her mother on her nerves. Coreen on the phone. Kerry calling and worrying. The lawyers. David. Whatever.

"Funny, I thought I saw you here Monday." Monty chuckled.

"Then why did you ask me a dumb-ass question, then?" Val snapped, finally looking over at Monty. He was brown and cute. Had deep dimples that probably could be annoying to look at sometimes.

"Hold on, boss lady!" Monty held up his hands like Val was about to hit him and she smiled. She could see the muscles in his forearms through his thin fall cashmere sweater. "Don't hurt a brother. All these young things in here and I see something sophisticated like you at the bar and I want to know what's up. I'm just trying to get to know you." He surveyed Val's plump torso resting in the seat.

"Ain't much to know, I'm afraid," Val said dismissively.

"Well, maybe I'm just trying to look at you, then."

Val stared at Monty again and there were those dimples.

He peered into her and she nearly felt his eyes peel her shoulder straps down and her dress up.

Later, there were more drinks and some laughs. Val loosened up some. Monty literally saw her shoulders fall and her frown dissipate. She told him nothing of herself and tried to seem disinterested whenever he spoke of himself. At one point a Jay Z song came on and she got up from her chair and started dancing really close on his lap. That was after he'd let it slip that he was a plastic surgeon and was opening a third clinic in Buckhead next year. She leaned back and let her Persian wavy weave fall on his chest, twerked her thighs in and out until his penis grew so stiff he could feel the blood vibrating in the tip as she bounced up and down.

"You're turning me on," he whispered in her ear and she blamed it on the alcohol. "What's your name?" he asked again for the third or fourth time.

"Does it matter?" Val laughed and downed the last of her drink so quickly it made her throat burn and her chest hot. "Hey, you want to dance?" She just grabbed Monty's hand and started pulling him toward the dance floor. They tunneled through a crowd of people ten to fifteen years younger than both of them. There were waitresses carrying buckets of champagne and vodka, outliers puffing marijuana. and little girls in heels so high they could hardly stand up straight.

Monty kept trying to pull Val back out of the party maze and smoke, but the more he pulled, the more Val protested, becoming more risqué and wild with her dancing. She'd pulled his arms around her waist and backed up against him on the dance floor. In the darkness, neon laser lights highlighted only slivers of her body.

"You fucking know you want this," she teased in whispers beneath the booming hip hop music that Monty didn't recognize at that point.

"You know that's right," he said in her ear. "Let's get out of here."

"Why you want to leave so bad?" Val snapped and her body suddenly became rigid and erect with no movement. She stood up straight in the middle of the dance floor and Monty felt she was about to make more of a scene.

"Oh, no, it's nothing, bossy lady." Monty put up his hands again and flashed his nicest smile. "We can dance some more!" He did a quick two-step that looked so out of place in the youthful crowd. He'd already told himself that the woman he'd been coming on to for over two hours when he could've been chasing some of the less bitter, scantily dressed targets around him would be some challenge; but somehow to a man like him, she'd be worth the extra energy in the end. There was that myth—the one about angry women in bed, how they'd be so forceful and wild. This made him look at Val like some kind of lioness with a broken paw. An animal whose behavior was at once unpredictable and all too predictable. Plus, he thought he'd recognized her from somewhere. And the alcohol muddying his thoughts convinced him that she must be a former model, maybe an old video girl he'd seen someplace before. That turned him on even more.

Val loosened up again and started dancing. The alcohol in her body made a mess of her thoughts, too. She wondered what the man's name was who was rubbing his penis into her thigh. She couldn't remember seeing her mother when she stopped at the house before leaving for the club. She tried to remember what Jamison's hands looked like when he was the man dancing behind her. What was the shade of red on those bloody sheets on the bed? Why had her baby died? What happens after death? What was a woman? A man? How long could hurt last?

"Let's go to the bathroom." Val pulled Monty through the crowd again, but this time he didn't resist at all. He felt around in his back pocket for a condom.

In the bathroom, Monty's back was against the stall door and Val was undoing his pants. She hadn't looked into his eyes once, but he'd caught glimpses of her icy stare on parts of him and somehow that thrilled Monty. He'd given a hundred dollars to the bathroom attendant to lock the door outside for twenty minutes.

Val kissed and sucked on his chest as she lowered his pants. She rimmed the tip of his boxers with her tongue and hummed into his middle so he could feel the promise of where her mouth was going next.

"Shit, you're so fucking hot. I knew this was going to be good," Monty said, like Val needed some of his encouragement and this thing was really about making him feel good.

Val giggled to herself at how silly all of these men could be. She wondered how long it would take for each one to turn from this helpless thing with his whole manhood under the control of her mouth, to something more like Jamison, so distant and unwilling to see her for anything else.

Jamison's cold eyes on her in the hospital room after the doctors had removed the last remaining pieces of their child from her uterus flashed in Val's eyes and erased the effects of any liquor in her bloodstream. But Val told herself to keep going. It would feel better soon.

Monty's pants began to slip down lower and then the top fell over, making the contents of his pockets fall out in familiar sounds. The wallet. The keys. The ChapStick. The *ring*.

The last sound was a *ding*, like something golden or platinum hitting concrete.

Even over the soft ricochets of music seeping into the bathroom from the club world outside, Val knew what that sound was.

She looked down and between the ChapStick and wallet was a little silver band.

"You're married?" Val was still on her knees, but she looked up at Monty like he was so far beneath her.

All he could say was, "So?"

"Nigga, you're married?" Val stood up for the question this time and poked out her hip, like a black woman who was about to curse a man out for some major transgression.

"What?" There were those annoying dimples again. "Come on, boss lady, don't act like you care about that shit." He held up his hands and smiled to bring Val back to him.

"Fuck that boss-lady bullshit. I don't fuck married men," Val shouted so loud the attendant and all the women arguing with her about opening the bathroom door could hear.

"Oh, suddenly, you have standards?" Monty's smile turned to an ironic chuckle. He tried to grab Val, but she slapped his hands away.

"Don't fucking touch me. You should've said something, motherfucker. Who you think you are?"

"Said something to whom? You wouldn't even tell me your fucking name. Fuck this!" Monty pulled up his pants clumsily and gathered his things from the floor before opening the stall. "Shit ain't worth it anyway," he said as he and Val walked out into the main area of the emptied bathroom.

"What's that supposed to mean?" Val asked angrily.

Monty went to the sink to freshen up like it was his bathroom vanity at home.

"You saw how many bitches were out there?" Monty quizzed with heat in his voice that didn't sound natural but still stung. "I don't have to do this shit."

"How many bitches? Fuck all those bitches. I'm the bitch in the bathroom and last I checked, I was the baddest bitch on the floor." Val's hand was back on her hip and all of her old attitude was in her voice.

"Yeah right, sweetie. Maybe it's time for a reality check," Monty said nonchalantly as he groomed his goatee with the bathroom attendant's dirty hairbrush. "You're . . . what . . . about fifteen years older than the youngest chick in there? And those is young titties. Young pussies. You fine as shit, but your shit ain't their shit. And you better know it. Any nigga fucking with you is being nice. Fucking charity case." He threw the brush down and proceeded to the door, where the attendant had started knocking. "I don't have time for this shit."

He threw a piece of paper towel into the trash and left Val standing at the vanity, where a gang of chicks with frowns on their faces stared at her when they entered the restroom in a line.

"You okay?" the attendant asked Val when she got into the restroom and found Val standing in front of the mirror, looking blankly at herself. "You need me to get security? I knew something wasn't right with that nigga. But you was with him, so—"

"I'm fine," Val said sharply before turning her back and walking out like nothing had happened.

Outside the club, the line was thick and still growing, though it was far past midnight. Fancy cars with shiny rims and rappers and athletes in the front seat inched past slowly, so whoever was inside the car could be seen by some desperate girl in line. It was an old trick that still worked.

The valet pulled Jamison's sparkling Jaguar around with the top down as Val had instructed.

She tipped him with a hundred-dollar bill and walked to the car, knowing everyone in line wondered who she was. Some did know, though. And she could hear them chatting, "Isn't that the dead mayor's window?"

Just when Val was about to get into the car, another valet pulled up behind her in a Porsche.

Monty came straggling out of the club with no one on his arm and headed toward the driver's-side door of the Porsche.

Val stopped and watched him with a frown that he happily returned. She reminded herself that back in the day, when she was one of those girls in the line with her feet hurting and nipples shivering in the cold, she would've cursed him out royally for saying just half of the things he'd said to her.

She was about to get into her car, but then something in Val made her turn and charge over to Monty. Maybe she was about to curse his name or slap his cheek or knee his crotch. Maybe all three.

Monty nervously tried to rush to his car, but Val was fast even in her heels, and she caught up with him just before the valet handed him his keys.

"You ain't shit," Val said to Monty. "You come here and you think you can say anything to me! Fuck you! Fuck you three times!"

Monty saw red in Val's eyes and he knew not to say anything. He stood there and tried not to look too apologetic or hopeless. He couldn't risk a scene. Getting arrested again wouldn't go over too well at home. His wife was actually the plastic surgeon in the family. He was her office assistant.

When Val was finished cursing, she didn't know what else to do. She told herself to back away, but her feet wouldn't move. Then she did something she hardly expected—well, that no one watching expected. All of the red in her eyes and the anger in her heart fueled a passion that literally threw her into Monty, where she wrapped her arms around his neck and kissed him. Full tongue down his throat and lips pressed over his, she tried to devour him in a second.

The valets standing there didn't know if they should cheer or tell the two to move on, as they were holding up the car line.

Monty didn't know what to do, either, but the confusion was certainly turning him on.

Before Val let him loose, she ordered him very loudly, "Follow me."

It was after 1 AM and the highways connecting downtown Atlanta nightlife to suburban sprawl were thinning out, but still active enough to provide some fantastic glow show of blinking lights and expensive zipping hot wheels along the interstate.

Val opened the Jag's engine up in the fast lane, doing 95 the entire way home with Monty struggling to keep up with her in his Porsche. His wife was calling and texting. His heart was beating so fast the balding forty-three-year-old who'd just had his bulging belly liposuctioned four months ago might have been having a heart attack. Still, he continued the pursuit and zigzagged through the traffic to keep up with Val.

When they pulled into the circular drive outside of the house where Mama Fee was hiding behind blinds in her top-floor bedroom window, Monty's heart was beating so fiercely, he feared he wouldn't be able to take his Viagra to keep up with whatever Val had in mind in the bedroom.

When Val pulled into the driveway, she noticed a familiar

automobile sitting in the space where she usually parked. It was a big, black truck that she'd seen recently but couldn't place in her memory. She wondered if maybe it was one of her sisters coming over from Tennessee to be nosy about what she was into, but then she noticed the Georgia plates.

Both Val and Monty got out of their cars at the same time.

Monty was walking toward Val, saying something about her driving speed and he was laughing, but all of Val's attention stayed on the truck.

"I've never seen a woman handle a car like that," Monty was saying when the driver's-side door of the truck opened. "You're like the black Danica Patrick." He laughed a little, but then he noticed where Val's eyes were focused and looked that way as well.

"What are you doing here?" Val said when she realized who was getting out of the truck. It was the man who'd been in her bed the night before.

"What? Who—who is this?" Monty said, stopping in his tracks behind Val. He was standing just inches away from the front of Val's car and a few feet away from the back of the truck, with the big man with the football player's body walking toward him.

"I wanted to see you again." Ernest spoke nonchalantly to Val like Monty wasn't standing behind her.

"See me? I didn't invite you here," Val snapped.

"I know. I was going to invite you out. Maybe to a movie at the drive-in or for some dessert in the West End. But you didn't give me your number," Ernest said, chuckling. He was wearing the black suit he'd put on to go out for drinks with some of the other former Falcons players he sometimes hung out with. But when he got to the bar, while all of the other guys were complaining about their wives and chasing young girls, he was thinking about Val.

"What the fuck are you laughing at?" Val said. "I'm calling the police." She went to pull her phone from her purse.

"What, you don't know this cat?" Monty interjected, trying his best to sound tough.

"Dude, don't say shit," Ernest offered, still relaxed and ironically sounding tougher. "You don't want it. I know you don't. You might as well just go back to your car and drive home to your wife and kids."

"How do you know I have kid—"

"Shut up, Monty!" Val shot and then she said to Ernest, "You don't have a right to tell anyone to go home. Your ass wasn't even invited here in the first place. What are you, a stalker?"

"Look, if there's a problem, I can go," Monty said with a sudden change of heart and already stepping away.

"That's right, partner. Carry your ass home. Probably have soccer with the kids in the morning, anyway," Ernest snapped at Monty. "Might as well call it a night."

"No! Don't you dare go anywhere!" Val ordered, turning around and pointing her finger at Monty like he was her teenage son.

He put his hands up again like he had at the club and tried to smile, but those dimples were looking very nervous as both Ernest and Val peered like they were about to attack him at any moment: one if he stayed, one if he left.

"I came here for some pus—" Monty started, but then he stopped when he looked at Ernest. "I'm sorry, bruh. I mean, I didn't come here for no drama. I think you two need to talk about some things."

"Yes, we do." Ernest stepped up and stood beside Val, who was trying to push him away from her, but he put his big heavy arm around her shoulders and forced her to look something like his lady.

"No, the hell we don't," Val complained, twisting away.

"Monty, don't you dare leave! I invited you here! Not this crazy fool!"

It was too late. Monty from the club was already two-stepping his way back to his car and jumping inside.

"Sorry! Tonight's not the night!" he said, slamming his door closed and turning on the ignition in a rush. He backed out of the driveway like the house was about to explode.

In all of her anger, Val actually was so pissed that she stopped struggling under Ernest's heavy arm.

"Look what you did," she said, like this was their routine.

"Nigga wasn't shit, anyway," Ernest said, waving at Monty. "Car wasn't even his."

"How do you know that?"

"It had sorority tags on it. You didn't notice that?"

"Hmm . . ." Val squinted to see a sorority plate right on the front of the car before Monty spun out into the street and sped off.

Ernest yawned dramatically. "I'm tired. Let's go inside and go to bed," he said casually.

"Bed? What? You're about to go to jail. I'm calling the police," Val argued again.

"No, you ain't." Ernest turned Val and her unused cell phone toward him and stepped up to her. "You don't want to make that call. If you wanted to, you would've done it already. You're the kind of woman who does exactly what she wants to do."

"You don't know me," Val said, but she was definitely putting the phone back into her purse.

"Maybe not. But I do like you." Ernest smiled. "And I really did want to see you tonight."

"Well, the night is over." Val rolled her eyes and crossed her arms over her chest. "You are too late."

Ernest looked up at the sky. "Moon's still out. Sun won't be up for a few hours." He looked back at Val so softly. "Can I spend those hours with you?"

"Doing what?" Val's eye-rolling and frowning was replaced with a suspicious blush.

"Sleeping."

"Sleeping?" She looked at him like he was crazy. "That's all you want to do?"

"Yes. I want to chat. And lie behind you and go to sleep. That's what I want to do. That's all I want to do." Ernest placed both of his large hands over Val's shoulders. "Will you let me?"

Chapter 5

Tyrian had observed two very important things about Thirjane Jackson since she showed up at his summer camp crying and saying he needed to come and spend another night at her house because his mother Kerry had "gotten herself in some trouble." First, his grandmother never did anything without first having a sip of her "special drink" that she kept in the silver bottle in her pocketbook. A trip to the grocery store, church, the doctor, tee off, or soccer practice—from the backseat of the car, he watched his grandmother take a few sips of her drink, sometimes say a little prayer or curse to herself while gripping the steering wheel, and then sliding the silver bottle back into her pocketbook before they made a move.

This didn't bother Tyrian much. Grandma was sometimes more funny and less mean after having the sips. The smart seven-year-old already knew it was alcohol, but didn't have the heart to tell her after she lied and said it was her "medication." She'd smile more and order him around less and not say so many mean things about Kerry. But still, sometimes things wouldn't go so well. She'd get really quiet and look tired in her eyes. And one day, when she was late picking him up from school and drove so far over the yellow line in the middle of the street a white man in a truck coming toward them gave them the middle finger, she just pulled over and started crying. He asked what was wrong. Why she was so sad. She hollered at him. Yelled. Screamed. Told him not to say another word and never to bring up what had just happened again. Her old-lady blush and foundation making waves down her wrinkled cheeks beneath streaming tears, she looked at him in the rearview mirror and made him swear, "Grandma's business is *Grandma's* business."

And that little verbal contract was the main motto of the second thing he'd observed: Grandma had a lot of business. Almost every day, sometimes twice in an hour, Tyrian would be sworn into these little secrecies. And sometimes they were little things or funny things. Like that Grandma's teeth weren't real. And that she almost always cheated at Pokeno when they played on Saturday night. And that she hated the pastor's wife at church. And when she went up front during the collection, the envelope she put in the basket was always empty. "All that money First Lady be spending on them tacky-ass Fashion Fair dresses she wears every Sunday, I'll be damned if I give a dime to this church," she'd said one day after church before turning to Tyrian and adding, "And don't you tell anyone what I said. Grandma's business is—" Tyrian had heard this so many times he cut in with the predicate: "*Grandma's* business."

As thin as the promises from a seven-year-old could be, Tyrian honestly intended to keep his promise to Grandma Janie. But there was one bit of business she was conducting that he was actually finding hard to keep secret. The bit was so juicy, so bold, that Tyrian promised himself that as soon as he got the chance he'd share the information with the only person who would care: his mother. As soon as he got her alone, he'd put his hand to his mother's ear and whisper so low that no one else would know: "Grandma's got a boyfriend."

Well, Tyrian wasn't exactly sure if the man was his grandmother's boyfriend. She'd never said he was and Tyrian never saw them kiss, but that was the only reason he could develop to explain why his Grandma Janie was so adamant that he tell no one, absolutely no one, about the white man with the black hat who met them at the park sometimes and sat on the bench to talk to his grandmother as he played on the jungle gym.

One afternoon, on a Thursday after school when Grandma Janie took Tyrian to the park, he decided to conduct an experiment when her boyfriend was walking toward their bench and Grandma Janie began to shoo Tyrian away. The precocious little one decided to record their conversation on the one device his grandmother would never suspect—his iPad. He'd seen it done on one of the animated pet-detective shows he'd watched on the Disney Channel. Sadie the Dog had launched a full investigation to discover where her owners kept her bacon treats. One night, she set up an iPad surveillance unit beside her crate in the kitchen and in the morning the video was filled with clues. Tyrian laughed innocently at the idea of being like Sadie the Dog, collecting clues about his grandmother's new boyfriend. He wouldn't tell his grandmother, of course. But he would tell his mother. As soon as they were alone, he'd whisper in her ear everything that was said and they'd laugh and laugh and laugh at Grandma's silly business.

"You go on and play, boy," Thirjane said sternly when the man was getting closer to her and Tyrian on a bench beside the playground. "Go on and play and don't come back over here talking about you're bored. Don't come back until I tell you to. You hear me?"

"Yes, ma'am," Tyrian agreed. He handed her the iPad he'd been playing a game on and smiled without showing his gap teeth—the way she'd taught him to. "Can you hold my iPad for me?"

"Not like I have a choice," Thirjane complained, to no one's surprise. "I don't know why you brought this thing out here in the first place. Act like you can't be away from this computer for five minutes. Not even to play."

Tyrian stood there and listened to his grandmother's tongue. He didn't know if he should stay or go and play. And he normally got more of a lashing if he chose incorrectly.

Finally, when the man was just five feet away, she said, "What are you standing there for? Go and play! And remember what I said. You don't come back over here until I call you."

"Yes, ma'am," Tyrian said. "And could you please hold my iPad on your lap? Don't sit it on the bench. It might fall and break."

"Boy, I'll throw this thing in the gutter if I choose! Now, go on and play!"

All that heavy talk and Thirjane did just as her grandson requested: Kept the iPad right on her lap like she was cradling a baby. She gave Tyrian a hard time, but really she loved him more than herself and his mother. The hard-time stuff—that was just her way.

Tyrian made good on his promise too. He stayed far away from the bench as his grandmother talked with her special guest, strategically biding his time on equipment that conveniently faced the pair. He tried to read their lips and guess what they were saying, and in his young mind the exchange sounded something like all those Lifetime movies his mother had watched on the couch at home. "Oh, my sweet love. I love you," his grandmother would say and the white man would respond, "And I love you too, darling."

But when Grandma Janie's boyfriend was gone and she called Tyrian back over so they could go home to cook and eat supper, he learned that their talk went nothing like that. In fact, hovering over the iPad in his dark bedroom closet after Grandma Janie had sipped her special medication and fallen asleep on the couch, he wondered if he'd need to launch a new investigation to get better clues about Grandma Janie's boyfriend. They weren't even talking about being girlfriend and boyfriend. And although Tyrian didn't exactly know what that meant, he listened and knew this wasn't it. He couldn't make sense of most of it, but before the charge went dead and the iPad had stopped recording, the conversation went like this:

Thirjane: You go on and play, boy. Go on and play and don't come back over here talking about you're bored. Don't come back until I tell you to. You hear me?

Tyrian: Yes, ma'am. Can you hold my iPad for me?

Thirjane: Not like I have a choice. I don't know why you brought this thing out here in the first place. Act like you can't be away from this computer for five minutes. Not even to play.

[long pause]

What are you standing there for? Go and play! And remember what I said. You don't come back over here until I call you.

Tyrian: Yes, ma'am. And could you please hold my iPad on your lap? Don't sit it on the bench. It might fall and break.

Thirjane: Boy, I'll throw this thing in the gutter if I choose! Now, go on and play!

[long pause]

Man: Hello. How are you today?

Thirjane: Could be better. Any news for me?

Man: Nothing much. Been making calls and—

Thirjane: Well, you can stop with the calls. They're not working. You want answers, you're going to have to go out there and shake some trees. That's what I pay you for.

Man: Actually, that's not what you pay me for. You paid me for—

Thirjane: Never mind what I paid you for. You fucked it up and look where we're at now.

[long pause]

I have to do something. We have to do something to make this right.

Man: I've been thinking. I know someone who put in work for the DA. You know when that guy from the church was trying to have him fired?

Thirjane: The pastor who drowned in Lake Lanier?

Man: Yeah, that one. Like I was saying, I know the guy who put in work for the DA back then.

Thirjane: You think he'll talk?

Man: Not a chance in hell, but he'll get us in the DA's ear. And then I'll get some phone calls returned. You know?

Thirjane: Sounds good. Make your move.

Man: Thing is, it's going to be a little more.

Thirjane: More what? Time?

[long pause]

How much?

Man: Twenty.

Thirjane: Twenty? I don't have that.

[long pause]

Man: She does.

Thirjane: No. No. I can't. She can't know. Not about this. She can't ever know.

Tyrian fell asleep on the floor in the closet after listening to these words more than ten times and making sense of none of it. Still, he knew it wasn't good. He'd never heard his grandmother sound so scared or being ordered around to do anything by a man—not any man. Suddenly, his plan for laughs with his mother about Grandma Janie's secret boyfriend sounded like trouble for him or trouble for someone. This was Grandma's business and Grandma's business was . . . *Grandma's* business.

Chapter 6

Kerry was on the phone, trying to fire her lawyer. There was a litany of reasons. Top of the list: She was still in jail.

"You should just be able to do something. And like, get me out of here, Stan. It doesn't make any sense. People come and go every day. Some with crimes worse than mine—I mean, who committed crimes worse than the one I'm charged with." Kerry pressed her mouth into the phone like she was telling a secret she didn't want the guard standing behind her and half listening to the conversation to hear. "One woman was in here for touching her kid. Like molesting him. She got out." She shouted louder in what was almost a scream, "But I'm still here!"

"I know. I know." Her lawyer, Stanley Lebowski, repeated what he'd said after each of the key reasons Kerry provided to explain why she felt she needed new representation.

"No, I don't think you do know. I don't think you really understand. You say you do, but then there's nothing. I have a child, Stan. I haven't put my son to sleep in three months. You have kids. Do you know what it's like not to tuck them in at night? Not to know if they're coughing in the middle of the night or having nightmares or just need you to hold them tight? Not to see them in the morning?"

"No, Kerry. I don't," Stan admitted.

"So, you can't know. You see? You can't know what this is like for me."

"I'm trying my best. And I know you think that's lip service, but it's true. I've called in every favor. I've shaken every tree, but nothing will turn up. The DA won't even see me to try to make a deal."

Stan was half-naked and laying on his back in the hot-coal steam room at the Jeju Day Spa just north of the city. It was his office away from the office. Where he came to clear his mind and see his most stubborn cases in a new way and maybe get a few glimpses at some hot Asian girls in their underwear, as well. He'd spent many days at the spa since he'd started working on Kerry's case. So many that one of his assistants had actually set up her laptop and Wi-Fi in the lobby. It wasn't because he was shrinking from his responsibilities or taking Kerry's lockdown lightly. Contrary to what Kerry believed, he was doing everything he could to get her out. But there was something stinking about the case. Something just rotten that wouldn't let his mind pull it apart. And no matter how many massages he got where he listed every single fact of the case in his head or sittings in the steam room he endured while considering those facts from every angle in the judicial system, he always came out feeling like he was back at square one. Kerry didn't do the crime. That was obvious. Kerry was in jail for the crime. That was obvious. Kerry shouldn't be in jail for the crime she didn't do. That was obvious too. It was base-level law-school logic. The same logic he'd thought would make the DA automatically release Kerry just hours after Val had called him in the middle of the night about taking the case. In his head, he imagined walking out of the courthouse with Kerry crying on one arm, Val crying on the other, a sea of cameras and reporters in front of them. He'd make a declaration—"Justice prevailed this morning!" Everyone would cheer for Lebowski. Another case won! That's how it always went. But not this time.

"The DA? Jamison went to Morehouse with Charles Brown. He won't even talk to you?" Kerry asked. "That doesn't make sense. Maybe it's *you*. Maybe that's why he won't speak to you."

"Why? Because I'm white?" Stan asked, sensing some hesitation in Kerry's voice. "No. That's not it. Listen to me, Kerry. You and I both know I'm not just the best man for the money for this job. I'm the best man, period. I win my cases. I don't lose. Val didn't get my number from some phone book or on Craigslist. I'm the best criminal defense attorney in the state. And I'm telling you I just need a little more time. There's something going on here and I need to figure it out. Don't give up on me now. You give up now, and I really don't know if you'll ever get out. That's how serious this is. That's how many doors are closed. Locked."

Kerry felt a bubble of anxiety burst in her throat and travel up to her tear ducts. This was a heavy load. Too much for her to bear and survive it sane. In 1997 she let her best friend talk her into going to Spelman's Valentine's Day dance and there she met Jamison. He became her best friend. He was the only one who understood her. Could make sense of her crazy mother and crazy upbringing. Could laugh at it all. Laugh at her. And still love her anyway. After the wedding it did all fall apart. But she knew the role she'd played. Jamison was no angel, but she wasn't innocent, either. And when it was all said and done, after they packed their bags and walked away from each other, she still loved him. And she knew he loved her. So what was all of this? How did this happen? How did she get here?

Kerry couldn't say another word. If she opened her mouth

she was afraid something like fire would come from her throat and burn everything in the world.

"I'll be there to see you next week," Stan said, hearing Kerry's soft sobs. "I think Val is stopping by there this weekend. You hold on tight until then, kid. You hear me?"

Kerry hung up the phone and dragged her body away on shuffling feet.

Still crying with memories of her past life creeping in, she went outside, hoping a last bit of sunlight or maybe the Georgia breeze that even the jail walls couldn't keep away would make her feel like somebody who was alive again. Or maybe the glimpse of the outside world above her head would remind her of some reality she was keeping from herself. She considered that maybe she was wrong and everyone else was right. Had she done it? Had she pushed Jamison from that rooftop? Why would she do it?

Maybe no part in the story had gone the way she was telling it. Jamison always needed more attention. Needed her to say things a certain way. Believe what he believed. Do what he did. The fragile black-male ego stuff. He hated her family and everything that it stood for. That old Atlanta. That old money. Black folks who acted like white folks and loved those white folks more than their own black folks. The poor black folks. "What does Jack and Jill do for the community? What does a cotillion do to save the lives of poor black children who can't read or write or think straight because they didn't have breakfast that morning?" Jamison asked one night when they first started dating and were hugged up in bed in his dorm at Morehouse. Kerry had looked up at the Lil' Kim poster hanging on the side of his bed and laughed. She was just telling him how much she hated being in Jack and Jill and hated those cotillions. "Why are you laughing?" Jamison asked her and she said, "No reason. I was a kid. I didn't know anything about that. My mother signed me up and I went. I had to." Jamison hopped off the bed and looked at Kerry like she was a thief. "You had a choice, Kerry. You always have a choice. Just admit that you liked it. You enjoyed it. Just say it." Kerry rolled her eyes and pulled Jamison's cheap, thin sheet up over her bare breasts. "Sometimes I did, I guess. It wasn't all bad. Sometimes it was fun." Jamison looked at Kerry with disgust in his eyes. "I hated all those organizations when I was kid. I hated them because I knew they hated me. Wanted me to go away and disappear. Come back a new Negro who knew how to act right. How to act like them. Sit at the big table and eat rare steak and talk about going to Morehouse and pledging the right fraternity and marrying the right woman and moving into the right neighborhood with just enough black people and vacationing in Martha's Vineyard." Kerry asked, "What's wrong with all that? You're at Morehouse. You pledged." She paused and added, "You're dating me." Jamison cut his stare from Kerry and his shoulders sunk down really low. He stood there and looked at Lil' Kim on the wall for a little while like he was in a trance. Her legs cocked open. Her crotch scrubbing the ground. Erykah Badu's new jam "On & On" was playing on his CD player. He suddenly became so aware of the contradiction in the room. He walked out and left the door wide open. Kerry would let herself out hours later.

That became the thing between them. Always the thing between them. Good girl and bad boy. Rich bitch and born hustler.

When Jamison started cheating, Kerry knew what kind of woman she had to be. Before she even met Coreen, she knew she was nothing like her. She was feeding that side of Jamison that Kerry could never touch. That he'd never let her see.

And although she loved him and he loved her, Kerry knew she'd never be enough. She could never be herself and someone else. Love wouldn't change that. And Jamison would never just accept that. She knew it and he knew it.

Maybe that was why she threw him off the roof. To quiet that constant quiz of who she was and what she could do to stop it.

With the Georgia breeze blowing over her skin in the jail yard, Kerry closed her eyes and imagined doing it. Being high up there on the roof over all of Atlanta around her. Her past a maze down below through the streets and highways. She could see I-85. Wasn't that the way she'd taken to Coreen's house that night when she was pregnant? When Tyrian was so heavy in her belly she could hardly walk? And she had to get up out of her bed and into her car, swollen ankles and all, to go out into the world to find her damn husband. Get him from another woman's house, smack in the middle of the ghetto. Make him see her. His wife. His first wife.

She imagined her hands pressed against Jamison's chest on that roof. Every question he'd ever asked her about who she was and how she could change, she turned on him. Who the fuck was *he*? How the fuck could *he* change? How the fuck could he do this to her? Promise her so much and then take it all away for some other woman? For Coreen? And a stroke of his ego?

She pushed.

She pushed.

She pushed.

She imagined pushing and pushing and pushing.

And he fell.

And he died.

And here she was, paying for it all.

Kerry opened her eyes and through tears, she looked out at what all her past had gotten her. Even though she hadn't really killed her ex-husband, she knew that where she'd found herself had to have been linked to that past. What she was guilty of . . . what she wasn't guilty of . . . none of it mattered. She only knew that if she wanted to change her future, to get out of that place, she had to change herself now. But how?

"What you doing out on the yard, sis? You ain't never out here."

Kerry turned and a woman she recognized as the leader of one of the groups sprinkled out on the yard had sat on the bench beside her. The social structure of the women on the jail yard was pretty much a mirror of the social structure they'd created as girls on the schoolyard. There were cool girls and nerdy girls. Good girls and bad girls. And then everything else in between clumped up in little gaggles around the open field. But now that they were women, the group titles had become more complex and even limited. There were the black women and white women. The lesbians and the straights. Rich and poor. Deadly. Marked for death.

The woman who'd just called Kerry "sis" belonged to what Kerry would describe as the earthy black chicks. The ones who probably wore head wraps up to the ceiling like Erykah Badu outside of jail and had likely gotten locked up for staging some kind of protest about legalizing marijuana or public breast-feeding. They all had dreadlocks and tattoos of ankhs and other symbols Kerry couldn't recognize on their forearms and at the nape of their necks. They prayed in a group facing the east, like Muslims, in the morning and read poetry in the library at night. That's where Kerry always saw them. And she'd heard the woman sitting beside her referred to as Auset. Sister Auset Supreme. She had a head of long, thick black hair that was a natural Afro, but from the back it hung below her elbows when she stood and walked across the yard. Her skin was a pale tawny and she had patches of freckles under each eye. She had a slender body that exposed her muscles and hinted at a lifestyle that probably included plant-based eating and lots of yoga. And while she looked not a day over twenty-five, something in her eyes and walk and the way the other "sistren" responded to her made it clear that she was much older—probably in her early forties or so.

"I come out here sometimes," Kerry said, answering Auset's question about why she was sitting on the yard. "Clear my mind. Get some air." Kerry wiped her tears and tried to look away from Auset like it was even possible or necessary to hide her tears.

"Clear your mind out here? Seems impossible." She smiled at Kerry. "I'm Auset." She nodded deeply, almost bowing.

"I'm Ker—"

"I know who you are. We all do."

"We?" Kerry repeated.

"The sistren. We know who you are." Auset nodded toward her group sitting out in the grass toward the back of the yard. Had it not been for their inmate jail jumpers, they'd look like they were enjoying some late-evening picnic in Malcolm X Park. "I guess everyone here knows who you are, though."

Kerry nodded.

"How are you holding up?"

"I'm not," Kerry said bluntly and she felt good for not lying to be pleasant. And for some reason, she felt safe sharing that little vulnerability with the woman sitting beside her.

"Well, that's okay, I guess. What you're going through can't be easy," Auset said. "But then I guess it isn't any more than what Sister Betty Shabazz or Sister Coretta Scott King went through. So, you can do it."

Kerry laughed aloud. "Well, I wouldn't dare put myself on their level. Not at all. Betty? Coretta? *Kerry*?" Kerry laughed some more. "Imagine that. Why don't we just throw in Winnie Mandela and Kathleen Cleaver?"

"Right on." Auset didn't laugh with Kerry. She pumped a Black Power fist in the air. "How do you figure you're not?"

"Not what?"

"Like them."

"Well, I'm just me. And if you mean Jamison . . . it's not—he's not like one of those men. He wasn't," Kerry explained.

"A lot of us thought he was. He did some great things for all of us. You know? The short time he was in office. Most of those fucking politicians—by the time they make it into office riding that black vote—they forget all about their people. He didn't. We had a lot of expectations for Brother Taylor."

Kerry hardly nodded, but she agreed with everything Auset was saying. Jamison had taken his run and win so seriously. When he'd first told Kerry he was thinking of running for mayor and offered to sell her 10 percent of his dividends from Rake it Up so he could have campaign funds, she thought he was just bored with running the company and wanted a quick out. Selling her that 10 percent would put her in control and he'd just be on the sidelines as they restructured and got a new CEO and president. But he stepped all the way back and when he emerged with his actual platform for mayor, she realized he was really going to do it. He wasn't happy with the sitting mayor's decision to shut down all of the midnight basketball programs in the city and use the money to build a new wing at the airport. Like most of the moves of the controversial "New Atlanta" mayor, the action felt like another nod toward the gentrification that was pushing all of the color out of the city. Where there was once public housing, there were now high-priced condos. Affordable and once family-friendly shopping centers and entertainment venues were replaced by urban "live, work, play" enclaves that attracted yuppies and buppies and anyone else who could afford a ten-dollar panini and eight-dollar craft beer for lunch. Jamison wanted to challenge this notion that a new Atlanta had to mean a white or rich Atlanta. The city had to be for everyone. All races. All classes. His campaign slogan: "For every resident, a new promise." He won. And when he got into office, he went straight to work and hustled his way through like the old Jamison Kerry knew and loved . . . before the divorce.

"A lot of people didn't like that stuff he was doing," Auset reminded Kerry. "Not those rich crackers trying to buy out the city. You know at the height of the recession they was setting us all up."

"What do you mean by that?"

"Mean?" Auset looked at Kerry, surprised by her question. "You don't know? They set it up. What happens when a good man loses his job? He can't pay his mortgage. He loses his home. Funny how when that happened, people showed up with cash, ready to buy those houses. They auctioned off half of Southwest Atlanta on the courthouse steps. Now they got this Beltline coming through the city. New everything. That ain't nothing but the big lockout and lockdown. Black people won't be able to move in this city in ten years without a fucking ankle bracelet on. That's why they wanted to get rid of Mayor Taylor." Auset looked into Kerry's eyes. "He was in the way."

"I don't think it was that deep. Yes, he was bumping heads with some folks, Governor Cade and those guys, but it was just politics as usual," Kerry said.

"Politics as usual? Is that what got Ras killed?" Auset asked, bringing up Jamison's old Morehouse roommate who'd become a community activist and was working with Jamison on some projects to get scholarships for college-bound black males from Atlanta's poorest neighborhoods. He'd been mysteriously gunned down after Jamison denied an indirect order from the governor to end the program in favor of labor-training initiatives he'd wanted to institute for black males in the city.

It was a sobering moment for Kerry. She knew Alfred Jenkins from the Atlanta University Center before he was "Ras" Baruti, before he'd grown out his dreadlocks and became a leader of local grassroots organizations. Though she and Jamison had already split when Jamison and Ras started working together, she didn't believe any of the charges the district attorney came up with to put Ras behind bars before he was killed. They'd painted him as a drug kingpin and an arms dealer.

For the first time, Kerry picked up that little dot and connected it to the line of dots leading to her current situation.

"What happened to Ras didn't have anything to do with what happened to Jamison," Kerry said, though she was really just thinking aloud.

"That's what they want you to believe, sis. But that's not what the people believe. We—and by 'we' this time I mean black people, conscious people, the community—know why they killed Ras. Why they wanted to kill Jamison."

Kerry got up from the bench and looked toward the door leading back into the jail. It was almost time for her to be in the kitchen to help start dinner service. But that wasn't why she'd suddenly felt prickled and wanted to go inside. She'd heard all of this before. When Ras died, there was a whole grassroots movement mobilizing that painted pictures of Ras and Jamison like they were starting some new Black Panther Party. There were even rumors that they'd both joined some militant organization that had camps in Israel, Cuba, even Venezuela. To Kerry, this was just as much of a myth as the idea Auset was sharing about "the man" and that old, haunting "they" who were out there trying to enact genocide on any black person with a brain.

"Look, I'm happy you believed in Jamison. He really did enjoy being mayor and if he'd stayed in office I know he would've done some good, but there is no 'they' in his case," Kerry said in her corporate voice. "I was there when he died. And there wasn't any 'they' up there on the roof. It was his past. That's what killed Jamison. His past. Saw it with my own eyes."

"But what if I told you your eyes haven't been made to see things the way they really are? That you're asleep to everything that's really going on? You've been programmed?"

"Programmed? Right." Kerry laughed like Auset had said something that was totally ludicrous. She started heading toward the door. "Maybe you and the sistren should stop smuggling weed into the jail. Makes you do and say crazy things, you know?" Kerry smiled at Auset once more and turned her back. "Programmed?" she repeated, still laughing. "Right."

After dinner, Garcia-Bell was in Kerry's cell. They were talking and laughing in what had become a kind of nightly routine since Kerry's fight with Thompson. Their once-convenient friendship had taken on a new depth and on some nights anyone listening outside the door might think the women were at an adult slumber party. They mostly chatted about their mothers. Their dreams. How their mothers had ruined their dreams. Talking to Garcia-Bell, Kerry remembered how badly she'd wanted to be a doctor. That she'd had her heart set on Cornell Medical School and when she didn't get in, she was crushed. So much so that she could hardly get out of bed. And though Jamison had gotten into Cornell, he decided to stay in Atlanta to wait for her. Garcia-Bell wanted to own a trucking fleet. Five or six haulers moving whatever from wherever to someplace else. She'd been a certified truck driver for ten years. She had a business plan and all the contacts she needed. But her criminal record made financing her own truck impossible.

Though the talks were quite therapeutic and actually often the highlight of Kerry's day—not that there was much competition there—there were some odd things she was noticing about her blossoming friendship with Garcia-Bell. Although they often talked about past loves, Garcia-Bell never sexed her lovers. It was never "him" or "he" and always "they" and "them." This wasn't a surprise to Kerry. Looking at Garcia-Bell's muscles and mannish way of taking up space and even hearing her voice, purposefully gruff and decidedly confident, it was pretty obvious to Kerry that she was not only a lesbian, but also a masculine lesbian—in Kerry's mind she'd identified Garcia-Bell as the "man" in any lesbian relationship she had.

Kerry really didn't care, though. She didn't have a slew of debutantes and sorors waiting to chat her up in her jail cell each night. She just wondered if Garcia-Bell thought she knew, how long she was going to hold out saying what she was, and if she ever intended on coming out to Kerry. Well, maybe she was already out of the closet. With those bright circus-themed tattoos of naked women on her arms, she certainly wasn't in the closet. Still, Kerry was willing to pretend she didn't see all of that until Garcia-Bell gave her some indication she wanted to be open about her sex life. But she knew it couldn't be far off. Because there was also the matter of how long the slumber sessions were lasting. That Garcia-Bell would wait until the very last call for bed before she'd leave Kerry's side. And she'd be grinning and giggling like a little boy leaving his girlfriend when she did. Things had gotten pretty awkward on some nights when Kerry had to break down and just say, "Go to bed," in her own gruff voice. They couldn't continue on like that much longer. Someone would have to say something soon.

"The crazy part was that she was dead serious. I looked into her eyes and I could see she believed what she was saying," Kerry said in the middle of retelling her account of what happened on the jail yard that afternoon with Auset. She was lying across the bed and Garcia-Bell was sitting on the edge. "It's like she's painting Jamison to be some kind of martyr. She actually called me Betty Shabazz. Can you believe that?" Kerry chuckled.

"She ain't too far from what other people be saying. On one of the video blogs on YouTube some guy calling himself 'the Green Pill' said Jamison was alive. A lot of people saying that now," Garcia-Bell revealed.

Kerry pushed up on her elbows and looked at her as the woman in the cell beside hers walked past, staring into Kerry's cell.

"People are saying he's not dead?" Kerry repeated.

"Just crazy rumors that people spotted him on One Hundred and Twenty-Fifth Street. One guy said he had a video of him," Garcia-Bell added.

"Was it him?" Kerry asked before she could remind herself that there was no way it could be.

"No. It was some dude who looked more like Fifty Cent," Garcia-Bell revealed, referring to the hip-hop star who had muscles like armor and a tough demeanor that Jamison had lost long ago.

The women laughed.

"I guess Jamison would like being compared to Fifty Cent," Kerry said. "Could you imagine if that fool was really alive? If he was hanging out on One Hundred and Twenty-Fifth Street in Harlem looking like Fifty Cent while I was in here just . . . dying?" Kerry looked off.

"Don't get all fucked up about it now. It's just people talking. You know that. I only watch the shit online because there's nothing else to do in the computer lab," Garcia-Bell said. "And whatever Auset was saying was that jail-yard talk. People in here blow things all the way up to make themselves look better. By the time they finish with a story, they can make themselves look like Martin Luther King or somebody."

After a long pause, Kerry said softy, "The thing is, she wasn't talking about herself; she was talking about me."

"Let's go with that, then. We can drop all that stuff about Jamison being in Harlem and just say the government or somebody else killed him because he was trying to help black people or something. Right? Isn't that what Auset was getting at? What then? What does that have to do with you?"

"I don't know." Kerry thought about it for a second. "I guess it would explain why I can't seem to get out of this place." She remembered her conversation with Lebowski. Everything he'd said about no one taking his calls and feeling like he was swimming upstream to be slaughtered. Then there was Jamison before he died and all of his suspicions about the governor. How he'd had Governor Cade locked up and hours later Jamison was dead and Kerry was in jail. "I mean, what if they framed me? They did it and they framed me"

"You really think so?" Garcia-Bell asked.

"Hell no!" Kerry laughed suddenly. "That's crazy. Crazy as hell." She looked at Garcia-Bell, who was clearly following along with her analysis. "I can't believe you were falling for it too. I thought you were the one telling me to focus."

Garcia-Bell laughed with Kerry, but really she was thinking that with everything she'd been reading about Jamison and Kerry online in the computer lab, what Kerry just said made sense. She'd only lied about one thing—her little Internet research had nothing to do with boredom. It made her feel closer to Kerry. Like maybe she understood her or could connect with her beyond the concrete walls and metal bars that ironically put them together.

"I'll tell you just like I told crazy-Auset: I was there—remember! I saw everything that morning. And there wasn't any white man or government in sight," Kerry said.

"Then who was?" Garcia-Bell asked.

"Coreen. I told you before. And I've told everyone else. Coreen was the person on that roof who threw Jamison over. Coreen."

The lights in the hallway flickered and quickly there was the sound of the footsteps of inmates returning to their cells before the final call for lights-out on the entire ward.

Garcia-Bell, of course, stayed in place on the edge of Kerry's bed, but Kerry poked her head out of the bunk to catch a glimpse of her neighbor spying again.

"All right. I'll see you tomorrow," Kerry started. "I'm turning in. Kind of tired."

"Tired? From what?"

"The day. Dealing with Auset and all of this. My brain is fried," Kerry complained. "I'll just see you tomorrow."

Garcia-Bell looked down at Kerry on the bed like a child about to throw a tantrum.

"Okay? I'll see you tomorrow," Kerry said jovially to hide the good-bye tension. "Okay?"

The lights flickered again, signaling that all inmates had about five minutes to make it to their cells.

"Okay," Garcia-Bell agreed finally, avoiding Kerry's eyes as she stood to head toward the door. "Tomorrow." She walked out without turning back to wave at her, something Kerry hadn't seen her do before.

When Garcia-Bell was a good ways down the hall, Kerry's neighbor showed up on her threshold, holding her hands on her hips and grinning.

"What are you smiling about?" Kerry asked, sitting back up on her elbows.

"You. Wondering how long you're going to torture that woman. You know what she wants. And I suspect you ain't about to give it to her," the woman said, shaking her head. "You're like a man stringing a woman along. Or a woman using a man. I swear, I see everything in here. Can't wait to get out." She turned back toward her cell and walked out.

Chapter 7

"Been a while."

The first wife was standing in the corner of the room, leering over at the second wife sitting at a table. The tension was too thick between them. Guards standing by whispered and watched for any signs of contention.

"Been too long. Too damn long."

"I've been—"

"No. Don't say it. Please don't say anything about why it's been as long as it's been. Let's just admit what it is and then . . . that's all." Kerry had cut Val off and sat back, annoyed and speechless, in her seat.

And these were two people who were supposed to be on the same team. They were, after all, sitting in the private visitation room where inmates commonly met with counsel.

After a while, Val said rather dismissively, "You think I want to be doing this? Doing any of this? But—" She looked around at the walls, with indistinguishable globs of this and stains of that decorating each cinder block.

Kerry cut Val off again. "Exactly, so you admit it. You don't care. And that's all there is to it. We can stop this right now."

She looked like she was about to get up, but she still needed to hear something else from her visitor.

The point no one would attack was this: Kerry thought Val was slacking at busting her out of jail and saving her ass. But Val thought she was doing the best she could, seeing as how part of her focus actually had to be on saving her own ass.

So what was all of the abstract talk about, then? Perhaps each woman was still trying to play with her cards held close to her chest, to gather the true position of the one who was once on the opposition. It was a sticky and stinky situation. But neither could walk away. Each had to sit and play. Kerry had her reasons. Val had her reasons.

"But . . ." Val continued from where Kerry had cut her off "I'm not going to walk away. I'm not going to just let this go." Val looked sharply at Kerry. "I meant what I said to you. I'm getting you out of here. Look, I know I've done some fucked-up shit in the past, but I keep my word—right or wrong. That has never changed about me. And you know it. I owe you. I owe you big-time. And I'm going to pay you back for what you did for me. I'm going to get you out of here."

Kerry sat back in her seat, caught off guard. What Val owed her was the only bond the two women shared. When Val was at her weakest, Kerry gave her the words to make herself strong. She'd showed up at the women's outreach center where Kerry was volunteering. Jamison had just kicked her out and Val realized something no woman who'd been put out ever wanted to admit: She had nowhere to go. Nowhere at all. And no plan. One of her old friends had told her about the Hell Hath No Fury House and when she pulled up out front she found *HHNFH* etched into a wooden sign hanging over a refurbished Queen Anne, with a huge porch decorated with potted flowers and swings and other beautiful things softer women might like looking at. When Val walked inside, shaking in her sadness and desperation, she assumed Kerry would turn her nose up at her as she always had in the past. Kerry was the first wife who'd earned the stripes, but lost the war. Val was the second wife who'd plotted and planned and eventually became prey. Served her right. Right? Kerry didn't follow suit with this belief pattern, though. She gave Val tissues for her tears. She gave Val a seat. She listened. She helped Val like she was any other woman in need—just as someone else had once treated Kerry. She said softly to Val, "Now is the time for you to stand up for yourself. Time for you to be a woman." It was the kind of grace a girl from the poorest part of Memphis hardly knew. She had to pay Kerry back for that.

"I spoke to Lebowski," Kerry said, remembering her conversation with the lawyer. "He doesn't seem hopeful. Feels like he's giving up on me." Kerry looked down at her chipped nails and the orange jumpsuit, which was no longer looking foreign on her frame that had once modeled Stella McCartney, Kate Spade, and Donna Karan in socialite circles where jailhouse meetings were the butt of the joke. She looked at Val's designer shoes and couldn't guess the brand. Maybe Prada. The suit was Hermès. Too much for visiting someone at a jail. It let Kerry know Val still thought she had something to prove.

"He says he's stuck. Says he can't get anywhere," Val added, echoing exactly what Lebowski had told Kerry on the phone.

"You think he's telling the truth?"

"I don't think he's lying. I've been trying to talk to people too. All I get is lip service," Val revealed. "Remember those news spots I was able to book last month to keep your name in the media? Well, they've all dried up. No one will even answer my calls."

"I don't get it. We all know who did this. And she's getting away with murder." Kerry's voice grew louder, where someone else would've whispered *murder*.

"I used to think that too, Kerry. I used to agree, but there ain't much evidence against her."

"You're starting to sound like them," Kerry said.

"No, I'm starting to sound like someone who's paying attention."

"To what?"

"The facts, Kerry. The facts." Val uncrossed her legs and inched her chair closer into the table. "I hate Coreen like the next bitch, and I know how much hell she was giving Jamison before he died. But, come on: There is solid proof that she wasn't there when he was killed."

"I saw her!" Kerry slapped the table with each word.

"You saw someone. You saw something. But I don't think it was her. Ever wonder why out of everyone who testified about who they saw on the roof that day, you're the only one who is certain it was Coreen? Everyone else switches back and forth, saying it was a man or a woman, or you or Coreen, or some people even said it was just a bird up there."

"It was her," Kerry growled.

"You want it to be her," Val offered sympathetically. "But it's like she said, she hated Jamison for what he'd done to her, but killing him wouldn't do anything but hurt her situation. Maybe you don't get that thinking, but I understand it. I get it."

"What do you mean, 'like she said'?" Kerry asked.

Val had to admit to something she hadn't exactly planned on telling Kerry. She told her about Coreen contacting her for money and threatening to go to the press.

"So, she's in Atlanta now? Is the boy here?" There was a little jealousy in Kerry's voice.

"I don't know. I don't care, so I didn't ask."

"I need to talk to my mother. I need to make sure Tyrian is safe." Kerry's voice was weighted with worry then.

"It's just about the money. I spoke to her; she's not trying to do anything stupid," Val explained.

"Val, listen. You can't trust that woman. I saw her myself. She's crazy. What she did to try to steal Jamison from me . . ." Kerry trailed off.

"Who hasn't done some crazy shit to get a man's attention?" Val asked. "So, she went a little screwball. That doesn't make her a killer. And I've been thinking. What Lebowski needs to get you off is someone else for the DA to put behind bars. If it's not Coreen, then who else could it be? Who else could've hated Jamison enough to do this?"

"You'd know better than me. You were with him then," Kerry said halfheartedly, still not convinced they really needed to have this conversation. "And from what I saw from far away, it seems like we could just give out numbers at the mall. Who didn't hate him? Jamison made a lot of the wrong kinds of enemies before he died."

"I mean plausible killers—people who could actually have done it." Val remembered her ex-boyfriend Keet threatening vicious retaliation against Jamison or Val in an attempt to cover up some of the dirty deeds the crooked cop had done for Governor Cade. As worthy of a candidate for murder as Keet was, like Cade and the rest of his cronies, he had the best alibi in the world the night Jamison had been killed: He was in jail. Also, Keet wasn't the kind of guy to dress up like a woman to kill a man. He'd want everyone to know his work. Want all of the credit and fame. If he'd done it, the streets would be talking. But, at that point, there'd been no word about Keet.

As if she'd been reading Val's mind, Kerry started slowly, "I've been hearing stuff in here about the government. People saying Jamison was some kind of martyr. That he was assassinated."

Val looked at Kerry like the jail had become an insane asylum. "You mean like Tupac or Biggie Smalls? Or like Malcolm or Martin?" Val asked carefully, like she was evaluating Kerry's sanity.

"Don't do me like that," Kerry said, picking up on it. "I'm serious. *They're* serious."

"They who?" Val whispered.

"The other inmates."

Val looked away and pursed her lips like she was trying to stop herself from saying something.

"I know. I know," Kerry said. "I was just talking to Garcia-Bell and she's also heard of—"

"Garcia-who? Who's that?" Val asked.

"She's my friend. And she said she's been looking online and that people—a lot of people—do see Jamison as a martyr and some even think he's alive. Like, alive and living in Harlem," Kerry blurted out.

"No, Kerry," Val said. "No. You don't make friends in jail. And you don't listen to anything anyone says online."

"I know, but—"

"There's no *but*," Val cut in. "No *but* at all. Yes, I've heard that crazy talk about the CIA killing Jamison because he had some great ideas for the people of Atlanta. And you know what that is? It's just what I called it: crazy talk. So what if Jamison was going to start some program with Ras? Who gives a shit? It wasn't going to change a thing."

"But Jamison had a voice and people were listening—"

"For real, you're sounding like those crazy folks saying the FBI killed Tupac because he was rapping about serious stuff in his lyrics. Really? You're smarter than this. It's that 'back to Africa' and hate-on-whitey bullshit that hasn't gotten black folks anywhere. It's that shit Ras was talking about. And you saw what it got his ass. Dead."

Tears came to Kerry's eyes and she tried to look off, ashamed at how desperate she was sounding.

"I'm trying. I really am. I just don't know. You know?" Kerry cried, crumbling under the pressure of her own questions of mental strength and clarity.

Val thought to reach across the table to grab Kerry's hand to comfort her, but she didn't. She just watched her crumbling. This was the woman who'd once laughed at Val. A woman who, no matter what she did or how she did it, would still be more respected than Val. In those seconds, watching those tears come down Kerry's cheeks, Val's friendly focus was clouded with something that tasted like revenge at the back of her tongue.

"I need more money," she said suddenly and thus getting to the point of her visit.

Kerry stopped consoling herself to lift her head and repeat, "Money? For what?"

"The case."

"But Lebowski's been paid. He's not expecting more money until next month."

"I'm thinking of getting a detective," Val explained.

"Lebowski has his own detectives on it. Right?" Kerry pointed out.

"You're the one who questioned if he's working hard enough."

"And you're the one who said everything was fine. You said you trusted him."

"Fine," Val said flatly. "If you don't want to do it, we don't have to."

Kerry wiped her cheeks to remove any traces of tears before the guards came to take her back to her cell.

"How much?" she asked, frustrated. "How much do you need?"

"Just ten thousand now," Val offered, giving the minimum amount she'd promised to pony up for Coreen when she'd spoken to her again in an angry telephone exchange following the Buckhead Diner meeting. "That'll be enough to get us started. We'll talk about more later."

Soon the guards came to get Kerry and after a quick and detached embrace, Val was left sitting in the room, alone. As she reached for her purse, she spread her prospects before her like a deck of playing cards. Weighing options. Predicting scenarios. While she was feeling a little twinge of guilt about what she was doing, she reminded herself that the promise she was keeping with Kerry was pleasure. And then there was business.

When Val walked out of the jail, her phone was out of her purse and pressed against her ear.

"Coreen. Let's meet. I have the money," she said after a nondescript voice informed her that the person she was trying to reach wasn't available and instructed her to leave a message on the voice mail.

She moved the phone from her ear and exhaled before putting it back into her purse. She kept telling herself that these were the kinds of decisions she had to make. The kinds of things she had to do. *Val* had to look out for *Val*.

When she stepped off the sidewalk at the head of the parking lot to walk toward her car, every street-smart sense Val had told her someone was watching her. She looked back over both shoulders and then just stopped walking altogether to survey her surroundings. There was nothing out of place or out of the ordinary: A mother walking toward the jail with a baby in a stroller. A bus loading passengers at the back of the parking lot. People getting in and out of cars. Val finally told herself it was nothing, but as soon as she took a new step a car sped to the front of the lot where she was and stopped behind her. It was one of those black Chargers police officers had started driving in the city years ago.

Val got angry quickly and was about to slap the hood of the car to let the officer know he'd almost run her over. But then the window came down and Leaf, the agent who'd worked undercover with Jamison, poked his head out.

"Leaf?"

"Get in the car. Get in right now," Leaf said.

"Where have you been? I've been calling you."

"Just get in the car," Leaf ordered then, rushing and looking over his shoulders.

Val was never one to be rushed or to ignore her own suspicion. Seeing the worry in Leaf's eyes, she pulled her purse in closer to her body and considered what he might be searching for over his shoulders.

"Trust me," Leaf offered evenly, trying to steady the nervousness in his voice. "Just get in the car."

"Fuck," Val cursed, rushing to the passenger-side door.

When she got in, Leaf pressed his foot to the gas pedal with such force, Val looked out the back window to see if someone was chasing him.

"What are you doing? Where are we going?" Val asked as the car raced out of the parking lot and into traffic.

"Nowhere. I'm just trying to make sure no one's tailing me." Leaf effortlessly whipped the Charger between lanes of traffic.

"Why would anyone be tailing you?" Sitting upright and facing Leaf, Val ignored the blare of the signal in the car instructing her to put her seat belt on. The collar of his business shirt was up and open and the sides of an undone tie flanked his shoulders. His hair was wet with what was obviously sweat, as Val could see droplets trickling down the back of his right ear.

Leaf ignored Val's questioning and zipped through lanes until he sped right through a red light at a busy intersection, where other drivers honked their horns in protest of the risky move.

"See anyone?" Leaf asked.

"No! No!" Val looked out the window, though she wasn't really sure what she was looking for. "No!"

Leaf drove a mile at top speed and turned onto a one-lane, cobblestone side street.

"Look, I know this cops-and-robbers shit turns on some of the girls you date, but it's not for me," Val joked as the car slowed. "Besides, I thought you *were* the cops, Leaf. Are we looking for the robbers?" Val added, looking at Leaf who was still searching over his shoulder.

"I need to tell you something. And I need to know that what I'm saying will stay between us." Leaf pulled into a space in front of a closed-down shoe store.

"What's it about? Jamison?"

Leaf looked at Val and nodded. She'd changed so much since he'd met her when he started working undercover as Jamison's assistant, just before Jamison married Val. Then, she was all fake nails and fake hair. Had an unapologetic bitterness about her and her ways that made him think she'd be nothing but trouble for Jamison. He was right. She was trouble. But she'd tried so hard not to be. He watched. She really did try. But she wasn't the kind of person who could be successful at escaping drama. All the cases he'd worked in all his years at the Bureau, he knew her type; he knew her well. As such, Leaf had preferred not to bring his news to Val. But with Kerry, his old ally, behind bars, he didn't have many other ears willing to listen and he wasn't sure how much longer he could go poking his head around in places and files where it shouldn't be without getting caught . . . or worse.

"Of course, you can tell me. Come on. You know where I'm from. You know how I get down. I won't—"

"Just promise me. Just promise me you'll at least keep things secret until the time is right to make a move."

In Leaf's panicked words, Val discovered the depth of the information he was prepared to share, and so she looked out the window again for an anonymous foe.

"I promise," she said soberly.

"Kerry's being framed."

Halfway through a plate of pepper ribs at Daddy O's with Delgado the other day, Leaf had heard himself "talking." Leaf realized he was giving information to someone who wanted him to expose, to reveal said information—in the Bureau, they called that "talking." In the Academy, he learned that there were three ways to get someone to talk: force, interview, talk. His lunch date had employed the latter tactic; Delgado was talking to Leaf to get Leaf to talk. But why? For what?

Leaf noticed the predicament when Delgado asked if he'd heard anything from Kerry. If she was making friends in jail. Talking to anyone about what happened. How she'd killed Jamison. These questions struck him, because while no one would suspect it, the other agents often indulged each other in the ongoings of each other's cases, almost as if they were soap opera narratives. However, Delgado seldom engaged. In fact, as Leaf spoke, he considered that he couldn't ever remember Delgado chatting him up about one of his cases. He was always talking about his family or some new BBQ joint, his high blood pressure, and his many exploits cheating on his wife. He also noted that Delgado was just insisting that Kerry killed Jamison. No agent in the Bureau could or would look at the public information out about the case and make such a finite judgment call. That meant Delgado was on the inside and likely sharing and trying to push an idea those on the inside wanted those on the outside to believe: Kerry was guilty.

Leaf didn't bother telling Val about all of this. Another thing civilians wouldn't ever suspect about agents was how often these kinds of internal infractions occurred. An agent's loyalty was to the department and the department alone. Not his comrades. Not his government. Not his country. Not his president. His mother, father, wife, son, or daughter. The department was where his truth began and ended and he could turn on any of the people beneath it and in the name of it at any time. Delgado getting him to talk was hardly a secret to share. It was the job.

The secret Leaf did tell Val was what he discovered when he decided Delgado's digging would require his own.

"The FBI had been watching Kerry way before we started our case on Jamison. Had files on her, taps on her phones, video. Some surveillance even included my initial meetings with her," Leaf said, informing Val of what his contact had discovered when he paid him to hack into Delgado's computer, break into his office, and search his files. "I didn't know we were being taped. I didn't know there was a separate investigation going on."

"An investigation? About Kerry? You have to be kidding me," Val said, covering her mouth in surprise. "What's in the file? Pictures of her having tea at Mary Mac's?"

"It started with her mother. She hired a hit man."

Val had lowered her hand, but there it was back up at her mouth again in surprise. "What?"

"Thirjane Jackson had contacted an undercover agent to have him kill Jamison. The Bureau has evidence to back this up and they were about to arrest her, but just before she was about to confirm a price and a date and time for the services to take place—the confirmation of intent we needed to make an arrest—she pulled out. Just like that. Stopped answering the agent's calls," Leaf explained as he mentally reviewed each of the copied files he'd been forwarded. "The agents thought they'd lost her. That she wasn't going to go through with it. But they kept up surveillance. And then weeks later, she hooked up with another guy." Leaf turned to Val. "And he didn't work for us. He isn't an agent. She hired him."

"She had Jamison killed?" Val felt like she'd been dragged down a really long and dark tunnel and then suddenly thrust into daylight. On many drunken nights, Jamison had told her about how much Thirjane hated him. That she was the one who vowed his marriage to her daughter would never last. That she'd been the one to whisper in his ear during a dance at their wedding, "You're her *first* husband."

"Actually, no, Thirjane did not have Jamison killed," Leaf said to Val. "Well, she thinks she did, but someone else got to it before her guy could. He's a real screwball, this guy. Took her money and has her thinking he was the one who did it, but he wasn't anywhere near the day of the incident."

"How do you know that? How do they know that?"

"He was in jail. Got picked up for driving with a suspended license, of all things. We wanted to hold him, but by the time he posted his own bail, Jamison had already been thrown from that roof."

"So you're telling me Kerry's mama thinks she had Jamison killed by some hit man, when he didn't even do it? He didn't finish the job?" Val laughed tensely at the absurdity and then sat in thoughts of Thirjane's constant frown and perfectly manicured, wrinkled hands. "So how did Kerry end up in jail? Do they think she did it?"

"No way. From what I can see looking at her surveillance, Kerry hasn't made a move indicating it was even possible."

"Then how'd she end up behind bars?"

"Isn't that the question we're all asking?" Leaf looked out

his rearview mirror and said softly, "Many ways of reading it. Many possibilities. None of which has to be that she's guilty."

"What?"

"It could be that they're waiting for Thirjane to turn herself in to get Kerry off. Maybe she hired someone else who went under the radar."

"For three months? They've been waiting for three months? Had this woman in jail that long? I mean, isn't it obvious at this point that if Thirjane was involved, she's not exactly about to give herself up for her daughter?" Val remembered how distant Thirjane had been about Kerry's case. She'd hardly spoken to the attorney and refused to go speak with media outlets to plead for Kerry's release, which was the lawyer's first suggestion and what he believed worked.

"Then there's the other possibility." Leaf turned to Val. "That it's a cover-up."

"For what?"

"Well, that's not exactly going to be in the file. That's going to require more . . . information gathering. Could be Governor Cade. Could be a number of things. Jamison had his hands in many places. Some I knew about and some I didn't. I'm realizing that now."

A black car with black tinted windows rolled past slowly and Val and Leaf's eyes were set on it until it was well up the street and stopped to let a woman and her dog out on the corner.

"Val, is there anything you noticed about Jamison's actions before he died, any information you have that you haven't shared with me or anyone else that you can think of?" Leaf asked. "And it could be anything. Something small that seemed odd, but could be explained away. Even something that's come up since his death."

Val scratched her temple and attempted to rub away tension gathering in her brow.

"You know how he was with me. You saw." She looked away from Leaf. "Always held me out so far. He was so secretive. Always. I can't say if those were the signs of a man hiding something. Or someone who just wasn't in love."

Had the situation been different and the lie Val wanted to believe about her marriage been true, Leaf might have reached over the console, grabbed her hand, and told her she was wrong—Jamison really did love her. But there could be none of that. There just wasn't anything nice to say. No comforting words.

Leaf actually leaned away before he repeated, "It could be anything" and gave Val some time to think.

"Nothing," Val said after a long while, where she rediscovered how little she'd really known about the man she'd loved so desperately. He'd let her in a little and then locked her all the way out, where she'd stand thirsting for any little bit of him until he saw fit to open the door again.

"Well, you can think about it some more and let me know," Leaf said. "In the meantime, I'm going to start looking into some other things. I just figured that maybe you'd know something. None of us are as mysterious as we think. We always leave clues. It's just a matter of paying attention. And I know you were. I know you—" He paused and patted Val on the shoulder awkwardly, but also earnestly. "I know you loved him," he said.

Leaf drove Val back to her car as he explained his next steps and clued her in on why he'd had to speak to her. He sensed some fear or desperation in Delgado's voice at lunch. That meant he didn't have everything he needed, but needed to close in on something soon. Val's name was mentioned in some of his notes. Delgado had been watching her. Leaf didn't want her to get caught up in the dragnet when things went down. If she helped him, if he could get her on his team, maybe he could make something happen to keep everyone safe, to get Kerry off and burst the case wide open. Get all the angles out in the open. Find out who or what the big boogeyman was behind the thing. And all of this could be for a good cause. To save the world. Or save someone. He'd grown close to Kerry when he was working with her undercover and even at least understood Val for what she was. It should be for them. But it wasn't. Deep down on Leaf's scorecard there was a check he needed to settle. If something wasn't right with this case, then something couldn't be right with his conclusion. It meant his resolution, his solution, and ascension were all a lie. He wasn't the kind of man who could sit in that and just be okay with it. Not if the lie was on his scorecard. He could be loyal to the Bureau, but if the Bureau wanted him to settle on a lie, then the Bureau wasn't being loyal to him. So then all bets were off.

Chapter 8

The same big, black truck that had been parked outside of Jamison's home was sitting in the driveway when Val got home. She jumped out of her car and stormed over to the door, so angry she could spit on whoever was sitting inside, but there was no one there.

Val switched her spiky stare from the car to the front door of the house and stomped up the walkway with the keys in her hand, pointed forward like a sharp knife ready to do some cutting.

Inside, she heard talking and laughing coming from the kitchen. It sounded like something delightful was happening and every echo of noise struck a sorrowful chord in her gut. It felt like she was being cheated. Like something inside of her was being stolen away.

Mama Fee was sitting at the kitchen table in an orange-and-tan caftan with a matching head wrap atop her head. She looked like a high priestess or maybe a genie. Her legs were crossed and she was holding a cup of steaming tea in her hand. One pinky pointed up. Smiling, grinning at who was seated across from her.

The man who drove the truck, who begged to sleep one more night in Val's bed and kept his promise of not seeking sex, was hunched into the table toward Mama Fee, talking like he knew who this woman was, like he was supposed to be there and this was a ritual. A cup of steaming tea was sitting on the table in front of him.

Val stood in the threshold and surveyed this picture. She knew they sensed her standing there. But they kept talking and laughing, trading these little intimate stares that let on that the visit wasn't brand new.

"What is this?" Val quizzed sharply, tossing her purse on the counter with a *thud*.

Mama Fee and Ernest turned to the doorway connecting the living room to the kitchen and displayed their best looks of surprise under Val's glare.

"Hey, baby girl," Mama Fee said sweetly, like Val had just walked in from getting off of the school bus and had twin pigtails dangling over her shoulders. She turned to Ernest, who was grinning, and added, "Did I tell you my Val is my baby girl? She got two sisters home in Memphis. Neither one is as pretty as—"

"Shut up!" Val barked at Mama Fee, but her stare was on Ernest. "What are you doing here?"

"Came to visit you. Your mother was kind enough to let me in. Made me some tea. What's this tea called, Mama Fee?" Ernest smiled wide at Val and then turned to his new ally.

Val could smell the Adam and Eve root and hibiscus leaves.

"Just some roots from the garden," Mama Fee answered. "You want some, Val? Why don't you come over here and have a seat?"

Val felt four eyes set on her with heavy expectation. Like she was a skittish horse or feral cat needing to be gathered in, in, in.

"No, I don't want any tea! I want you out of here—out of this house!" Val said, looking at Ernest.

"Why he need to leave?" Mama Fee asked, like this was the most absurd directive she'd ever heard. "He was just telling me about his days playing football and how he retired from sports altogether to start his very own trucking business." She smiled at Ernest like he was a piece of cake she was about to put on a plate and present to her daughter. Before Val had gotten there, she'd already recited Genesis 2:18 to the man as she'd served him the tea. His impression on her had been that strong.

"Mama, shut up. You never should've let him into this house," Val charged, pointing her finger at Mama Fee.

"Damn, you need to stop talking to your mother like that," Ernest said, getting up from his seat and half-empty cup of tea. "Now, if you want me to leave, I will, but ain't no reason to speak to this sweet woman like this."

"Good. Great. Get the fuck out," Val said, clearly unaffected by Ernest's valiant effort to defend her mother's honor.

Ernest turned and bowed slightly to Mama Fee in her caftan and turban. "It's been a lovely afternoon. Until we meet again?"

"That'll never, never, never happen!" Val cut in before her mother could answer. "Now get out!" She'd stepped into the kitchen and came up behind Ernest with fists balled at her sides.

A series of slurs shot from Val's mouth at Ernest's back as she stayed tight on his heels, following him out of the kitchen, through the living room and into the front foyer. Mama Fee knew not to go along for the sad stroll or else Val would turn on her too. She just sat in the kitchen, sipping her tea and listening. Soon, she'd grab the teacup Ernest had been holding and set it on her altar upstairs.

Old folk would say Val had called Ernest "everything but a

child of God" on the way to the front door. Still, the behemoth of a man kept his mouth closed and, more importantly, his hand in his pockets, because these were fighting words, clauses, and phrases that had led many men to wrap their hands around a quick-tongued woman's mouth, push her into a wall, and holler, "Shut the fuck up!" But Ernest was unmoved.

Annoyed that her words weren't leading to a response, Val said, "You ain't got to say shit! You ain't fooling nobody with this good-guy shit! You're up to something, just like every other nigga!" right when Ernest had his hand on the doorknob in the front foyer.

He stopped.

Val stopped behind him.

He paused.

She looked at his hand on the knob with more expectation and desire than she was willing to admit. When she was little, she'd memorized every angle and curve of the front doorknob in the home she'd grown up in. She'd sit on the creaky wooden floor, her knees held into her chest, just feet away from the door, and wait for the knob to turn. In her mind, in her imagination, always on the other side of the knob would be her father's brown, rough, workingman's hand. He'd push the door in. The sunlight would make a crown around his head and so Val couldn't really see him until he'd get up close on her. But she could hear him saying, "I'm home, baby girl. Back from the dead, just for you. Not ever leaving again. Nothing no one can do to make your daddy leave you." He'd pick her up and kiss her cheeks and count her fingers and toes like the white people did their newborn babies on television. Take her into the kitchen, where a table filled with different kinds of ice cream would be waiting for a feast that would end with laughing and full bellies.

"What you waiting on?" Val said to Ernest. "Open the door! Leave! Leave!"

Ernest was about to turn the knob. He really was. But something made him stop.

"Why you so fucked up?" he asked, looking at Val over his shoulder. He turned to her.

"Shut up and get out!"

"Who did this to you?"

"Shut the fuck up and get the hell out!"

As Val spoke, Ernest spoke beneath her. "Can't you see what I'm trying to do? Why I'm here? I want you. I'm here for you. Nothing else."

"You know what?" Val was saying over Ernest's words. "You want to know why I'm so fucked up?"

"Why?"

"Because of niggas like you. Niggas. I'm so fucking tired of this shit I don't know what to fucking do. You say you want me, but for how long? How long? Huh? You don't know me. You don't know where the fuck I been. What the fuck I been through!" Val was screaming so loud her mother had covered her ears in the kitchen and was praying aloud.

"That's what you're missing, Val. I do know you. I know exactly who you are."

"No you don't."

"I do. Look, I didn't know when or how I was going to tell you this but, I knew you before."

"You knew me?"

"We . . . um. When I was playing for the Falcons, we—I slept with you," Ernest admitted, afraid for sure of what Val would do or say next. He hadn't wanted to tell her, but also feared not telling her.

"Get out," Val said bluntly, like all emotion in her had been turned off at the clear mention of the reality of her past.

"I didn't say that to embarrass you. I was just—"

"Get out." She cut him off.

Ernest chose to ignore her again and kept up his explaining.

"I just wanted you to know that I don't care about your past. I have a past too. We all do."

"So I'm your charity case now?" Val posed. "What? Because you slept with me you're supposed to just slide right back in and get it again? Sorry, the kitchen is closed." Val tried to reach past Ernest to open the door, but he blocked her.

"I'm not here to get anything from you. I'm here to give something to you," Ernest said.

"Like what?"

"Well, what do you want?"

Val crossed her arms over her chest like she was holding something in. "I don't know. Okay? That's it. I have no fucking clue. Thought I did. Thought I wanted all of this!" She held her hands up and looked around the foyer. "But now I know it don't mean shit. 'Cause I got it and you know what, the only thing I can think about is that it ain't mine. None of it. Because every time I pull into that driveway in *his* car, I look at this house and think, this is *his* house too. And he ain't even here! He ain't even here!" Val started crying inside, but she wasn't the kind of woman to let those tears pooling up fall to her cheeks—not then and there.

Ernest wrapped his arms over her arms and around her body and pulled her into his chest, where his big frame made her so small, discounting years and years and years of growth and dissipating the sad occurrences on a timeline marked up by a brokenhearted little girl. And he felt that energy transferring into him the way a father does when he kisses his daughter's fresh bruise and causes the crying to instantly cease. It was what he'd felt that first night they'd slept together in that bed upstairs. When Val had finally fallen asleep—not when she'd faked sleeping by closing her eyes and breathing hard through her nose, but when she'd really left the world and her worries—she actually rolled over toward Ernest and threaded her hand through his arm and around his back. She leaned her head into his chest like he was a pillow. Ernest leaned back and slowly moved her body on top of his before wrapping his arms around her waist, making a cradle of himself. Into the night, he laid there still and listened to Val's slow heartbeat. It might have been the most beautiful thing he'd ever felt. The closest he'd ever been to someone. Still, he knew it wasn't for him. It was just for her. All of this pleasure in rest, she needed it. That second night when he'd returned, it was for Val to get some sleep. Not him.

"He may not be here," Ernest said to Val. "But I am."

"But I don't want you to be. Don't you understand? I don't want you to save me. I don't want to be saved. Please just go," Val said, hardly holding onto those tears.

"You really want me to go?" Ernest asked.

There was silence at first.

"Yes," Val answered soon. "Just go."

Ernest released her and backed up to the door. He could see the water in Val's eyes and reached out to cup her cheek.

"I will be back," he said firmly. "When you know you need me, I'll be back."

"Just go," Val repeated with all of the bite out of her tone.

Ernest nodded in defeat and removed his hand from Val's cheek.

As he backed his arm away, Val noticed a symbol of some kind on his inner wrist. It was a big, black square with spikes that looked like daggers on the four corners.

Val grabbed his wrist and turned the palm up, facing her. She'd seen the symbol, but not on him.

"What's this?" she asked.

"What? My tattoo?"

"I see it's a tattoo. What is it?"

"If I tell you, can I stay?" Ernest joked and Val shot her eyes at him like bullets. "Okay, shit. Just playing."

"What is it? Tell me."

"It's the *fihankra*. An *adinkra* symbol. I got it a few years be-fore I left the league. Actually, a couple of the other players got it too," Ernest explained and Val remembered when he'd men-tioned that he used to play for the Falcons.

"Why? Why get this tattoo?"

Ernest looked at the tattoo with Val. "It means protection, security. Every time I look at it, it reminds me that I have to take care of my own—that includes me and everyone I love. No matter what. By any means necessary. Have you seen it be-fore?"

"Yes," Val said, remembering the symbol on some of the paper-work with Jamison's will. "I have."

"Where?"

"I don't think that's any of your business." Val's rigid com-posure returned. She dropped Ernest's wrist and looked at the door.

"I'm going," Ernest said. "You don't have to say it again."

He dropped his head low and turned to walk out, hoping Val would stop him and knowing she wouldn't.

Val slammed the door behind Ernest and walked into the kitchen, ready to fight.

"Why would you let him in here?"

"Child, don't start again. You won the fight. Can't you see? You done drove him away." Mama Fee was standing at the sink, with her hands in the cold water. She'd been waiting for Val to come for her. Underneath her breath, she mumbled, "Drive everyone away from you. That's what you do."

"No. This isn't about me. This is about you letting him in here and you don't even know him. He could've—"

"His name is Ernest and he been here twice. I know him plenty," Mama Fee said, pulling the stopper out of the sink bottom and letting the water rush between her fingers as it headed down the drain.

Val came and stood beside her. Stuck her hip out and leaned into the counter.

"Oh. So you been spying on me now?" she asked, sounding less than flabbergasted by her mother's actions.

"Can't spy on what's done out in the open. May be done at night, but not all of God's creatures go to sleep with the sun." Mama Fee looked at Val. "Besides, somebody got to keep an eye on this doorway. Too many things moving in and out, seen and unseen."

Val remembered Jamison's mother falling to her knees, dying in the stairwell right in front of her after their last fight.

"Well, I don't need you keeping an eye on me or the door. I ain't bring you here for that," Val said. "Not that or Ernest." Val reached into the draining sink and pulled out one of the teacups. "What were you doing, Mama Fee? You trying to put some kind of spell on him? Make him love me? You think he's gonna love me?" she listed sarcastically.

"Can't put a love spell on a man that's already in love," Mama Fee revealed knowingly.

"Please. That nigga just whipped. One night and he thinks he's about to be up on me. Probably broke. Probably saw this house and thought he'd hit the jackpot. Well, he can have it if he wants it so bad, and he can have you too, since y'all so damn close."

Val dropped the cup and walked away from the sink.

"*Obatala! Obatala! Eni Orisa!*" Mama Fee cried out. "Please help my child. Help my blind child to see!"

"Oh, stop with all that shit! Cry out to Obatala, Jesus, Jehovah, whatever and whoever, ain't nothing going to change."

Mama Fee was compelled to rush toward her baby with her finger pointed out at her. "You know what I can't stand about you, girl? You always angry about the broken parts. Can't focus on nothing but what you don't have and what ain't yours. Want something from everybody's plate on your plate. World ain't right unless something wrong. And the worst part is that you can't even see when you got it all. When you got a good thing."

"What's my good thing, Mama Fee?" Val cried, with her tears coming down then. "You? This house? Ernest?" Val laughed like a madwoman. "My dead baby? My dead husband, who didn't even fucking love me? What, Mama Fee? What's my good thing? What can't I see?" Val rushed toward her mother in her anger and the women met in the middle of the floor in a standoff neither of them was expecting, until Val said the words, "My father?"

"Don't you bring up my dead. Now, you called on yours, but mine is resting in peace and I don't reckon he needs to be woke because his child is having some tantrum," Mama Fee said in a rare order to Val.

"Resting in peace? How?" Val asked. "When the people who killed him are out in the world, walking around free and probably got grandkids and retirement homes and Cadillacs? How is he resting in peace?"

"I couldn't do anything about that. You know that. Those white folks: They killed my husband and there wasn't nothing—"

"You could've done something," Val cut in.

"What?"

"Fight," Val said. "Fight! Fight! Fight with more than your roots and herbs and chanting and prayers. Burn down their fucking houses and fight for me!"

Mama Fee was crying at the shame of the past.

"I had you girls. I had to carry on. Had to show you how to move on," Mama Fee defended herself.

"Did we? Did any of us move on?" Val asked, staring into Mama Fee's eyes for an answer. "Two of your daughters are afraid to leave Memphis, one is married to an ex-con, and the other got so many babies neither one of us can name them. And the third—" Val grinned sadly and pointed at herself. "Look at her. Just look at her, Mama Fee!"

An arm straight out, Val cleared everything from the kitchen counter in a fit, sending glasses and silverware and trinkets crashing to the floor. She looked at the damage, turned, and left the room and broken pieces behind. In the middle of the mess was a Post-it note with a number Lorna had taken from a man who'd called the house that morning when Val was away. *Agent Delgado* was written above the name.

Mama Fee hadn't noticed it before, but she felt an itch beneath her left breast and thought she should pick up the little note. She took it upstairs and burned it in a pot with poke root at the foot of her bed.

That night was something like many others for Val, like déjà vu, the "already seen," lived and relived. She'd gotten out late and vowed to stay out until there was some warm body she could find to break the chill on her own. And though that was an accurate accounting of her most recent activities, it wasn't what made the behavior so familiar. The aching that drove her into a pair of killer platform stilettos and the tightest dress with oval cutouts at the hips she could find in the closet, hot pink lipstick and enough eye shadow and concealer to hide the dark circles around her eyes long after midnight, had been riding her for a long time. It always seemed like something wasn't right. Couldn't get right. Be just right. Not for her. And what was she supposed to do about it? Lie in bed all night and think? Cry? Feel? For what? She had to keep moving. And within the four walls with vibrations from an unending stream of music and bodies moving to it all around, just for a little while she wouldn't have to think, cry, or feel anything. She could focus on what she could do to fix things. Numb herself just enough to come up with a plan. Because that's what she needed.

So, she was back at the bar. Well, a bar. This one was in one of those updated, chic lounges that hosted cliques of professionals who preferred to hide the heavy drinking and dirty dancing they'd consider immature or reckless once they exited the city and started making the long drive back to the suburbs, some place more upscale than a nightclub. It was the kind of place where thirtysomething single ladies sat at the bar in boring Ann Taylor LOFT dresses with two layers of shape wear beneath them, praying some "good catch" would speak to them, and fortysomething "good catch" guys walked in with their porky chins up and portly chests poked out, praying some "easy catch" would actually fall for their weak lines. Because of this ironic mix of corporate desperation, the drinks were strong and the service was friendly. Val sat at the bar and turned out toward the room with her third drink in her hand. While this mix of entertainment and attention could usually settle much of what was on Val's mind, she couldn't seem to get herself together that night. Maybe it was the parade of information that strung her through the day. The last twelve-plus hours led her from Kerry to Leaf to Mama Fee and whatever Ernest was. Every situation had a new problem she couldn't solve easily or without guilt. She couldn't understand how she'd actually felt bad about asking Kerry for the ten thousand dollars to pay Coreen. It was what was best for both of them, for all of them. But why was it so heavy on her heart? And just when a few sips made her cover up her feelings with lies or slick sentiments, she'd move on to Leaf and his suspicions about Thirjane and who really killed Jamison. She told herself she didn't care who did it or why, but she wondered. Could feel Jamison's lips on her back and wondered. Why? More sips. More lies and slick sentiments, but then there was Mama Fee and all of the issues Val could never solve between them. She loved her mother as much as she could, as much as she knew how, but it was so much to hate her for, to box on her, to blame. Val knew this was wrong; she always did. But who else could be the punching bag? Who else would know the exact role to play to drag out all of Val's emotions and help her line them up as crosses to bear? It was a dramatic affair that had tired most everyone else in Val's life. Friends. Family. Lovers. It certainly ran Jamison off. But Mama Fee always stuck around. Two more sips and lies about that relationship would come. Then slick sentiments about how bad of a mother Mama Fee was, anyway. Then there was Ernest. And Val needed a shot for that one. Who the hell was he? Who the hell did he think he was? Talking about he'd be back when she needed him. He'd already come back—from the past or whenever. And anyway, she didn't care to remember when or how she'd known him. The point was, she was sending him away again. Why couldn't he get that?

"I see you have some things on your mind, sweetheart," Val heard from behind.

She didn't move, though. Took two breaths before glancing over the wrong shoulder purposefully.

"I'm over here, dear," the voice called in her right ear, sounding surprised at the slow and incorrect reaction. This was a game of patience and anticipation.

"I know where you are," Val said, trying to sound aggravated, annoyed. "I was looking to see if you were maybe talking to someone else. I hoped you were."

Across from Val's seat at the white lacquer bar that looked like it was shipped from some closing nightclub in Miami, was a table filled with white women. She studied them hard to see their reaction to whoever was sitting beside her. One glanced over and then whispered something to her friend, who then glanced over and then whispered something to the woman on her other side. This chain went on until all eyes were on Val's neighbor, each dragging behind them a sliver of thirst and unmistakable interest in the inhabitant. Val knew one of two things must be true about him without even looking: He was either very rich or very famous. She could tell from his voice that he was black. As such, fortune and fame would stand as the only reasons a table full of white women would be looking at him.

"Oh, shit," he joked. "All the women in this club, and I come up to the one who's going through a breakup! Just my luck."

"Please, I haven't been through a breakup since I was sixteen and had Raisinets for tits. Now, I'm full grown. I just cut my losses and move on," Val said, rather seductively.

"Guess my luck is finally paying off, then. I'm Chuck." A light brown hand slid right into Val's point of view, begging for attention and connection.

Val laughed at how easy this game always was and ignored the gesture. Instead, she turned over her right shoulder for a first glance.

Her heart nearly stopped at what she was seeing. That brown hand was connected to a brown body in a blue, moderately priced and poorly tailored suit. The man was handsome, though. The face was familiar. Too familiar.

"What, girl? You're looking at me like I'm a dead man walking," Chuck said, looking perplexed, but entertained, by Val's reaction.

Val wasn't exactly looking at a dead man walking: It was the DA walking, as in the district attorney walking, as in Charles Brown, who was sitting beside her, calling himself Chuck.

Her eyes were wide as she tried to figure out why he was talking to her. Surely, he knew who she was. They'd been in each other's company on too many occasions for him not to—when she was married to the mayor and after. She was about to smile and call him by his proper name to make it clear that they both knew who they were running into at the bar, in a hidden lounge when folks their age were at home avoiding sex with their spouses and praying their children didn't wake up before their favorite reality show went off, but then Chuck grinned and looked into her eyes like he was meeting someone new.

"I'm not trying to scare you. I only want to make you smile. Maybe we should begin again." He held out his hand and Val noticed him kind of step back on one heel a bit, almost falling. "I'm Chuck," he slurred out that time.

Val shook his hand and felt a wobbly grip. She glanced at his empty drink glass on the bar.

"And you are?" he pushed. He wouldn't let go of Val's hand and peered down at it like he was about to lick it.

"I'm—" Val looked into his eyes and searched for any recognition. There was nothing there. Just drunken commotion. "I'm Cinnamon," she let out, though she wasn't yet sure why she was lying or where she'd go with the lie. What she did know was that the man leering down at her through glassy eyes was a known drunk and skirt chaser, who'd divorced his first black wife after she gained a limp following a stroke and then married the state attorney general's blond, blue-eyed daughter to secure his selection for district attorney. All of that and he was the main man behind the machine keeping Kerry behind bars. And, together, that made Val mad as hell. She felt something wicked needling her thoughts.

"Cinnamon?" Chuck laughed a little too loud and the bartender came over to gather his empty glass from the bar. "That's not a name, baby; that's a flavor."

"Actually, it's a spice," Val said.

"Okay! So, you're telling me your mama named you after a spice? Like that's your real name? 'Cause if it is, I love it." He whispered his last line in Val's ear and his breath reeked of cheap cognac and maybe a little marijuana.

"She sure did," Val said confidently. She looked at the table of white women and they seemed to be following their exchange and whispered to each other as they guessed at what was happening.

"Hmm . . . I think I need to see some ID to prove that." He shot Val a sharp, accusatory side eye.

"ID? Why would I show you my ID? You could be a secret agent, working for the government, or just a thief," Val said. "You a thief?"

"No, Cinnamon. I'm just a hardworking brother out here looking for a queen to spoil."

"Really? What a coincidence. I'm out here looking for a king to spoil me. Can you spoil me, Chuck?" Val licked her lips and looked right into Chuck's eyes without saying a word for fifteen seconds. She saw the blood flush out of his face as it flooded down to his private parts.

She knew his type well. Probably came from an upper-middle-class family. Grew up in a neighborhood where azaleas framed manicured lawns and bikes cluttered the sidewalks. She could look at his thick neck and tell he was likely chubby then. The scars on his cheeks were from bad teenage acne. Those straight teeth were the result of years in thick, complicated braces. Nothing had been cute about him. But he was smart. Always smart. Maybe too smart and in his head, because he couldn't get any girls and only had two good friends who were just as unattractive and nerdy as he. He masturbated right through high school. Went to Morehouse. Lost a little weight. Got the braces off and hormones took care of the acne. And then he became the man—the ladies' man. He probably only went to law school to keep the attention coming. To get the girls. And when he got the one he married, she was so beautiful he felt lucky. Then she had a stroke at thirty-five and a limp that reminded him of his past.

An hour or so later and Val had used this catalog of inklings to draw her male suitor to a cozy, make-out couch at the back of the lounge. It was after one AM and the place was clearing out, as the reality of work in the morning made ghosts of the would-be partygoers who'd long ago accepted defeat and willingly walked to their cars to head home. The only folks left in corners and tucked-away in the place were either new couples who were negotiating an evening of casual sex or drunks waiting for their alcohol to wear off. The DJ had switched the nineties hip-hop music to techno drivel that sent inebriated minds swirling.

Chuck was whispering every bad line Val had ever heard in her ear. It was actually laughable. He'd mentioned wanting to get married. And planning his "next" trip to Dubai. He'd dropped some hints at his salary and even threw in how "Magnum Trojan condoms were too small" for him. These were all things that were supposed to matter to Val. She was supposed to imagine that she was the wife he was seeking, dream of her trip with him to Dubai, imagine what he could buy her with that salary, and what he could do to her with his big old penis.

All of this wore Val out psychologically, as she wondered how he'd ever gotten any women with his weak games, but still, she smiled at him, played with the fat at the back of his neck seductively, and let her spandex dress inch up a little bit more each time she crossed, uncrossed, and re-crossed her legs.

He placed his hand on her thigh and licked her ear.

At one point Chuck laughed and said he knew who Val was. He'd seen her somewhere. He knew who she was. Her name "wasn't no Cinnamon!" He took a sip from a new cup of alcohol that promised there was no way he'd be driving himself home that night.

Val couldn't tell if he was serious, playing, or just drunk.

She was ready to come clean and curse him out for feeling her up, but then he said, "You used to work at the Pink Pony. Baddest sister in the strip club. Knew I recognized you." He looked at her waistline. "Got those butterflies tattooed around your waist. I'll never forget that shit. I remember you."

Val laughed and nodded along, though she'd never danced at the Pink Pony and despised the contradictions in butterfly tattoos.

Chuck leaned into her. "Can you show me those tattoos?" he asked softly.

Sitting there with his hot breath and sweaty hands on her, Val just couldn't believe this was the man who was in charge of prosecuting the city's criminals. He was just a man. Fragile like any other. Stupid. Blind. Troubled. Maybe like her.

Val put her head back on the couch and let him slide his hand between her thighs. Her drinks were wearing off. She wondered what time it was. If Mama Fee was up in the window, waiting for her to come home. Then Val remembered why she was there. What drove her out of the house, same as it had on so many other nights.

Chuck was saying something stupid, so she looked at him and smiled again.

She wondered what had driven him out that night too. And how in the world God saw fit for the two of them to be out that night together. What were the odds that this drunken man—of all of the drunken men in the city—would come chirping in her ear? Mama Fee would call it *àyànmô*, saying it was both of their destinies or fate to be there at that exact time and in that place together. But why? The drunk and high DA who was so wasted he couldn't recognize the dead mayor's ex-wife as he tried to fondle her vagina? And who was Val? What was her role? The dead mayor's ex-wife, who was trying to get his first wife out of jail and had the DA's hand locked between her thighs . . . literally?

Val heard a weak voice that sounded something like a little girl inside of her say *no*. But it was barely audible, just barely. Val knew what she was supposed to do then. She quieted the little girl and told herself this was what she had to do. What she'd always done.

"You taking me home, Daddy?" she purred in Chuck's ear so sensuously he blushed and stuttered out a response that made him sound like a teenage boy preparing for his first orgasm with a pretty girl. Val loved that reaction. It reminded her of how every man she ever met used to respond to her. Blushing and stuttering. Jamison had been that way once too when she had her stiletto in his mouth.

"Ho—ho—ho—home?"

"Yes, Daddy?" She looked into his eyes. "I'm kind of tired of this scene."

"Ho—home. *O-o-o-kay*. I need to come clean about something right now," Chuck said, starting a rehearsed excuse as to why he couldn't have a woman at his place—and not one bit included the fact that there was a petite blonde with his last name waiting inside.

He asked if they could go to "Cinnamon's" place and she came up with her own list of excuses that included a busted pipe and dead cat. Then there was talk of a hotel. Chuck said he'd need to go to the ATM to get some cash to pay for a room. He asked if they could go someplace outside of the city, outside of the perimeter. Val laughed and said, "I'll go anywhere with you, Daddy."

The sex was uneventful. There was probably a better word to describe it, but even taking the time to think up one would give the sad series of bedroom fumbles too much energy. Suffice it to say, it was at every possibility a waste of gas, money, hotel-room time, and even the walk of shame through the hotel lobby to get to the room.

First, Chuck couldn't get out of his pants. Val laid on the bed in bright-red lace crotchless panties, spread-eagle and watching this man stumble to get down to his boxers, which were some cheap, checkered Walmart discount undies that made him look fifty pounds overweight.

Then he tiptoed to the bed, making promises about everything he was going to do to Val—where he was going to put his penis and how he was going to "pound" it into her and make her scream for "mercy." And he did put it here and there and pound it all around.

And Val responded with the requisite "Give it to me, Daddy" and "Harder" and "Oh, baby, yeah."

When it was done, when Chuck was done flipping Val all around and pretending he was a porn star, he put her on her back and hunched over her like they were their most primitive selves, having sex in a cave with animal sketches on a wall. He heaved and thrust, dug his knuckles into the sheet and then just suddenly fell into Val's legs, wrapped around so hard he could've broken them both off.

That was it.

Val as Cinnamon laid there in the middle of the bed with bleached, white sheets strewn all around for no good reason and the district attorney already passed out between her legs. His stinking spit oozed out onto her breasts as he fell into a deep, coma-like sleep.

Val peered up at the dusty chandelier that looked maybe too grand to be in the dank hotel room Chuck drove right to out by the airport. Those cries of *no* from the soft voice inside were growing louder and sounding so sad, hurt, betrayed.

"Just do it," she said to herself. "Get it over with."

Val laid there for a minute until Chuck started snoring and talking in his sleep, then she dragged herself from beneath his body and stood over him, looking. She held her cell phone in her hand with the camera focus pointed at his naked, pimpled black behind. She left the hotel room with fifty self-styled pictures presenting various levels of incrimination. That and the platinum wedding band she found in his pants pocket.

When Val pulled into the driveway in the back of the house that always made her remember Jamison, she was shaking and a crying mess. While the little excitement she'd felt capturing the DA in some act that would have him ready to do anything she requested, made her feel like she'd really done something special as she strutted out to her car in the hotel parking lot, by the time she made it to the highway to head home, she regretted something. Not necessarily that she'd slept with him. But something. Like that she could do it. That people could expect that from her. That it was her part.

She went back to the question she'd asked herself on the couch before she'd went to the hotel. Who was she? Who was Val? And why was she always in this position?

Those tears came out so easily with no one other than her to see them. Then, sobbing like a baby pulled from her mother's breasts just when she was about to fall asleep, Val banged on the steering wheel and cried out, "Why?"

There was no black truck waiting in the driveway. No mother snooping in the window.

Val looked at both empty places and felt the despair of loneliness. Nothing seemed attached to her in any way. Not even her own hands on the steering wheel. She looked at them. They were removed. Away. Disconnected. Just not there for her. Then she sensed that maybe she wasn't real. Maybe none of this was. It was all a dream. She wanted it to just go away. All of it. And herself too. Go away with her baby into the dark night.

More tears were falling and Val was about to scream out for anyone to hear her when two lights pulled into the driveway of the little mansion. They glowed like stars hanging down so close on the Earth.

These were the headlights on that black truck.

Val jumped out of her car. She ran to the truck. When Ernest got out, her arms were reaching toward him.

"What is it? What?" Ernest asked. He opened his arms and let Val and her worries crash into his massive covering. And he held her.

"I'm here. I'm here, baby. I'm here," he assured Val, though she hadn't said a word. "I got you. I told I'm going to be here, right? You don't have to cry."

He rocked her in his arms and repeated his soothing words.

"Where were you?" Val asked through crying, like he'd always been there and she hadn't just banished him hours ago.

"I was thirsty. I went to get a slurpee. Had some onion rings too," Ernest said nonchanclantly, but Val could tell he said it to make her laugh.

In his arms, she looked up at him.

"You're crazy," she said, laughing a little.

"Yes. I am. I was crazy thirsty sitting here waiting for you to show up with another one of your busters," Ernest said.

"And what were you going to do if I did? Beat him up?"

"If that's what it takes."

"And what if there's some new buster every night?"

"Then I'll fight every night." Ernest kissed Val on the forehead, like she was something precious, and tears she didn't expect and couldn't control fell out of her eyes.

"You can't be serious," she said, "about me." Her voice quivered in anxiety.

"You bring more busters here and you'll see how serious I am," Ernest said. He then swept Val off of her feet and carried her to bed for restful sleeping.

Mama Fee, of course, saw this from her perch.

Chapter 9

Thirjane wasn't resting easy. Though she'd taken a little Prozac, had her evening sip as she watched the news, had lain in bed and closed her eyes, her sleep was less than restful.

Somewhere between real life and a real nightmare, Thirjane tossed and turned under her sheets, reliving a past she wanted to forget.

From his bedroom down the hallway, Tyrian could hear her crying, "No! No!" and "Stop! Stop!" He sat up and thought to go and wake his grandmother, but he'd done it before and gotten two licks on his backside for getting out of bed without permission. So, instead he did what had become a kind of directionless hobby with his grandmother's odd actions: He climbed out of bed, grabbed his iPad, and went to sit outside of her bedroom to record the strange cries. But what he couldn't record were the heartbreaking memories his grandmother was forced to visit in a lifelike retelling of her history with his mother.

"I'm so sorry, Zachary, but my Kerry can no longer chat with you. We have to leave. Come along, dear." A young Thirjane was sliding on her overly prissy day gloves and beckoning for Kerry to gather her things and follow her out of the Fullerton house, just doors away from their summer home in Oak Bluffs, Martha's Vineyard. Kerry, just seven or eight at the time, had accompanied her to an afternoon tea at the Fullertons'. Mrs. Olivia Fullerton was the wife of a respected surgeon from Old Westbury, New York, whose family had been vacationing with Thirjane's family in the Bluff before Labor Day weekend for as long as either family could remember. While Olivia was a newbie to the group and had none of the legacy of either the Fullerton or Jackson clans, her marriage to the good doctor, with his lineage and impeccable training, made her at least acceptable in the vacation enclave, where the ilk of Martin and Coretta King and later Bill and Camille Cosby made friends with other black elite and, more importantly, new family ties. As Thirjane's mother had told her, *"A woman ought to marry above her station, Janie. Never equal. Never less."* As such, when the Fullertons announced that they were expecting a boy when Thirjane and her husband were expecting a girl, Thirjane couldn't have been happier. She delighted at the idea of connecting her Kerry with their Zachary. Of course, he'd go to Morehouse when Kerry was studying at Spelman. He'd follow in his father's footsteps and go to Morehouse Medical School, become a surgeon, and then marry her daughter. The teas the women had were to casually bring their children together as friends first and then, over the years, through strong suggestion and careful planning, a romance would develop that would lead to a ring and a wedding at the Summer White House.

This sensational scenario came to a hard halt that afternoon, when Thirjane had to so expeditiously fetch her daughter from the Fullertons' parlor and escape at once. Just seconds before, Thirjane had been sipping Darjeeling on the back porch with

Olivia. The two were laughing and talking about the ways of their growing children, when Olivia had consumed just a little too much brandy in her tea and asked if she could open up to Thirjane—who accepted such an invitation, knowing full well the woman was drunk and probably about to tell a secret she should never tell another soul—especially not in the Bluffs. But, Thirjane wasn't one to pass on the opportunity to hear juicy gossip, so she assured Olivia of her sincere secrecy and listened up. Olivia Fullerton was having an affair. She'd been sleeping with the gardener. She blamed the blues of being a housewife in boring Long Island and an afternoon brandy habit. She was certain her husband either knew or was about to figure it out. She didn't know if she could stop—if she wanted to stop. She wanted Thirjane's advice.

On the surface, Thirjane was a pillar of support for her Bluff buddy, but inside, the little Janie who'd been coached by her mother never to involve herself in such activities that could ruin not only the family's name, but also the chances of good connections moving forward, was screaming that she needed to get herself and her daughter out of that house as soon as possible. The Fullerton ship was about to sink and she wasn't going to allow her child to go down with it. Marry some Zachary Fullerton who'd soon be from a broken home and raised by a single, pedigree-free, drinking mother.

Thirjane nearly dragged Kerry out of the house.

"Why do we have to leave now? Zachary and I were having fun," Kerry said, pouting, as they made the short walk back to their smallish bungalow.

"Never mind that boy. You'll never see him again, girl, so don't ask me another word about him," Thirjane said in her strict voice that was pretty much the same as her relaxed voice.

"But he's my friend. My only friend in the Bluffs. Why won't I see him again?"

"I said, don't ask me about him. Now, that's it. You are never to talk to him again. You hear me?" Thirjane stopped and turned to Kerry. "Do you understand?"

"But he's my friend. He's my—"

Thirjane stopped Kerry's back talk with the back side of her right hand up against the little girl's soft lips.

She pointed her index finger between Kerry's eyes.

"You bring that boy up again and I'll tell your father. You hear? You don't understand it now, but he is not good enough for you. He never will be. One day your mama will find a husband for you and he will be suitable and he will be perfect. Do you understand?"

"But he's my—"

Thirjane cut in with, "Answer me yes or no, girl, or I swear I'll spank your behind right here, right now."

A spring of tears erupted from Kerry's eyes and she sobbed out, "Yes, ma'am," like a good Southern child.

Thirjane grabbed her by the wrist and dragged her the rest of the way home.

This history was followed by similar scenes—boys Kerry wanted to love, friends Kerry wanted to make, places Kerry wanted to go, things Kerry wanted to know—all squashed with the heavy hand of a mother who did the honors in the name of love.

"I love him, Mama. And he loves me." This was Kerry speaking more than ten years after the situation in the Bluffs. Then she was graduating from Spelman and she'd met some boy who

was on scholarship at Morehouse. Thirjane had met the boy a few times. He was rather dark. Didn't know which forks to use and spit in her begonias.

"I can't believe you said yes to this man and accepted this ring—without speaking to me first." *Thirjane looked at the sad little ring and decided that there was no way she'd let her child go showing that thing to her people around town.*

"What is there to talk about? We're getting married."

"He's not good enough for you, Kerry Ann. And you don't understand what I'm talking about now, but someday you will. He's going to bring you down. This man is going to ruin you; ruin us—this family—our legacy. You're my only child. Please!"

Kerry rolled her eyes like her mother didn't know anything about anything.

"Mama, please stop. You've been telling me that since you forbade me to talk to Zachary Fullerton when I was eight years old. And he's on his way to medical school."

"Well, why don't you call him up then? This Jamison isn't going to medical school."

"That's because he's staying here with me until I can get into school. And he wants to marry me."

"This is going to be the biggest mistake of your life, girl. I'm telling you. Listen to your mother. I know best. That boy isn't from anything and he's never going to have anything. You're going to struggle and struggle just to have a little bit, just to keep up. You will have to work. You will have to clean. You will have to pretend it's all okay, but it won't be. It's going to be hard as hell because you married down and you married the wrong man. And I am not going to help," *Thirjane said so nastily her words dug into Kerry's tear ducts and produced the crying Thirjane was seeking.* "I will not let that nigga have a dime of my husband's money!"

If the situation in the Bluffs with the Fullertons set the tempo for the dream, then this later scene about Jamison was the chorus and so many other similar situations filled in the rest of the brain noise that had Thirjane tossing and turning in bed. Soon she was sweating and popped up in the bed like a mummy waking during the zombie apocalypse. She looked around, surprised at her surroundings. It was like she'd been returned to the waking world, with all of her worries packed on her shoulders ten times heavier.

When her feet hit the floor on the side of her bed, Tyrian was about to get up and run back to his bed, but he sat for a minute and kept his recording going.

In the bedroom, his grandmother was walking around, talking to herself. He held the iPad to the door to capture the angry mumbles and fear-tinged declarations.

"He was ruining everything! Everything! I worked so hard. Gave her everything! What was I supposed to do, just sit by and watch him hurt my baby? Not again! Not my baby!"

Tyrian dropped the iPad and pressed his ear against the door. He couldn't tell if the sounds were coming from his grandmother or the television, which she sometimes left on at night when she'd gone to bed.

But then there was: "Jamison was never right for her. I told her. Why couldn't she listen to me? Why? If she'd listened to me, none of this would've happened. I never would've done this!"

What had she done? What? Tyrian pressed his head closer to the door and wondered this. Why was she talking about his father? She never liked him. Tyrian knew that and quickly learned when he was just a baby and noticed just by watching the two that whenever his father walked into a room, his grandmother walked out. And if she stayed, soon there would be arguing.

On the other side of the door, Thirjane was standing in the middle of her bedroom beneath an antique Tiffany light fixture. She was wearing a simple, white cotton nightgown and her long, silver hair had slipped from beneath her nightcap and was hanging down her back. She wrapped her arms around her waist like she was holding some agony down in the lower part of body and was afraid to let go, or else it would rise and rise and drown her as it filled the rest of her.

"Why, God? Why?" She shook and looked up at the ceiling. She kept imagining Kerry's sad eyes that afternoon in the Bluffs. "No! No! No!"

Something got into her and she rushed to the little baby blue bathroom in her bedroom, flipped the light switch, and planted herself in front of the mirror.

She squinted at her reflection. At the drama of the years in lines beneath her eyes and sagging cheeks. Where was the tight chin and piercing eyes that used to send people into fear and trembling? That chief of chiefs, who'd walk into a room and put everyone into a corner? She'd lost her power day by day when she wasn't looking. Every ounce of it. And her child was sitting in jail and there was nothing she could do about it. All she ever wanted for that little girl was for Kerry to be better than her. Happier, maybe. Softer. To have everything and not have to fight. Not to have to enter into the world with boxing gloves on every single day.

"Kerry!" Thirjane cried at her reflection. "Kerry!"

And then seconds later she was sitting on the edge of her bed with an ivory house phone pressed to her ear.

"In the morning, I'm going to turn myself in," she got out through sniffles. "I'm going to turn myself in, so my child can go free. I did this. I can't stand by and watch Kerry suffer because of it."

"No need, Mrs. Jackson," an ominous male voice said on the other end. "The DA is making a statement in the morning. He's releasing her."

"What? What? Why?"

"Change of heart, it seems."

Thirjane hung up the phone and fell to her knees in prayer.

In the morning, she'd find Tyrian asleep on the floor, cradling his iPad in front of her bedroom door.

Part 2

Chapter 10

"*While recent rumors tell a tale that Jamison Taylor is alive and working with underground militant groups in Harlem, New York—some even claiming to have spotted the Atlanta mayor who faked his death to escape a CIA plot to have him murdered—reliable sources who preferred not to have their identities revealed, due to government agents working undercover in the publishing industry, say Taylor has actually been connected with the growing African Liberation Army camp in Cuba, where he now resides.*"

Kerry read this passage from a blog aloud. She was sitting at one of the computer terminals in the library at the jail. Garcia-Bell was seated beside her, hunched over and listening.

Kerry scrolled down the screen and read some more, before turning to Garcia-Bell for a response.

Kerry's eyes were so big and excited. This was a different Kerry than the one Garcia-Bell had met when she shuffled into the jail looking like she'd just landed in hell.

"So, what do you think?" Kerry asked, pushing for some confirmation from Garcia-Bell.

"I don't know. It sounds like all the other ones. Same thing.

I don't know," Garcia-Bell said, trying to sound even and not dedicated to believing or disbelieving what Kerry had read.

Kerry had been reading those blogs for days since she talked to Auset on the jail yard. While she'd started a skeptic and claimed she was just looking into it to see what Auset was talking about, after a while it seemed like Kerry believed some of the stuff—and Garcia-Bell . . . well, she didn't.

"I found this site this morning. Some guy who lives in Atlanta publishes it. He says he has contacts with ALA," Kerry said, clicking to the *about the author* tab on the blog. She'd started using the lingo and jargon writers used on all of the sites and her eyes popped with enthusiasm that also registered in her voice.

She'd been clicking from site to site for almost two hours, dragging Garcia-Bell through a story that began with the CIA plotting to kill Jamison because he was the next perceived leader of young black males seeking success in the South, him connecting with whatever militant group could free him from the ill-fated plot, faking his death, and fleeing to wherever any blog would claim.

"What's the ALA?" Garcia-Bell asked.

"The African Liberation Army. It's in Cuba—well, that's where it's based, but there are camps everywhere," Kerry explained and then she read lines from the author's biography. "Baba Seti. Founder of the Fihankra Center in the West End." She looked at Garcia-Bell. "Well?"

"Well? What?"

"What do you think? I mean, he sounds very confident."

"Think about what, Kerry?"

"Do you think he knows—like, about Jamison?"

"What about him?" Garcia-Bell was trying to push Kerry, so she could hear how crazy she sounded even considering what she'd read on some blog. Kerry frowned at Garcia-Bell like she'd missed something and lowered her head down to Garcia-Bell's level to whisper as if anyone was listening: "If he's alive?"

Garcia-Bell looked away.

"What?" Kerry asked. "What?"

"I don't know. I think—" Garcia-Bell paused and looked down to avoid the hope in Kerry's eyes. "I think it's just like all the others. The other conspiracy theory—"

"*Conspiracy* theory?" Kerry stopped her with an accusatory tone.

"Yes." Garcia-Bell looked up and into Kerry's eyes. "I do. All of it is and I don't know why you're reading this stuff," she said. "No, I guess I do. I guess I do know why, but you can't believe it. You said it yourself. You saw it happen. You were there. Right?"

"I was, but what if I didn't see what I think I saw?" Kerry asked. "What if what I saw was what Jamison wanted me to see and—I don't—he's . . . ." Kerry looked off to consider the seduction of her frazzled ideas. "He's alive."

Kerry released the computer mouse and kind of sulked at her words.

"He's alive and you're in jail? You said he loved you. And you think he's in Cuba. So, he's over there and he knows the woman he loves is in jail for killing him? That doesn't even sound right. None of it does. It sounds crazy. Too far out there, you know?"

"Maybe he had to do it. And he knows I'm in jail, but he's preparing to come and get me. To get me out," Kerry said.

Garcia-Bell wanted to shake Kerry and ask her if she heard herself. But she didn't and she couldn't. She'd actually seen this inside before. Women who'd gone delusional or half-crazy about everything going on outside once they were locked up. And it was usually about men, all to explain why this or that had happened or wasn't happening. Prostitutes who believed their pimps loved them and hadn't come to bail them out because they were "teaching" her a lesson. Girlfriends locked up for crimes committed by their drug-dealing boyfriends, all taking the rap for their lovers, claiming they'd get the easier sentence and do the time in the name of love. But Kerry, how was she falling for this? What was with this sudden change?

She thought to tell Kerry all about the other women and what the bars could do to the desperate mind, but she didn't think it would do Kerry any good. Maybe these theories could actually help Kerry with her time. Put some bandages over her broken heart.

"Baba Seti?"

Garcia-Bell and Kerry turned to find Auset standing behind them, reading the words on the computer screen over their shoulders.

Garcia-Bell rolled her eyes instantly.

"You ever hear of him?" Kerry asked, seemingly happy to have another potential believer there.

"Yes. Of course. He's a good brother. Works with the ALA," Auset said low.

"Really?" Kerry looked at Garcia-Bell. "I guess that's how he has his sources."

"Sure," Garcia-Bell confirmed shortly.

"I'm glad you're finally seeking the light, sis. Good to know we have more sistren like you," Auset said.

Kerry smiled back a response. This wasn't her first visit to Baba Seti's Web site. Since her conversation with Auset that day on the yard, she'd been thinking of Jamison constantly, dreaming of him, daydreaming of him and remembering every little moment they'd shared up until that day on the roof. Then, one afternoon, as she peeled potatoes for dinner in the kitchen, her thinking went past that moment and she saw something that felt more real than anything around her: Jamison alive after the incident. He was in the middle of a crowd of brown faces in Cuba. He was wearing a Havana shirt, holding a microphone and telling the listeners the next plans for the revolution. They were to unite and then they'd come up from underground to reclaim their power. Reaching the bottom of the box of potatoes snatched Kerry from her little pondering. She chuckled off the idea at first. Chalked it up to having been on Baba Seti's Web page all morning and looking at several other blogs. But then, when she went to her cell and looked up at the picture of Jamison and Tyrian hanging over her bed, she felt something so deep in her being that told her it was real, it was true. He was alive.

Sister Auset put her hand on Kerry's shoulder. "Don't be surprised if the enemy starts to do things to make you give up your search. Like, now that you know the truth is out there, things will start happening to you. Trust me." She leaned in and cocked her head to the side, making her long locks cascade over her shoulder. "There are undercover agents everywhere. Even behind these bars. Don't be fooled."

The three women suspiciously looked at the librarian, a svelte white girl with red curls who was a volunteer from Georgia State University, and then over at the black inmates who never spoke to anyone else, sitting at another computer.

"Jesus, Auset! Agents? Who are these agents?" Garcia-Bell said, annoyed. "And *the truth is out there*? Isn't that from *The X-Files*?" She laughed.

Auset looked over at Garcia-Bell like she was a child engaging in a conversation far beyond her level of comprehension.

"My Latina sister, I am not expecting you to understand what we are talking about," Auset said.

Garcia-Bell laughed again like Auset was crazy. "Because I'm Spanish?"

"No, your people have led many revolutions. It's just that you're not conscious."

"Conscious of what? The agents you claim are lurking around the jail? Spying on criminals?" Garcia-Bell snapped.

"No, conscious of the white-supremacist regime and how it remains in power in the world. That this is the beginning of the New World Order—you can't see it? The G Eight taking over the Middle East, killing any African leader who opposes their power? And it's nothing new. It's what they did to every true freedom fighter and revolutionary since the beginning of time. Patrice Lumumba, Che Guevara, Fred Hampton, Malcolm X, Jesus Christ."

Garcia-Bell held in a sarcastic chortle. "You can't be serious."

But Auset and Kerry kept straight faces. Kerry nodded. This was the sort of enticing information she'd been reading about on the blogs.

"Laugh if you want, but it's real. And it's serious. Now, they tried to get Sister Assata Shakur, but she fled to Cuba. They even tried to get Sister Angela Davis. And then Jamison Taylor." She put her hand on Kerry's shoulder again. "They tried. But we're getting stronger. And we protected him."

"From what?"

"The CIA was going to kill him."

"Why?"

"Because like everyone else I mentioned, he was going to do something revolutionary to help brown people. You know what was on the line with the scholarship program Jamison was working on with brother Ras Baruti? Getting black boys educated and not just working? An entire generation? Jamison was talking about getting people in his community to stop tithing to churches and instead donating time and resources and money to schools. No way they were going to let that happen. And with the help of the basketball teams? All million-

aires? Black men with money putting that money up to edu-
cate other black men—not spending it on dumb stuff like cars
and chains, food and houses, but in the community? Some of
the Falcons were signing up too. It was all coming together. By
any means. Now, they couldn't let that happen in this city. In
this city? The busiest airport in the world is here. Atlanta is
about to become the center of the universe. Educated black
men here means new business. Means black business. Competition in the marketplace—competition they can't control. And
imagine if that idea left Atlanta and all basketball teams did
that? And then all football teams in all the cities in the country? What would white supremacy look like then in ten years?
Twenty years? They wanted Jamison dead. It's easy to see if
you're conscious of the truth."

"You know what I'm conscious of?" Garcia-Bell asked slyly
and didn't wait for a response. "The fact that your ass is really
crazy."

"No, Garcia-Bell," Kerry said, trying to stop her friend, but
it didn't work.

"And you have some nerve coming over here feeding all of
this crap to this woman. She needs real help, not fake hope.
You know what? I think you should probably get away from
here and sit your ass down." Garcia-Bell stood and her imposing frame might have made Auset, who was a couple of inches
shorter, look weaker, but Auset clearly wasn't intimidated.

She only stared blankly. Her crew of women, who were sitting at a worktable nearby, noticed Garcia-Bell's move and
stood, ready to defend Auset.

"Oh no!" Kerry stood and tried to step between Garcia-Bell
and Auset.

"No need, sis," Auset said, waving off her crew. "I only come
in peace," she added, mocking Garcia-Bell's stance and subse-
quent stare down.

"Well, *go* in peace too, then," Garcia-Bell said.

Auset rolled her eyes at Garcia-Bell and popped out an encouraging smile at Kerry before stepping back.

"Remember what I said, Sister Kerry." She looked at Garcia-Bell, but kept her words aimed at Kerry. "And beware of people trying to keep you from the truth. You never know who the agents are." She bowed with a nod that Kerry awkwardly returned and then went back to her circle, who gave Garcia-Bell averse stares.

When she was gone, Garcia-Bell turned to Kerry, ready to laugh at the mystical, righteous dialogue with Auset.

"Chick is crazy," she said.

"She's not crazy. She just sees things differently than you. Things you can't see," Kerry countered, borrowing some of the words Auset had used the first time she spoke to Kerry.

"*I* can't see?" Garcia-Bell scrunched up her face at Kerry in disbelief. "So, *you* see it? You're saying you really believe this stuff? Like Auset and this Seti character?"

"Why not? Why shouldn't I?"

"Because it's a silly conspiracy theory and they're just playing with your emotions," Garcia-Bell argued. "I'm just saying. What proof do they have that any of this is true?"

"I guess I'll find out soon."

"How?"

Kerry glanced down at the computer on Baba Seti's page. "I e-mailed him," she revealed.

"What?" Garcia-Bell's mouth widened.

"I contacted him. Told him who I am and said I wanted more information. I wanted to know if he could put me in contact with Jamison," Kerry said. She'd already e-mailed Baba Seti that morning from her inmate e-mail account.

"You what? Why would you do that? I don't get it. You know this stuff is all lies. Just let it go."

"I can't," Kerry said with glassy eyes. "I love him. He was my husband. And I feel like if I let this go, then I'm letting him go. And I won't do that. Not if there's a chance. Because if there is, I'm going for it. Because I'd want him to do it for me. Because I'd want him to know the truth."

"Kerry Ann Jackson," someone called from the door and the librarian, Kerry, and Garcia-Bell looked, expecting to see Auset, but instead it was one of the female guards.

"Yes," Kerry answered, wiping a tear that had fallen when she was speaking.

"Warden wants to see you on main right now. Follow me. You're going home," the guard announced with no feeling.

Everyone in the library, including the redheaded librarian, Auset and her crew, and the two silent sisters looked from the guard to Kerry, who grabbed Garcia-Bell's hand tightly for support as she worked to understand what had just been said.

"Home?" Kerry repeated, like her three months on the inside had felt like three lifetimes—and it did, to her anyway. "*I'm* going home?"

"Yeah. Something about the DA. Think he was on the news this morning. Your lawyer's already here. I'm sure they'll tell you all about it. Let's go," the guard said in an explanation that sounded like a riddle to Kerry.

Kerry looked at Auset, who threw a tight revolutionary fist in the air, and then at Garcia-Bell, and repeated, "I'm going home."

Kerry returned to her cell to get some things she wanted to take home: Just some pictures, Tyrian's artwork, a few letters she'd gotten from her best friend Marcy, and some newspaper articles she'd collected about Jamison's death.

Garcia-Bell was standing against the wall in the cell watching Kerry organize her things and the guard was in the hall talking to another guard about some fight that had broken out on the yard between two women who shared the same baby daddy.

"I can't believe this is happening. Like, just like that," Kerry said, peeling the tape from one of Tyrian's pictures from the wall beside her bed. "Just a day or so ago and the DA wouldn't even take my attorney's calls and now he's letting me out."

"Hmm," Garcia-Bell let out, nodding in agreement.

Kerry was finding it hard to tell if her only jail friend was happy for her leaving or what, and in her own happiness and surprise she didn't have time to sort out Garcia's-Bell's feelings. She kept thinking of seeing Tyrian. His smile again. Letting him know they'd never be apart again.

"It's kind of fishy. Don't you think?" Kerry said.

Garcia-Bell nodded again, but kept silent.

"But I don't even care. I'll take my freedom however I can get it," Kerry added, stuffing the painting and some pictures into the box of her things. "I wonder if my mother is here with Tyrian? Who am I kidding? Of course not. That would be too much like right for that woman." She put a picture of Tyrian and her mother into the box after looking at it for a second. "Let me not be so mean. My mother has her bad sides, but she's done what she can to support me through this. Taking Tyrian in—that was big for her. And I know she loves him." Kerry looked around and shrugged her shoulders. "Guess that's all," she said. "Got everything." She went to pick up the box, but Garcia-Bell stopped her.

"Wait," Garcia-Bell said.

"What?"

"You forgot one." Garcia-Bell went to the bed and sat down, leaning under the top bunk to pull the picture of Tyrian and Jamison from beneath the springs.

"Oh, thank you."

Garcia-Bell got back up and handed the picture to Kerry. "I know it's your favorite," she said.

Kerry looked at the picture for a second. "Got me through some tough nights." She walked the picture to the box and slid it in.

Garcia-Bell was behind her, feeling like she wanted to say something just in case she never saw Kerry again.

"Okay," Kerry said, still facing away. "Guess I'm ready to go."

"Ke—" Garcia-Bell stopped herself. Funny how she could fight for anything, but when it came to matters of the heart, she was always trying to find the right words. "Kerry!" she forced out.

"Yes." Kerry turned around to see Garcia-Bell looking at her with red eyes. Quickly, she remembered everything the woman in the next cell had said about her teasing Garcia-Bell, knowing the woman had a crush on her. "What's up? What's wrong?"

"It's nothing. I'm fine," Garcia-Bell said. "I'm just . . . I just wanted to say—" She reached out and grabbed Kerry's hand. "I wanted to say thank you—thank you for being my friend. You know? I'm grown and I think you're probably the best friend I've ever had. And I'm kind of sad that you're leaving."

Afraid at what was coming next and not wanting to embarrass Garcia-Bell by turning her down, Kerry tried to thwart the emotional outpour with "Don't be sad—"

But Garcia-Bell stopped her. "Wait, let me say this. I'm sad because I don't know if we will ever meet again. But I want you to know that I learned a lot from watching you. How you carry yourself. How much you love your son. And I think what I really like about you is that I never felt like you wanted anything from me. Everywhere I go, everyone wants something. No matter what, they plotting to get it. But you just—you wanted a friend, I guess. And I'm happy I got to feel what that's like. And that you didn't judge me, you know, because of how I looked. I know I don't look like other women, but I am a woman. And you always treated me that way. Never worried about me trying to come on to you or accused me of trying to get with you. I respect you for that. I'm going to miss you."

"Wow!" Kerry said, now returning the grip Garcia-Bell had on her hand. "I'm going to miss you too. And thank you for being my friend too. You helped me. You really did. I wouldn't have made it here without you. I mean, my best friend is like on the other side of the world, but with you here, I never felt like that. I felt like I had someone right here for me."

Kerry opened her arms to Garcia-Bell and the women hugged and cried on each other's shoulders and promised to stay in touch.

After meeting with the warden, Kerry was led to a small room near the exit of the jail where Lebowski, his assistant, and Val were waiting for her. It was awkward to see Val at that moment. Kerry was looking for someone to hug, to connect with in the excitement of what she'd been waiting for, but she and Val had been enemies for so long when Jamison was alive, it actually felt funny to be happy to see her. Or that this was the first connection she'd see to her old life.

Still in her jail jumpsuit, Kerry hugged her enemy-turned-friend anyway, and then Lebowski, who instructed her to change into a brand-new gray conservative suit and matching heels his assistant was holding in a garment bag.

"I tell you, I didn't see this coming at all. Not one bit," Lebowski admitted as Kerry was handed the garment bag and with nowhere else to go, she began to change right in front of them. "When my phone rang at seven AM, I thought it was a joke. No negotiations from the DA for weeks and suddenly he's making a move? And this one? Who knew? You'd think someone was bribing the man, the way he's moving so quickly.

Wouldn't be a surprise with the sort he hangs out with. You know?"

Val shrugged her shoulders and smiled. "Just a change of heart. Even the devil reserves the right to change his mind and do good sometimes. Right?"

"What happened? What did he say?" Kerry asked, stumbling into her new clothing. In recent months she'd become accustomed to undressing, showering, and dressing in front of total strangers.

"He held a press conference at his office and said there were no findings to the charges held against you and that you would be released immediately. It was over as soon as it began," Lebowski explained still sounding stunned by the move. He was wearing his navy blue suit with the dated padded shoulders that made him look inches taller, wider, and stronger. On his lapel was his Masonic pin. He knew every television station in the city, including the national news networks, would have journalists and cameramen waiting outside the jail to see Kerry released. While the case had lost most of its traction due to all of the eccentric conspiracy-theory talk, it was still a good headline: Girl from the right side of the tracks marries a guy from the bad side and then she kills him.

"So, that was the only reason? But that's always been there. What's the change for?" Kerry finished buttoning her suit jacket with echos of Auset's charge in the library just hours ago coming to mind somewhere in the background of her thoughts.

"Probably the same politics that got you here in the first place," Lebowski whispered, though no guards were in the room. "I told you, this whole thing smelled like a cover-up from the start."

"What do you think, Val?" Kerry asked, noting how quiet the commonly loud and central Val was.

"I have no idea. Maybe it's just a blessing," she answered. "Have to take them as they come. Right?" Val smiled and shrugged again uncertainly.

"You know what? You're right. Who cares?" Kerry chirped with a smile bigger than Val's. "I'm free. I get to go home to my—" Kerry paused. "Is my mother here? With Tyrian? Did anyone call her?"

"First call I made," Lebowski said before his voice waned with, "you know . . . I think Thirjane just felt—"

"I know," Kerry cut in quickly to hide her disappointment. "It's probably not the best place for Tyrian, anyway. I'm just happy he's safe with his grandmother."

"I'm sure you two have a lot to talk about," Val said rather dubiously, but Kerry was too busy sorting her feelings to pick up on it.

"You sure do," Lebowski said, unaware of the unique meaning behind Val's declaration. "But not before we get you out of here, dear."

Kerry slid on the heels and handed the garment bag back to Lebowski.

"It's going to be a circus out there when we leave these doors. All kinds of people with all kinds of questions. You stick with me. You stick behind me and say nothing. Now is not the time for comment. We're out of the woods on this, but I have a feeling more is to come and I don't want the DA switching things up on you. You understand?" Lebowski ordered.

"Sure," Kerry confirmed. "I get it."

One of the guards showed up at the door and opened it so Lebowski could lead the women out of the room and into daylight, but Kerry grabbed Lebowski's arm just before he stepped over the threshold. Val and the assistant were behind them.

"I almost forgot. Did you get the ten thousand dollars you requested?" Kerry asked him. "I know it's an odd time, but I just want to make sure it's taken care of."

"What ten thousand dollars? My office didn't send a new invoice," Lebowski declared, looking at his assistant.

Kerry turned to Val. "But Val said she was—"

"Don't worry about it," Val stepped in. "I must've gotten the invoices confused. We'll check on it. Okay?"

There was this long, distressing silence as both parties, Kerry and Lebowski, added up the inconsistency, felt that something must be wrong, but then assured themselves that they were just being suspicious. Still, notes were taken. Dispatches received. Ears and red flags raised and that was clear in Kerry's tone when she said, "Sure."

The guard holding the door said something to rush the party along and Lebowski grabbed Kerry's shaky and sweaty hand like he was leading her into the doorway at the senior prom.

"It'll be fine," he said to her with Val looking over Kerry's shoulder. "Just fine."

When the doors of the jail finally opened, the media and a crowd of onlookers swarmed in from every angle. There were cameras and flashing lights, microphones, and people hollering out questions that sounded like charges to the two Mrs. Taylors.

"Did you kill your ex-husband and now you're getting away with it?" Kerry heard.

"How could you support the woman who killed your husband?" Val heard. She felt eyes digging into her from all angles. Like they all knew what she had done. Knew her part.

Kerry glanced over her shoulder at Val and grabbed her hand knowingly as Lebowski led them, pushing through the crowd en route to a blacked-out SUV waiting by the curb.

From the cameras hovering from the news helicopters above, it seemed like people were just everywhere. Tightest at the nucleus where the little group was moving and then thinning out from there. On the outskirts, people held up signs that read "JAMISON IS ALIVE" and "THE CIA KILLED TAYLOR," contradicting ideas that somehow seemed to unite certain groups.

While Lebowski hadn't intended on saying too many words to the media and wanted to wait until his client was safe at home before releasing a statement, as the crowd tightened around them, he knew he would have to say something to wet their tongues before he asked for privacy or they would follow the SUV across town, on the highway, and line the street outside of Kerry's home.

Nearly at the SUV, he stopped and signaled for Kerry and Val to stay behind him.

"While my client is very excited and anxious to get home to her son and family, we know that you are all equally excited and anxious to hear something from us. I'll answer a few questions and then we'll ask for privacy until we release an official statement."

Ready with questions, reporters jumped right in, organizing their microphones in front of Lebowski to be sure to capture every utterance.

Lebowski ignored most of them and pointed to one of the journalists he knew in the crowd.

"Please, tell us how you feel, Kerry. Over three months in jail, and now you're released. What does it feel like?" the reporter asked.

The crowd went quiet, anticipating Kerry's response.

"I'll speak for Mrs. Jackson," Lebowski said. "She just told me that she's only thinking of her son right now. A good Southern mother, she wants to be home with him so they can eat dinner as a family tonight, she can tuck him into bed and say prayers with him. While tragedy has struck this family, they thank God that they have a lot to be thankful for."

Lebowski nodded to another reporter he knew.

As he listened and answered the second reporter's question, Val pretended to listen, but she was busy looking through the crowd. In the faces before her there were people she knew who hadn't been so nice to her when she was the first lady of the city. Some who'd put pictures of her online and made her the punch line of jokes about the mayor marrying a stripper. One who'd plastered her face on the cover of a magazine and put the headline "THE LADY IS A TRAMP" over her forehead.

Kerry could feel Val drifting away and looked through the crowd too, as Lebowski was doing a fine job with answering each question aimed at her.

Kerry noticed some of the protestors who'd been there when Ras, Jamison's old roommate, was killed, seemingly after the grassroots leader signed up to help Jamison with the community project and was jailed and released just like her. There were also some of Jamison's fraternity brothers there. Some still held alliances with Jamison when he died. Others had stabbed him in the back when the governor flashed checks and promises of promotions before their eyes. Behind one was a black man with a boy toddler perched on his shoulders. The baby was wearing one of the old *Free Ras* T-shirts people had been wearing when Ras was locked up in the jail right behind them. Kerry had pushed Jamison to do everything in his power to get Ras out of jail. She broke one of her rules after the divorce and got into Jamison's business, telling him Ras was only being persecuted because he was trying to do something right in the community. After all, he had been the one who'd rolled up his sleeves and come up with the muscle behind Jamison's big plans. These were his ideas. His connections. His theories.

Jamison was the one with the metaphorical megaphone who'd gotten all of the attention and glory and accolades, but Ras was the catalyst. And because of that, he was a target. Kerry remembered this—and what Auset said happened to targets—when the man with the boy on his shoulders caught Kerry's stare and pumped a black fist into the air.

Something in Kerry quickened. It was like a butterfly in her stomach, only more fierce and tugging at her gut for a response of some kind.

Kerry blinked and looked back at Lebowski, to find that he was quiet and listening to something his assistant was whispering into his ear. In fact, as she looked and listened, she realized that everyone was quiet and looking down at their cell phones. Something had happened—was happening.

"What's going on?" Kerry heard Val ask.

"I don't know." Kerry looked back at Lebowski, whose once-confident stare had turned distant and obscure.

He looked out at the crowd. The crowd looked at him. There was an air of solemnity all around.

Kerry could see Lebowski's Adam's apple roll down his throat as he struggled to swallow. This was bad news. Very bad news.

She looked at Val and shrugged.

"I've just received the news and a confirmation, I suppose like most of you at this point," Lebowski started softly, "that unfortunately and sadly, the DA was just found dead in a hotel room by the airport of an apparent suicide. While reports are still forthcoming, I do have confirmation that a suicide letter was found with the body and his wife has confirmed that the pistol found in the room belonged to him."

Chatter erupted everywhere.

Val felt like everyone had turned and looked at her. Suddenly the sun above became mercilessly hot.

Some news teams united and raced to their trucks for the fastest lead to the hotel.

"What?" Kerry looked at Lebowski as he spoke.

He said, "My client has also just learned of the news and we are not prepared to comment at this time. Right now, we can only hope that God is with District Attorney Charles 'Chuck' Brown's family in their time of need. That is all."

Lebowski began pushing through the crowd toward the SUV again.

"He's dead? He died?" Kerry looked at the assistant frantically; honestly not knowing what she should be doing or saying.

Noticing again that Val was quiet, she turned to her and saw that her face was blank and her cheeks were flushed like she'd just seen a dead body. She looked like Tyrian always did just before he vomited.

"You okay?" Kerry asked Val as Lebowski got into the SUV.

"I'm fine. Just feeling a little light-headed."

The driver held the door open and Kerry let Val get into the SUV first.

While most of the news crews had already left to check in on-location about the DA's suicide, a few loyal, ambitious, and militant crews had stayed.

"Wait, Mrs. Jackson, can you let us know how you feel about all these conspiracy theories that maybe your ex-husband is alive and in Cuba?" someone asked just as Kerry was about to get into the car behind Val. "Do you think there's any connection to the DA's suicide?"

Kerry stopped in her steps and searched the crowd for the voice.

"You don't have to answer that," Lebowski said. "Best you don't." When Kerry didn't move, he added, "Just get into the car."

"No. I want to," Kerry said and then that quickening in her

body cleared her throat and vocal chords and pushed out sounds that gathered in the air as words she had no idea she intended on speaking.

"I believe it," Val heard Kerry saying outside the car, so she inched over and poked her head out to look at her.

"Shit!" Lebowski grumpled beside Val in the SUV as he scurried to get out. "What is she doing?"

Kerry went on speaking so loudly that the now smallish crowd could hear her as clearly as if she was speaking through a bullhorn. "I believe Jamison is alive and wherever he is, he went there because he was trying to escape."

"Escape what?" someone shouted.

"This system," Kerry said, setting her eyes to the back of the crowd where the man with the toddler on his shoulders was still standing. "The system that originally had him under investigation by the FBI and the same system that had me in jail for his murder."

"No, stop!" Lebowski urged Kerry through his teeth as he smiled for the cameras and tried to force her into the SUV. "Okay, that's all," he said, trying to speak over Kerry, but she only got louder.

"I didn't believe that for a long time; I didn't want to listen to people who were saying it," Kerry shouted. "Like everyone else, I called their thoughts 'conspiracy theories,' but now that I am listening and I have my ears wide open, I think it's no coincidence that the DA chose to release me from jail. I don't know what happened to him, but I think he knew exactly what's going on here and soon, soon, we'll all know."

"Okay!" Lebowski snipped, nearly tossing Kerry into the back of the SUV at that point.

But it was too late again. Amid cheers and fists in the air from the people in the back of the crowd with the banners and a few supporters up front, Kerry had stepped onto the floor-board of the SUV and was hollering along, "Revolution! Revo-lution! Revolution!"

"That'll be all." He waved at the crowd.

Once Lebowski had finally gotten Kerry into the SUV and they were about to drive off, her little scene brought out the Brooklyn Jewish boy in the now-distinguished attorney.

"What the fuck was that? Fuck! Fuck! Fuck!" Lebowski cursed at the end of a series of worse expletives that had his as-sistant very nervous in the front seat with the driver, but the black women seated beside him in the back hardly moved and were more focused on how red his face was getting as anger consumed his body. "I told you to follow my lead—let me talk. The fuck was that, Kerry?"

The driver tried to pull away from the curb, but he couldn't move too quickly or he'd hit some of the bystanders who'd en-circled the automobile.

"I wanted to answer the question," Kerry said, still high off of the electric response the crowd had given her. She'd felt like a superstar: Betty. Coretta. Winnie. Kathleen. That night, lying in bed, she'd imagine that Auset was in the jail watching her from a window with a fist in the air.

"Why would you want to answer that question? It was a dumb-ass question. A crazy question! What were you think-ing? Were you even thinking?" Lebowski fired.

"I was thinking about the truth," Kerry said boldy.

Val and Lebowski and the assistant and even the driver looked at Kerry like she'd pulled out a crack pipe.

"What?" Val asked, with her tone matching the concern on her face.

"Okay, listen," Kerry said, noting the stares. "I've been read-ing about Jamison's death online and, I know it sounds like a stretch, but there is proof out there that he's alive."

"Oh shit," Lebowski said, tapping his assistant on the shoulder. "Contact our guy at the *Atlanta Journal-Constitution* and tell him we are retracting all of the statements Kerry just made outside the jail. Tell him . . . she's obviously mentally drained and possibly suffering from depression." He looked at Kerry and added, "and likely delusions."

"I am not delusional. I am not depressed. I'm smart and I know what I'm saying," Kerry countered.

Lebowski ignored her and tapped his assistant on the shoulder again. "And get in contact with that trial psychologist—the one from Emory—and get an appointment for Kerry. First thing tomorrow morning." He turned to the driver. "And why are we still sitting here?" he asked. They'd moved only a yard or so from the curb.

"I'm sorry, sir. There's nothing I can do right now. We have to wait a second until the crowd gets out of the way." He pointed to the many militant bystanders who'd started chanting, "*Torkwase! Torkwase!*"

"What is that? What are they saying?" Kerry asked.

"Don't know. Don't care!" Lebowski answered. "My only focus right now is getting you out of here and getting you some help."

"Help? For what? I'm not crazy." Kerry looked at Val, whose expression had changed. "Why is it so hard to believe that he's alive? And that there might be more to what happened at the hotel than we know?"

Val asked sharply, "Why is it hard to accept that he's dead. Is dead and been dead?"

Sensing that Val's abrasive words and tone might lead to further conflict, Lebowski jumped between the brides with, "Kerry, you've been through a lot, more than any of us. You haven't had time to mourn the loss of someone you loved. Someone who loved you. And if you need more time, we understand. But let us help you."

The driver was about to pull off from the curb but there was a solid fist banging on the window.

"Just one more question for Kerry Jackson," the group in the SUV heard a woman's voice say.

"It's a reporter," the assistant said, before signaling "no" to the final visitor.

As if she hadn't heard any of Lebowski and Val's pleas for silence, Kerry pressed her finger on the button to lower the back window beside her.

In what seemed like slow motion, poor Lebowski went to stop the tinted glass from disappearing into the door frame, but his effort was in vain.

"Driver, put your foot on the gas and get us out of here," he ordered, seeing these indiscretions adding more distance between him and his imagined victory. "If we move, they'll move!" he added, pointing to people in front of the car.

"No!" Kerry barked behind the driver with so much power that he had to listen to her. "We can't leave!" Sitting beside the lowering window, she was the only one in the car who could see the face on the other side of the door. It was no reporter. Just a familiar foe with red hair and a long history with Kerry.

"So now he's alive and on the run from the CIA?" Coreen said, looking over at Kerry with all of the contention between the two women, the first wife and the first mistress, clear in her stare. "That's funny. That's really funny. Because a few months ago you were so sure that I was the killer. Had every detective in Georgia down my throat." Coreen was pointing her index finger at Kerry and this got the attention of a few cameramen who immediately started recording the incident.

"I was just telling them what I knew. What I heard and saw that day," Kerry said in what sounded like an apology but could never be. The last time she'd seen Coreen the two women were in a church and Kerry was still trying to fight to save her marriage. She'd given Coreen a sharp warning that was more like a threat. She'd told Coreen to stay away from her husband "or else"; well, Coreen clearly hadn't listened, and that threat was still there.

Realizing who Kerry was talking to, Lebowski was back to his foul language and begging the driver to plow over the bevy of photographers and whoever else was blocking the SUV's trajectory. All of that while simultaneously trying to keep Val from jumping out of the truck and charging at Coreen herself because she was all curses and threats too. He was a seasoned veteran, and so he'd expected some of these little bumps in this escape plan, but nothing like this. Nothing like this at all. Later, while replaying the circus of Val trying to claw her way out of the SUV to get at Coreen and thus nearly tearing the collar off of his shirt, he'd tell his brother and best friend, "It was like a bunch of black woman with baby mama drama. These girls wanted blood." While he'd admit a part of him was entertained being in the center of the melee, he said he had to maintain only two goals: keep his team in the car and get out of there as fast as possible.

"You killed Jamison, Kerry. Period. You threw him from the roof because you were jealous of his relationship with me and his relationship with his son. Admit it!" Coreen said.

"What did she say?" Val asked Lebowski, trying to get out of his hold.

"Jealous? Do you really think I could ever be jealous of you? Some random ass he flew across the country to see and then left?" Kerry said to Coreen. "His little secret?"

"His little secret who ruined your marriage," Coreen replied nastily.

"You did. Sure you did," Kerry admitted. "Does that make you feel good? Make it easier for you to sleep at night? Does it? Knowing the only way you could ever get a man like that was by stealing him? That you had to get on your back and open your legs just to have him? And that even then, you still didn't get him? He still wasn't yours? Right? Because after all of that—after taking him and trapping him with your bastard son and even after our divorce—he still didn't marry you. He married someone else. Does that make you feel good?"

The commotion in the car had silenced as Kerry, once demure and sweet, tore into Coreen with all cylinders smoking. Even the driver had given up on the escape and was peering at Kerry from the front seat, wondering when Coreen was going to spit on her or hit her or something—because those words were fighting words.

Meanwhile, the onlookers on the outside of the car had already made the first seconds of the argument a viral event. The bombshell news Kerry revealed in her rant had dropped on social media—Jamison Taylor had a "bastard" son. But what was the boy's name?

"You can call my son a bastard if you want to, but remember to also call him Jamison," Coreen said. Her invoking the boy's name sent chills up Kerry's spine. She'd heard it before, but every time she even thought of the name it made her hot with fury and scorn all over again. It was the most aggressive thing Coreen had done to slap her in the face. Coreen flicked her hair behind her ear and went on, "And while you're at it, don't forget to call my son, Jamison junior, rich . . . because all that money you bitches got when his father died, some of it is his and I'm going to make sure he gets it. That's the only reason I'm here. I don't even care who killed Jamison. I just want my money." She looked at Val, who was back to fighting to get out of the SUV after hearing Coreen call her a bitch. "I told you not to play with me. Don't play with my son's money and don't play with me."

Val had gotten away from Lebowski and now Kerry was holding her back. The poor assistant in the front seat had seen the damage done to her boss's shirt, so she was less than anxious to help out.

Kerry let out a surprising laugh that would be noted in the viral reports.

"What the fuck is so funny about what I said?" Coreen asked.

"You just played your last card," Kerry said. "Without even knowing it, you played your last weak card. You let the secret out and now you have no more cards to play. You want money? Fine. But you won't get it from me the way you got it from Jamison. We'll see you in court."

When the SUV made it to Thirjane's house where Tyrian was waiting in the front window for his mother, Kerry insisted that Val come inside to talk about what had happened at the jail with Coreen. But really, everything was clear to her about the incident. She'd put the pieces together about the ten thousand dollars and decided she would wait until Val brought it up. In truth, the somewhat forced visit wasn't about Coreen or the money or Val; it was because Kerry felt right then that she needed a friend. Some bestie or buffer, a third party to mediate the one thing about getting out of jail she wasn't sure about facing: her mother.

Reminding Kerry of why she so desperately wanted Val there, when Thirjane opened the door to let Kerry in, she was all tears and cries of joy. Her arms were extended toward Kerry and she made Tyrian stand there and wait as she hugged Kerry.

"My child is home!" Thirjane cried. "Thank you, Jesus!" she added, rocking Kerry and blocking Tyrian from getting to her.

Kerry looked over her mother's shoulder and smiled at Tyrian as tears began to fall from both of their eyes. And maybe it was more touching, more meaningful than it might have been had they been in each other's arms. Because the gaze, the look on his mother's face from inches away was something Tyrian would remember for the rest of his life.

In his memory, so quickly he would then find himself in her arms. He could smell her again. He'd thought he'd forgotten what she'd smelled like, but there it was. His mother's scent. Indescribable but so immediate and fused into his being. Then the feeling of her tears wetting his back.

She released him and she was busy wiping his tears as hers fell.

"Hey you," Kerry said. "I've missed you so much."

"I've missed you too, Mama," Tyrian said, with his grandmother standing behind him then, and Val behind Kerry.

Thirjane was, of course, eyeing every inch of Val and wondering why she was in her house. That and how she was getting home—that black SUV had rolled away.

"You know what I was thinking when I got the news that I was coming home?" Kerry asked Tyrian. "That I was going to see you. That's all I was thinking. That's all I wanted."

Kerry pulled her son into her arms again.

"I love you so much, baby," she said to him in his ear. "And I'm so sorry for all of this." She looked into his eyes again. "But your mama is back home now and I'm never leaving again. Not ever."

"Company? I didn't know we were having any company," Thirjane said with her eyes still locked on Val, who was returning the stare, but had something else hidden in the scrunched-up frown aimed at Thirjane. The two had been in each other's presence a little over a handful of times when they'd bumped heads, trying to get Kerry out of jail and then in a brief struggle for power at Rake it Up before the CEO less than politely told both women he wouldn't be taking direction from either of them. The company was just remaining afloat with the scandal concerning Jamison and Kerry and if they wanted to keep it from drowning, they needed to step back and off.

"Yes, Mama," Kerry said to Thirjane. "I invited Val to stay to have lunch with us. I figured we could show her a little Georgia hospitality for everything she's done for our family."

"Lunch? I let Ethel leave for the day. I guess I could pull something out of the freezer," Thirjane said drily.

Val rolled her eyes and stopped herself from saying something nasty, for Kerry's sake. Thirjane didn't like her and that was okay with her. This was about class and Thirjane thinking she was better than Val. If only she knew that Val had gotten word of her murder-for-hire plot, she'd snap in line and run to the kitchen to heat up whatever Val wanted to eat to keep her secret from Kerry, who obviously had no idea about what her sweet Southern mama had been up to. Thirjane should've been serving up steak and potatoes. Veal and fresh tomato sauce. Whatever. Val thought that and smirked.

"Mama, I want to show you something on my iPad," Tyrian said, jumping up and down with excitement in front of Kerry.

"On your iPad? What is it? A new game?" Kerry smiled and picked a piece of lint from Tyrian's hair.

He looked at Thirjane and then back at his mother to say softly, "It's a secret. I can't tell you in front of everyone."

Thirjane jumped in with, "Boy, you don't have any secrets in my house. I've told you that. Children don't get to keep secrets. When you get a job, you can have secrets." Thirjane laughed, but Kerry kept her attention on Tyrian.

"Oh, Mama, he's just wanting to show me something. That's all he meant by it." She took Tyrian's hand. "Where's your iPad, sweetheart?"

"In my room," he replied, pulling her toward the steps that led upstairs to the bedrooms.

Excusing herself, Kerry asked Val if she minded if she spent a few seconds with Tyrian and then followed him upstairs to find the tablet.

Val watched Thirjane boil as Kerry and Tyrian played freeze tag up the stairs and then loud thuds could be heard from upstairs as they padded toward the bed.

"Sounds like a whole football team up there," Thirjane said, getting louder with each word, so they could hear her upstairs. "And Kerry knows better. I didn't raise her to walk like an elephant. Not in my house."

Val listened and noted how Thirjane sounded like she was talking about a little girl or someone she could control. She giggled, but not because she thought anything Thirjane had said was funny. She giggled *at* Thirjane. There was a difference.

And Thirjane, a person who specialized in conversational shade and knew too well how to make someone the butt of any joke, knew that difference.

She eyeballed Val to consider what she could be laughing at.

"Hmm," Thirjane offered, pursing her lips at Val. There was a time when someone like Val, with a dress so tight and with earrings dangling so close to her shoulders, wouldn't be allowed in Thirjane's house—or at least they'd know never to come. Thirjane eyed Val's long nails and the ring on her index finger and announced quite uncomfortably, "Guess we should go sit in the parlor and wait for Kerry."

"Sure," Val agreed smugly. "Sounds like a plan to me." She followed Thirjane to the parlor (which was really just a living room), looking at the assiduous decorator's elaborate collection of interestingly placed antiques and cultural trophies. Everything looked so expensive and delicate. A huge painting of a black female slave being baptized in a river hung over a couch loaded with so many pillows Val had no choice but to sit on the edge.

Thirjane sat across from her in a chair with wooden eagle talon feet and crossed her legs like she was beginning an interview.

"So interesting how this all turned out. You getting Kerry out of jail," Thirjane started speaking and her tone was so flat it sounded like she was just trying to fill the silent moment with sound. "You know I've been meaning to be more helpful with things, but having Tyrian here—that was a lot. I'm saying if you had children, you'd understand. It's a lot of work. A mother's work is never done. Raised one and here I am raising another."

"Well, now that Kerry's home, you won't have to worry about that anymore. Right?" Val quizzed.

"Oh, yes I will. That boy needs more guidance in his life. My Kerry is a good mother, but she's no disciplinarian. Neither was that Jamison. And with things the way they are now, all Tyrian's got is me and his mama."

"Yes. It is sad that Tyrian lost his father under such—" Val stopped and grinned at Thirjane for effect "—circumstances. Good thing he had a good grandmother like you at home to help take care of him. Especially since the killer is still out there."

Thirjane looked at Val like she'd peeked under her dress.

"What?" Val followed up. "Haven't you thought about that? The reality that whoever killed Jamison may be an insane serial killer planning to kill off everyone Jamison loved?"

"I doubt that. It was just an isolated incident," Thirjane said, obviously perturbed by Val's morbid analysis.

"How do you know? Hmm?"

"Someone said it—on the news or one of those detectives, maybe. Someone," Thirjane stuttered out.

"How could they know that? I mean, come on—they don't even know who did it. No leads." Val leaned toward Thirjane in the chair and spoke so low and sharp she sounded like a witch whispering a spell into a cauldron boiling over with remnants from a magic potion. "The killer could be planning anything. He could be anywhere. At any time." She sat back and looked around. "Could be in this very room."

"What? Hunh?" Thirjane looked flustered—like she was sitting in the stand in a court of law and going through cross-examination for a crime she committed.

Val had decided she wasn't going to tell Kerry about her mother's plot to have Jamison killed. She figured she would leave that to Leaf. But with Thirjane and her constant airs and putting on sitting in front of her squirming, she thought she could at least have a little fun. Especially since Thirjane had no idea her plan had failed and really thought her actions had led to Jamison's demise.

"We could know the killer. It could be one of us," Val announced shadily. "How do you know it's not *me*? How do I know it's not *you*?"

Thirjane started coughing and looking around the corner for Tyrian and Kerry. "Where are they? Taking so long up there." Thirjane tried to change the topic, but Val ignored her.

"It could be anyone. The killer is out there."

Thirjane looked back at Val and started getting up from her chair. "You want some tea? I want some tea," she asked erratically.

"I'm not thirsty," Val said. "But you look like you could use something to drink."

Thirjane was out of her chair and had her back to Val as she took steps toward the foyer that led to the kitchen on the other side.

"A drink . . . or a priest," Val added.

Thirjane stopped straightaway, but did not turn around.

"I know," was all Val said.

"I didn't do it." Thirjane turned around.

"No. But you ordered the hit," Val said, getting up from her seat and walking toward her.

"Who told you that? How do you know that?" Thirjane asked.

"A little birdie told me," Val joked. She got in close to Thirjane. "It whispered in my ear that you had Jamison killed. Hired someone else to do your dirty work. Not a surprise, either. I bet you have someone clean this house too. Make your bed. Clean your ass. Bail your daughter out of jail—I did that for you."

For the first time in her life, maybe, Thirjane worked as hard as she could to look innocent and maybe weak. "Did you tell her?" she asked.

"No," Val revealed. "Not going to. I thought you could handle that dirty work yourself. You should be the one to tell your daughter you had her ex-husband, the father of her son, murder—"

Before Val could finish, Kerry came bouncing around the corner, all smiles.

"Hey!" Val switched her tone and looked at Kerry. "How'd it go upstairs? What did he have to show you on the iPad?"

"I didn't get to see it. The darn battery was dead," Kerry answered. "We plugged it in. It'll be up in a minute." Kerry looked at Thirjane, who was standing right beside her in the entryway to the foyer. "You okay?" she asked. "You look like you just got bad news. Come on, I'm home! That's the best news ever."

"I know. I'm just worried about lunch," Thirjane managed. "Just wondering how we're going to feed our guest."

"God, Mama. You're always worrying about stuff like that.

I'll split mine with her," Kerry said. "Come on. Let's go eat. I'm starving. I haven't had a decent meal in months."

Everyone laughed. Val laughed the loudest.

"Come downstairs to eat, Tyrian," Kerry hollered upstairs as she led Thirjane and Val to the kitchen. "Wash your hands and leave that iPad upstairs."

Chapter 11

Something bad was coming. Or something bad was going. At least that's what Mama Fee thought. Val knew this because a few days after Kerry was released from jail, she woke to the smell of sage, cedar, and sweetgrass burning in the house. It meant Mama Fee was smudging, burning dried herbs in tiny terra-cotta bowls in the corners and side spots everywhere to fend off some negative energy or bid it farewell. When Val was a little girl, she'd witness her mother wrapping the furry, soft green sage sprigs in her prayer closet sometimes after a funeral and other times days before someone had died. Mama Fee was young and beautiful then, and she'd pin some of the herbs in her bun. Like her mother, Mama Fee taught her daughters about burning and smudging when she'd finished combing their hair and forced them to collect every single fallen nap from the floor, comb, or brush to add to her smudge bowl and be burned immediately.

One time, Val asked Mama Fee how she knew trouble was coming or going and what she should burn. When and where. Mama Fee was braiding sweetgrass then. She leaned over to Val. An extra braid of sweetgrass was dangling from a feather at the base of her scalp. Val's older sister had always told people they were part Chippewa to explain the ornaments neighborhood kids witnessed hanging from their mother's hair. "I smell kitten's breath and hear the drum in my sleep, baby," Mama Fee said to Val. "That's how I knows what to do. The world tells me."

Val had gotten a cryptic and shaky phone call from Leaf the night before the smudging scent filled the house. He wanted to meet with her and Kerry. He had new information, something big that led him to lock himself up in his summer cabin in the woods in Dahlonega up in North Georgia near the Chattahoochee National Forest. On the phone, Val was half asleep and complained about the hour drive out to the middle of nowhere where black people hardly went and white people probably still hung the Confederate flag on the front porch. She'd asked him why he couldn't just come meet her and Kerry in the city over a cup of coffee, but Leaf insisted on it and told Val to make sure she told no one else about the meeting and ensured they weren't being followed on their trip up to the mountains.

In the days since Kerry was released from jail and the media was going crazy trying to figure out why the DA would kill himself in a hotel room, leaving behind only a note to his wife that read *I'm sorry*, Val was telling herself there was no reason for her to continue to be involved in the mystery behind Jamison's death. She'd done her part. Paid her debt to Kerry in a sleazy airport hotel room with her legs in the air and forwarded all of the photos she'd taken of the DA to his cell phone with the words *Let her out or I'll let these out*. Her part was done. And though she was still grateful for Kerry helping her when she was at her lowest after Jamison kicked her out, she knew in her heart that neither Jamison nor Kerry would have gone that far for her had she been the one behind bars or thrown from the top of a building. While her baby was dying in her stomach and Jamison was out in the street drinking and calling Kerry all times of night, she realized she was just a point in their love triangle. But with Jamison gone from the top of the geometric shape, Val was made far more important in Kerry maintaining her own balance. It seemed like Kerry now thought of Val as a friend, an ally, a confidante. Since she'd been out, she'd been calling Val, seeking her out, telling her secrets. And again, Val explained to herself that Kerry was out of jail. There was no reason to answer the phone or listen to annoying mothers and boys who were just like their fathers. But there was something about Kerry's attention that made Val feel less alone in her predicament. They were both grieving the same loss in different ways. Missing the same man. There was something kindred in that. Something sisterly. It was a feeling Val, even with two sisters all her own, never knew.

But still, why should she care about what happened to Jamison? She certainly didn't believe he was alive like Kerry had been telling everyone. And, like Lebowski, she thought Kerry was simply listening to those underground theorists who crowded Internet shows, blogs, and podcasts with theories of Jamison's every move that Kerry was now tracking in a notebook, because she couldn't accept that he was dead. But he was. Val had gone to the hospital. While the coroner said there was nothing left of his face that could be identifiable and what he could show Val would give her nightmares for the rest of her life, she did see Jamison's bloody clothes, his wallet, his hands, his feet. It was him. She was sure of it. He was dead.

However, knowing that and disagreeing with Kerry did nothing to answer what had happened to Jamison. And her reasons for caring were becoming quite personal.

While the old Val had lured drunk Chuck to the hotel so she could get those pictures and bust Kerry out of jail, that old Val was nowhere to be found when the news of his death felt like a knife straight through Val's throat. Standing beside Kerry outside the jail, Val encountered what had felt like a panic attack or heart attack or both. She kept her cool and held it in until they were climbing into the SUV, but inside she was feeling like she'd killed a man. A weak man, yes. But, a man, no less. Old Val might have laughed at that. Claimed it as collateral damage. But it was now keeping Val up at night, even with Ernest as her pillow. She couldn't accept that she was the body bait that led to a man ending his life. There had to be something else.

"Shit, Mama Fee!" Val cursed when she emerged from her bedroom fully dressed and nearly stepped into a terra-cotta bowl of ashes set right outside her door. "Why is this here?" she shouted, stepping over the bowl and heading for the steps, where another bowl was waiting on the bottom landing. "God! It's everywhere."

She fanned some leftover smoke from her face and turned the corner off of the steps to head toward the kitchen, where she could hear the dishwasher going and voices speaking Spanish coming from the television.

"Lorna, please get these bowls up from all over the house. That woman is about to burn the house down or suffocate all of us," Val said when she found Lorna in the kitchen, standing on the top of a stepladder with a rag in her hand cleaning the ceiling-fan blades. "And where is she, anyway? Got it smelling like a Catholic church on Christmas Eve up in here."

"You know." Lorna nodded toward the garden.

"Again?" Val rolled her eyes and walked to the window over the kitchen sink to see Mama Fee back out in the garden. "Lord, she's in one of her moods again."

"Been like that a couple of days now," Lorna pointed out.

When Lorna got to work at sunrise, Mama Fee already had her seven bowls placed in doorways and turning points throughout the house and had just started her burning. Lorna didn't bother to ask what she was doing or why. She had her own Santeria-practicing mother at home and knew not to touch a thing.

"Yeah, she has been like this a few days," Val confirmed. It seemed like since Kerry had gotten out of jail, Mama Fee was sinking deeper into her practice. She'd never leave the house, always kept her hair covered, and went searching for spiders; morning, noon, and night. "You keep an eye on her today?" Val added. "Make sure she doesn't burn anything else."

"*Es impossible,*" Lorna replied. "Doctor's appointment at noon. I told you I leave early today."

"Early? Are you kidding?" Val turned to her. "I need you here."

"I tell you, I no babysitter. You help her. She's your mother. She needs you. *You,*" Lorna said and her tone wasn't gentle or forgiving. "You're going out." Lorna looked at Val's clothing. Every day, each suit looked more expensive than the last. One of Lorna's paychecks had bounced a month ago. Val had given her the money to make up for the mishap immediately. But Lorna knew it was a bad sign and started looking for a new job. Her "doctor's appointment" was actually a meeting with a woman who'd fired her maid after she'd caught her sleeping with her husband. "Take her with you."

"I can't. I'll be gone most of the day and . . ." Val's voice trailed off as she imagined Mama Fee sitting in the car with Kerry all afternoon to and from Dahlonega, how she'd be looking at Leaf. All of her superstition and suspicion about everyone and everything. "I can't," Val repeated, picking up her purse and slinging it onto her forearm. "Let's just hope she keeps herself busy in that garden and doesn't burn the house down." Val turned on her heels and started clicking toward the front door like she couldn't be bothered. "And make sure you get all those bowls up. It's like a damn temple in here."

That garden had been keeping Mama Fee very busy. Busy, indeed. For weeks. And before that another garden had kept her busy for months. Years. She was sowing and reaping and reaping and sowing in a febrile effort to quell the insidious labor pains that had been punishing her womb since her last child came into the world. Like any other mother, Mama Fee always wanted what was best for all of her children. Maybe she couldn't always give it, didn't always have the means of providing it, but she knew what it was and sometimes, the magic of motherhood was that just knowing it and wanting it was enough to make such things materialize in her children's lives. This instinctive desire was commonly easy to resolve with her first two children, sometimes requiring little-to-no will on her part. But the last one, the one who'd bit clear into her tit when she realized she could get more milk by dragging her brand-new bottom teeth beneath the nipple while sucking, was just insatiable. And, as Mama Fee's own mama had told her, Mama Fee was bound to spend the rest of her life quenching that unending thirst for more.

By the time Val was a grown woman, every ounce of milk in Mama Fee's breasts, both literal and figurative, had been used and abused. Still, she stayed wanting the best for Val. And when she set her eyes on Jamison Taylor, Jamison Taylor's house, Jamison Taylor's car, and Jamison Taylor's money, she thought she'd finally found the thing that might surfeit Val's yearnings for more. The morning of their near-shotgun wedding, the day she'd actually met the man who'd impregnated her child, she stood in the window in that rich man's house and made a vow to give it all to Val. And she knew how she'd do it too.

Her mother had taught her the good and bad of the roots in her backyard. How to cure her baby's cough; how to make a man go blind and stumble off of the roof of a building. The good was simple. Uncomplicated. Those were the charms based in truth and righteousness. Light. But the bad was usually messy. Very complicated. Those were the incantations based in hexes and curses. Dark.

Mama Fee knew the charms she wanted for Val would require incantations. None of it was deserved or owed. It was just wanted. And would need to be taken, stolen away. There were two problems with that. Mama Fee never liked Jamison and did not want Val to have a child with him. How was she to get everything else in the beautiful picture Val wanted, while losing those two things? The answer was in the bottom of a dark pot that would make a slave of Mama Fee forevermore.

At the end of Mama Fee's lessons on the bad, her mother left her with the most important truth of the work they did, what others called conjuring, voodoo, roots work, hocus-pocus, evil, paganism, witchery, and it was that when one casts condemnation, she is forever tied to condemnation. One dark spell begets another dark spell. If you wanted your enemy in the ground, your spell might make it happen, but then the next was to keep him in the ground. And the one after that would be needed to take care of anyone who loved him and hated you enough to want you in the ground. Castings could be endless and costly. It was how the old voodoo women made their money. It was the only way Mama Fee could get that house, those cars, and the money for Val.

So, she used it. For the first time in her life, with full advisory, she used it. When she got back home to Memphis from the disaster of a marriage at the courthouse in Atlanta, where Jamison's mother looked at her and Val like they were some barnacles stuck on the bottom of a Louisiana shrimp boat, she sat a rock before her front door, slid off her shoes, and marched right to her garden with the sounds of a *djembe* pounding her ear. Yes, it was she who created that sudden and great and impenetrable divide between Val and Jamison right after the wedding. It was she who possessed Jamison's mother and made the hot stew that poisoned the unborn child in Val's stomach and led to the blood on the sheets and the baby's death. It was she who then stole Jamison's mother's breath away at the bottom of the steps in the house, killing her slowly and painfully as she begged Val for mercy.

Her next step, and it needed to happen quickly before Jamison and Val ended their short marriage on paper, was to get rid of the groom. Well, then, everything would be perfect. The house, the cars, the money. All for Val forever. Ironically, she never got to that. Jamison's tumble from the top was wanted and wanton, but not of her work. Maybe it led to the completion of her work, but she'd had no parts in what Val reported had happened to Jamison. It was a mystery that she'd charge to fate, had it not been for the fact that her invisible third eye tucked away in the pineal gland, the conarium or epiphysis cerebri, in the middle of her brain could never see Jamison falling from that roof or any of the events that led up to it. That could be explained by her distance from the man or the hard work some other fate fixer was busy putting in.

But Mama Fee had little time to worry about that. Her own fate fixing had her busy trying to find more precious milk in her old, flattened tits for her grown-up daughter. As she knew, once they moved into the house, they had to keep that house. And every incantation Mama Fee had breathed into a bowl since she set foot in that house was toward that complex cooperation. The whispering to ancient flowers in the garden, the dried roots she was collecting for the glass jars in her bedroom, rings with gems on her fingers, the terra-cotta bowl at the bottom of the stairs, the cluster of salt on the doorstep . . . she was exhausted with work and worry. And worse, she felt all the way to her bones that something was still on path to take it all away. Because of that, she could never, ever rest. She could never, ever leave that house. Not until she could be sure she could get back in. Until she stopped feeling what felt like spiders trumping up her back at night, pricking and stabbing along the way. Letting her know something was coming.

"Excuse me, ma'am," was what Mama Fee heard coming from behind her as she sat on the ground in the garden. She'd already seen the shadows of a man's frame cast in the dirt long before she heard the voice, so the male voice didn't startle her as she'd pretended.

"Oh, Jesus!" She turned and looked up and worked to appear surprised and sound simple. "You nearly scared me to death, young man!"

Val and Lorna were long gone from the house.

"I apologize! I wasn't meaning to scare you at all," the man with dark hair, eyes, and luscious, turmeric-colored skin said. "I probably should've announced my presence sooner. I actually tried to go to the front door, but there was one angry-looking cat waiting for me there. Then I noticed you out here." He extended his hand. "I'm Agent Delgado."

"I'm Marie Antoinette, but everyone calls me Mama Fee."

Mama Fee shook Delgado's hand, noting the heat and slight shaking, and used the grip to hoist herself to her feet.

"Thank you, young man," she said for the quick lift. "And I apologize for that no-good neighborhood cat. You'd think a place like this wouldn't have strays. Seems that old feline answers to Bast—at least that's what I call her. She means no harm—unless you mean her harm." Mama Fee smiled. "So how can I help you, Agent—" She paused.

"Delgado."

"Yes. How can I help you?"

After asking Delgado to retrieve a basket of what looked

like weeds from the soil, she led him to the back door of the house, chatting the entire way.

The cat Delgado had seen at the front door came racing around the back and flicked her ratty tail against his leg before he entered the house.

In the house, Mama Fee ordered Delgado to take a seat at the kitchen table the way only an old Southern woman could—with a smile he couldn't turn down.

"I'm actually here looking for a Mrs. Val Taylor. I've been here before and spoke to another woman. I left my card with her," Delgado said. "Do you know if she got it?"

Mama Fee had carried the basket to the sink and had her back to him. She didn't acknowledge his inquiry. She started humming some tune.

"Ma'am, it is very important that I speak with her. Do you know where she is?"

"No clue. She comes and goes. You know these kids." Mama Fee looked up from the sink and turned around to Delgado. "Maybe you don't. Nothing but a kid yourself."

"She could be in trouble, ma'am. Serious trouble."

"I know about trouble."

Delgado pushed the chair he was sitting in back like he was about to get up, but Mama Fee stopped him with a loud voice.

"Been getting ready to make this special tea all morning. Was wondering why I needed to make it. Suppose I knew company was coming. Won't you stay and have some?" she asked.

"I really can't. I was just looking for Mrs. Taylor. Do you know when she will be back?"

"I'm actually thinking she'll be back soon." Mama Fee carried a pot of leaves and water to the stove. "How about you indulge an old woman's desire for company and have some tea with me as we wait? It'll really just make my day. And I promise you'll love my tea. Everyone does. See, I'm an old woman. From the backwoods and I know how to work these herbs. Can cure just about anything. And I can hear in your voice that you could probably use some healing. What's that, high blood pressure? I see it in your color."

Delgado was taken aback. "Well—I—sometimes it is high. My wife, she cooks a lot of food with salt—and—do you know when Mrs. Taylor will back?"

Mama Fee turned the fire on at the stove and it seemed like a ball of fire shot up in the air, turned blue, and disappeared. "Soon," she said. "Really soon."

Mama Fee went on with her humming, stopping every so often to compliment her gentleman visitor about his appearance and build. She spoke of her loneliness and more of her tea he'd have to try.

While Delgado could feel himself being conned into a corner, that blue flame that had disappeared was still dancing in his pupils and he couldn't move. He just nodded and felt the room closing in with the humming and talking.

Soon came and soon left. And Delgado imagined that he was walking out of the house, but there he was, sitting, and soon there was a cup of dirt-brown tea in front of him.

"Drink it, baby," Mama Fee offered with her voice sounding like the refrain in a spiritual. "Drink it up, my baby. It'll make you feel better. Make it all better, baby."

Delgado had left his mind, but Mama Fee was there, holding the teacup up to his mouth, humming and talking to him, coaxing, conning, hypnotizing.

He sipped.

"I'm looking for Mrs. Taylor," he said, the cadence in his voice matching Mama Fee's.

She wrapped his hand around the teacup.

"Just sip, baby. Sip. Drink." She smiled and rubbed some sweat from his temple.

"She's in trouble," he whirred.

"I told you, I know trouble. I know it well." This was whispered from an old woman who now looked young and beautiful and dreamy in Delgado's eyes. "Now drink. I told ya you'd love it."

Soon the tea and even the dirt was gone from the little teacup.

Mama Fee was sitting in the chair across from Delgado, watching. The cat was in the house, rubbing her entire torso against his legs, back and forth and between, purring and sometimes even roaring.

Delgado's eyes were wide open and bloodshot. His face was red too. Sweat was pouring down his forehead and wet his collar. His teeth chattered. His brain was awake, but asleep.

Mama Fee stopped her humming and posed a question.

"Dear, are you okay?"

Delgado looked at her and looked and looked and then blinked in a snap of wakefulness that was marked with one final rub by Bast on his inner legs.

"Oh!" Delgado jerked. "Oh!"

"You need anything?" Mama Fee asked, concerned.

"What?" Delgado looked around the kitchen like he was waking from the longest dream. "What?" He looked at Mama Fee.

"I was asking you a question," she said. "You look like you dozed off. I was telling you that I didn't think Mrs. Taylor was coming home. Maybe you should leave and come back at another time." Mama Fee smiled.

"Yes. Maybe I should," Delgado said, taking the suggestion into mind like a prescription. "I should come back."

"You look so tired. You young people, you work so hard. Maybe you should go home and get some sleep. Let that beautiful wife of yours make you something to eat." Mama Fee grabbed the teacup from Delgado's side of the table. "I'll be sure to tell Mrs. Taylor you came by. Right?"

"Yes, ma'am."

Delgado was on his feet and wondering what had happened. He couldn't recall when he drank the tea or how Mama Fee had even ended up in the chair across from him. The last he knew she was at the sink or maybe the stove. Something that felt like peppers or maybe his breakfast gone bad was boiling in his stomach.

Mama Fee got up and took his hand to lead him to the back door, talking again and thanking him for keeping her company. What a pleasant chat it was about his work with the GBI and Jamison's case. About how Delgado had been cheating on his wife and wasn't sure if that little boy with his name was actually his son, anyway. Mama Fee laughed. "No worries. I'm just an old woman. I won't tell anyone your secrets."

"I told you all of that?" Delgado said, now on the outside of the threshold, looking in with Bast at his side.

"Of course you did," Mama Fee said. "Now you go on home. Come back soon. I'll let Mrs. Taylor know you were here."

"Don't you want my card?"

"No need. I know how to contact you," Mama Fee assured him. "I told you, I know trouble."

Chapter 12

Before Val could pick up Kerry, she had to make a drop-off for Coreen. Though she'd already given her the first sum, Coreen quickly called back requesting more and had a higher figure and worse attitude. It seemed like since Kerry had gotten out of jail, Coreen was more demanding and daring. Her threats now included Kerry and the business and every bitter dispatch was tainted with what Val knew was jealousy for Kerry and disdain for the fact that Coreen had never been in that position in Jamison's life. Val understood, so she took much of the fiery venom Coreen spat in her direction with the same kind of ambivalence and pacifying that Jamison had applied. She kept reminding herself that she was in control of Coreen and that at any moment, when she was ready to, she could and would handle that woman. Val was thinking that maybe Jamison's lawyer was right and she'd just have to let Coreen do everything she was threatening to do. If she did, then she'd end up splitting what little money she had with Coreen when the old contacts and contracts at Rake it Up shriveled up with the demise of Jamison's reputation. But Val wondered if there was another way to deal with Coreen and everything that came with her. After Coreen threatened that she'd next contact Kerry about her financial needs, Val knew she'd have to figure out something fast and final.

When Val pulled up outside of Thirjane's house, she honked the horn and waved at little Tyrian standing in the doorway. He was holding his iPad and looking at Val's car sitting in his grandmother's long driveway like he wanted to run out and say something to her. When Val thought about it, she realized that she was sitting in Jamison's old car and that Tyrian probably remembered it and was thinking of his dad.

Just then, Thirjane showed up in the doorway and pulled Tyrian away, snatching the iPad away, and saying something that didn't look kind from Val's perspective in the car.

"That bitch is crazy," Val said.

Kerry showed up at the door in country-club worthy khakis and a plaid shirt with a ruffle collar. She was back to looking sophisticated and neat and the beige tote tucked beneath her arms and Dockers on her feet were the final declaration of her return.

Val spied as Kerry seemed to parade to the car like an everyday Black American Princess who'd never been arrested, locked up, and charged with anything other than a traffic ticket.

Kerry walked up to the driver's-side window with a welcoming smile to greet Val and kissed her on the cheek before climbing into the car. It was like they were college sisters apart for years, going off on a trip where the other "sistergirls" were waiting with lemon-drop cocktails and tales of kids in private school and husbands who couldn't get enough of them.

Driving out of the complex, Val imagined that the above-mentioned might be the case. Her past and present erased in a new reality, where something other than the current situation would cause Kerry to befriend her. Val had two parents at home just around the corner from Thirjane's house. Their names were

Milton and Marjorie Wilshire. They were retired. Aging with gray hair, but graceful, elegant. They drove an old Mercedes-Benz. Contributed to the local Negro College Fund, especially to those girls attending Spelman College, where their only daughter, Valerie Bethanny Wilshire, had graduated with honors, earning a degree in art history after pledging whatever sorority Kerry belonged to. That's how Kerry and Valerie met. Sorortity sisters. Sorors.

"Thank you for coming to get me out of that house," Kerry said. "My mother's positively driving me crazy. Everything is always a problem with her and she seems even worse right now. I don't know what it is. But Mrs. Janie Jackson is about to make me kill her."

"Careful what you speak into existence," Val replied. "Has she said anything to you about Jamison? About the case?"

"Not really. She's been glued to those news stations all day and night, trying to get information about the DA. It's like she's addicted to every little detail about the investigation. Funny how she's so interested now, but when I was in jail, it was like she was too busy." Kerry's tone dallied in disappointment.

Val pulled onto the highway, driving in the direction of Dahlonega.

"If she's so bad, why not leave? Just go home," Val said.

"I am—I will. I'm working on it. Just want to take it slow for Tyrian. He was already forced to leave his home when I went to jail and for three months his grandmother's house was all he knew. And she moved all of his things there, so it's kind of like home for him. And he just stopped wetting the bed again. I want to give him some time to adjust to me being home and then we'll go back," Kerry explained. "And I'm not really excited about being in the house anyway."

"Why?"

"Oh, well . . ." Kerry hesitated.

"What? What about your house?"

"Jamison—he was there before he died. He came over." Kerry looked out of the window. This happened when Jamison was still married to Val. After his mother had died, he'd come to her house for consoling, a shoulder to cry on that would turn into him confessing his love for Kerry—his being in love with Kerry—a love that he'd said had never left him, not after their split, not even when he'd married Val.

"Oh," Val half-verbalized. She could still hear the pretext in Kerry's voice, her withholding or fear of letting something out. They drove a mile or so in silence as they remembered those days before and after Mother Taylor's death. Though they were far apart, it was shared history. Soon Val spoke. "We haven't talked about it—about Jamison, but I know. He loved you. And that's fine. I know that. And I know you loved him too."

Kerry couldn't deny these charges.

"Of course, he went to you when his mother died," Val went on. "He was tied to you in a way he was never tied to me. You two were friends. We never were." Val stayed in the slow lane as she spoke; still, cars were moving from behind her car and passing in the next lane. "He trusted you. You know? Like there were times when things were going on with him in the mayor's office—with that whole Ras thing, especially—I knew he needed someone to talk to." Val glanced over at Kerry. "I always wondered if he was talking to you."

Kerry remembered Jamison coming to her with the information about Ras when he was arrested. She'd been so coarse with him, so angry she could hardly look him in the eyes. She was still so angry with him.

"And if he wasn't talking to you, I knew it was only a matter of time before he did," Val said. "And then, only a matter of time before he—" Val looked over at Kerry suggestively.

"What? Sex? No—never." Kerry sounded surprised by the suggestion. Like no ex-wife had ever slept with her ex-husband after he'd remarried. "Fooling around? When he was married to you? No." She laughed. "Our connection was never really based in that. We . . . like—we had good sex, but not like—what I'm sure he and you—like you—" she stumbled.

"What? Sex with me?" Val didn't look surprised. "Jamison was crazy in bed. Like a madman."

"What? Really?" Kerry remembered Jamison lying on top of her—that was how they commonly had sex. He always kissed her neck softly. He'd whisper about his love in her ear. Then he'd have an orgasm. She did sometimes.

"Girl," Val said, sounding really chatty, "that man would get some coke in him and turn into a porn star." She laughed at a memory of Jamison tearing out every single hair extension glued to her scalp as he held her from behind in a parked car.

"Coke? Jamison used cocaine? Drugs?" Kerry asked.

"Yes," Val confirmed. "But not like a drug addict. Just like once a week, maybe twice, so he could—you know."

"No. I don't," Kerry said awkwardly. It was like she was hearing about someone she didn't know.

"Coke is the original Viagra. Long and strong. Men like Jamison use it to keep it up. That and to forget who they are, their limitations. You want a happy man? Put a line of coke between your titties and let him snort it up. That'll keep his ass at home."

"Okay. Too much information," Kerry said.

"I'm just sharing tips," Val said, unashamed. "It's not like he was your man then. He was single and for the taking. And I took." Val paused to be sure she was getting out everything she wanted to in the needed exchange. "Something I never understood about you was how angry you were with me."

"What do you mean, angry with you? I was never angry with you."

Val scrunched up her face at Kerry. "Chile, please don't lie. You can't save the devil from the jury," she said, repeating one of Mama Fee's old sayings.

"What?" Kerry laughed. "I am not lying. I never hated you."

Val rolled her eyes playfully to make it clear she wasn't taking this exchange too seriously, but she had to let Kerry know how she'd felt. "You were acting like I was the woman who stole him from you. Like I was some kind of side piece. And I never was. I was a lot of things to Jamison. I wasn't a lot of things to Jamison. But a side piece was never one of them. And I wasn't his mistress."

Kerry nodded along. "Good point."

"So, why were you like that? Why did you act like that to me?"

Kerry thought for a minute. "I could say a lot of things. Maybe I didn't like your long, fake nails—"

"What? Wasn't nothing wrong with my nails!" Val declared.

"Girl, French tips on dragon-lady nails? It was just horrible. And I didn't even get to the clear heels you wore to the office. And your titties hanging out everywhere! Dear God!" Kerry pretended to clutch imaginary pearls around her neck.

"Umm, your ex-husband loved those nails and those heels and those breasts," Val countered and they both laughed.

"Really, though, if you want the truth, I think maybe I was just jealous of you," Kerry admitted sincerely and maybe to herself for the first time.

"Jealous of me?" Val was admitting something to herself for the first time with irony in her voice. It sounded something like, *How could the woman I was so jealous of have been jealous of me?*

"You're beautiful," Kerry blurted out.

"I'm just—"

"No, wait." Kerry stopped Val from trying to lower her compliment. Now she was the one who had to let something out. "You're not just beautiful. You're stunning. Alluring. Sexual. Just sensuous."

"But look where that got me."

"Let me finish. But you're not only that, Val." Kerry reached over and placed her hand on Val's leg for a second to emphasize the candidness in her speech. "You're also free. And daring. And bold. You give a fuck!" Kerry shouted that last line in the car and they laughed together again. "You cursed me out. You cursed Jamison out. You cursed Mother Taylor out! You play by your own rules and I admire that so much." Val said the words from her heart, but she wasn't thinking of a single one before it came out. "And I know all of that daring is the only reason you could even think to help me when I was in jail. Funny, right? All the reasons I hated you early on were the reasons you could try to help me get out. Who else would help their dead husband's ex get out of jail?" Kerry frowned at Val. "Come on. Only someone who makes her own rules and doesn't care what people have to say about it."

"Plenty of people would," Val revealed.

"But you kept your promise to me. As crazy as it was, you kept it. And I don't even think I could've. I'm sure I couldn't have," Kerry said. "Thank you."

"No problem," Val said.

"Right."

"Right."

"Good."

Val looked at Kerry and repeated, "Good."

Kerry shifted her weight on her seat and looked at the highway sign for clarity on where they were in their journey. They were nearly halfway to Dahlonega.

"Damn, this is a long way out," Kerry said, changing the

subject. "Why do you think Leaf wanted to meet us way out here?"

"Who knows. Poor little white boy sounds like he thinks the world is about to end. All I know is what I told you—he had some big news about Jamison's case and he wanted to speak to both of us," Val replied. She'd already told Kerry most of the other stuff Leaf had revealed to her—everything except for the information about Thirjane.

"Well, it better be good," Kerry said. "Got us driving all the way out here. He knows black people don't venture this far out of the perimeter. No telling what kinds of crazy folks are out here. Might run into a Klan meeting and have to call Reverend Markel Hutchins to come and get us out of the country."

When Leaf heard footsteps coming up the front steps of the old woodsy cabin he'd been locked up in for days, his instincts automatically told him they weren't from the company he'd invited. He noted one tap on each wooden step and that indicated one person was arriving to the utilitarian tuck-away he often knew as a summer home as a child. There was also no talking or chatter—which would be odd for the two black women he was expecting. He hadn't heard tires turn into the drive, the sound of a car's engine humming and then shutting off, or the doors opening and closing. This was a problem.

Standing in the back bedroom of the cabin, just getting ready to slide his shoes on, he looked to the corner beside the bed where he'd set his shotgun, but then remembered that he'd left it downstairs in the bedroom in the cellar after cleaning it.

"You move and I'll blow your head right the fuck off!"

The above command came with the feeling of a cool bit of steel pressed at the back of Leaf's cerebellum.

"How'd you find me?" Leaf turned around slowly and was face-to-face with Delgado.

"Does it matter?" Delgado immediately started searching Leaf's body for weapons.

Leaf noticed that Delgado's hair was so wet he could see his scalp and it was pink, nearly red. The coloring matched the feverish tint on his forehead and cheeks too.

"I guess it depends on why you're here. If you're here to take me in—"

"I'm not here to take you in," Delgado replied quickly.

"Then there's no harm in telling. Not if I'm a dead man. Dead men don't tell secrets," Leaf said. "Who sent you?"

"I sent me," Delgado answered through bated breath. He looked haggard. Unsteady.

"Come on. I know you have orders."

"I do. And you had orders too. You shouldn't have gotten involved. There was no reason for you to go poking your nose around places where it doesn't belong. You know that."

"Taylor was my case. I was responsible for what happened. I couldn't just walk away," Leaf said, following Delgado's directions to sit on the bed. He could hear him breathing.

"You were supposed to walk away when they told you to walk away. But you didn't listen. I told you—I tried to tell you to just leave it alone." That heat Delgado had felt in his stomach after drinking Mama Fee's tea was now lava flowing through his veins. When he left the house in Atlanta, he knew he had to get to Leaf before Val did. He drove north at top speed with the windows open, telling himself he wasn't as sick as he felt. He popped one of his blood-pressure pills; said he'd give it time. After a few minutes, he felt a little better, but then the heat started its havoc again and when he got to the dirt

road leading to the cabin where the ping the Bureau had sur-
reptitiously hidden in Leaf's second secret phone sent out a signal, the pulsating and throbbing had overtaken nearly every
sense and function he had—all but duty. He had to finish the job.

"Leave it alone?" Leaf shook his head. "This was the one
time when I couldn't. You know, I keep thinking about that.
Why I couldn't. Why I can't just walk away. And I'm realizing
that after all my years in the Bureau, all my calls, all the secrets,
all the lies I've kept under lock and key, I couldn't do it with
this one because of how anxious everyone seems to be about
me doing just that—letting it go. It's almost like they assumed
I wouldn't. Like they knew I couldn't. That promotion. The
office. The accolades. All to try to pacify me. And then I'm
like—why? What's so important that the man tracking a man
had a man tracking him? You ever wonder who's tracking you?"

"Cut the shit," Delgado said. "No one's tracking me."

"You sure? Or you just think you're sure? Want to believe
that?"

"Maybe someone is." Delgado wiped his forehead and then
readjusted his grip on the gun. "Why does it matter?"

"Because this can't fail. Because something big—bigger
than me; bigger than you—is at stake. I read through all those
files. Every one. Mine and yours. This has nothing to do with
Taylor or Cade. This isn't some sting or probe. That's just a
show to get you and me going. Get us to lock people up. Shoot
each other and walk away thinking we really did something,"
Leaf said and added sarcastically, "That we contributed to our
society. Saved our society from each other. But that's not what
this is. See, we're really saving *their* society for *them.*"

It was impossible for Delgado to unravel these high ideas,
speculations based on an untenable mythos that was in no way
a part of the very solid foundation that structured his thoughts.
That wasn't helped by the foggy mind where Leaf's speech

sounded something like an old black woman humming. Delgado blinked. Pointed the gun and nearly pulled the trigger.

"Stay still," he ordered, though Leaf hadn't moved. Delgado staggered left and right.

"You okay?" Leaf asked, watching his captor and trying to figure out when and how he could make a move to turn the tables and get away.

"Shut the fuck up!" Delgado spat. "And stay still!"

The gun waved at three and four different versions of Leaf moving around in the room.

The heat in Delgado's veins pushed up, over, around, and through his heart and made it shudder like he'd just jumped off a building.

"Get up!" he said to Leaf.

"What? Where are we going?"

"I need the files. The ones you had stolen from my computer," Delgado said. "Where's the zip drive?"

There was no sense in denying having the files. Of course, Delgado knew Leaf had access.

"Downstairs," Leaf said, remembering where he'd set his shotgun. "In the cellar. Follow me downstairs and I'll give you everything."

Kerry and Val passed Delgado's abandoned car on the side of the road a mile from Leaf's cabin. It looked odd, sitting out there in the dirt on a road that was populated only by sky-high Georgia trees and signs warning of deer. Kerry noticed the Fulton County, Atlanta tag on the car, but had no true purpose in considering how that clean Pontiac had come to be left in the dirt. Not wanting to alert Leaf of his presence, Delgado had left it there and cut through the woods to get to the cabin.

The Jaguar's GPS led Val to the driveway with the thrice-painted and chipping metal mailbox. She turned into the property and all the chatter in the car stopped as she and Kerry surveyed the winding path through a small grouping of trees that led to an open area, which featured in its center a little cabin that had obviously passed its days of beauty and glory twenty or so years ago. This and that was broken and tacked back into place. The flower beds were overrun and only made apparent by slanted bricks that had been pushed into the ground to create enclosures. The face of the cabin had either never been painted or every inch of color had faded. The front door was wide open.

"You think this is it?" Kerry asked Val, who looked just as worried by the sight as she felt.

"GPS says so," Val said and then she pointed to Leaf's car that was parked right in the grass on the side of the house. "There's his car."

"Why is the front door open?" Kerry pointed to the front door.

"I don't know. We're in the country. You know people do things like that. Maybe he left it open because he's expecting us."

Val had driven as close to the cabin as she could and then turned off the car. Neither she nor Kerry moved, though. They just looked out at the cabin like it was a haunted house.

"Guess we need to get out," Val said soon, as if it had just occurred to her.

"Maybe we could just blow the horn or text him—let him know we're out here," Kerry suggested.

"Oh, Lord, let's just get this over with." Val reached behind her seat and grabbed her purse.

Outside the car, Val and Kerry climbed the steps, fully expecting Leaf to pop out at any minute, or hoping he would. Something just didn't feel right about the situation.

"Leaf?" Val said, leading Kerry into the house. "You in here? It's Val and Kerry."

Kerry looked on the wall just inside the front door, found the light switch, and flipped it up.

Startled by the new light in the shadowy room that somehow seemed extra-spooky at that point, even with its backwoods location and dank interior design, Val turned to Kerry and quipped, "Why'd you turn on the light? You don't know if he wants his lights on."

Kerry shrugged and went to turn the switch down.

"Just leave it," Val said, looking around the room at cobwebbed paintings of hunting scenes on every inch of wall space and antique hunting weaponry.

"Where's Leaf?" Kerry asked to avoid saying something about how eerie the room felt. She'd never been a particularly intuitive person, but there was a sound radiating through the middle of her brain telling her to get out of that little woodsy cabin. "You think he's here?"

Val stepped further into the house. She looked down a dark hallway that seemed to lead to bedrooms. "Leaf?" she called again before turning back to Kerry after there was no response. "He said he'd be here," she said to her.

"Well, it's not like him to say he'd be somewhere and then not be there," Kerry replied.

"I know."

The women instinctively moved in toward one another.

"Leaf!" Val called again, but only echoes of the sound of her voice returned.

Kerry pointed to the open door leading down to the basement that was at the top of the hallway. "Looks like there are steps in that doorway. Maybe he's downstairs."

"Okay," Val agreed, nodding. "Go on and check it out."

"What? Why me?"

"You found the doorway."

"But you're closer to it." Kerry pointed to Val and then the doorway.

"Come on and stop being a pussy," Val said, avoiding the pangs of flight in her brain. "He's probably just down there doing some high-level FBI-type shit, like sharpening swords or something and that's why he can't hear us."

Kerry frowned at Val. "Fine. Look, let's just go down there together."

Val rolled her eyes dramatically. "I don't think so. The way I see it, we're two black girls visiting a white man's cabin in the middle of the woods and he's not answering us."

"What does that have to do with anything?"

"Since when do black women go search for clues for missing white men in dark basements?" Val put her hand on her hip and awaited Kerry's answer.

"You can't be serious with that superstitious black stuff." Kerry pointed out. "We drove all the way up here and you want to leave because going downstairs wouldn't be the 'black thing' to do?"

"Yup."

Kerry grabbed Val's hand. "Come on." She started pulling her toward the basement and spoke the whole time to cut the haunting silence around them. "Like you said, he's probably down here working." She pulled Val down the top two steps. "Probably has on headphones." Two more steps. "And is listening to something like Pink Floyd or R.E.M." Two more steps.

"I hate R.E.M.," Val said.

Kerry looked back and up at her at the bottom of the staircase. "What? I loved them! Are you kidding me?"

"Your music taste just sucks."

The women were hand in hand when they peeked around

the corner and saw a light on in a room toward the back of the basement. There were couches and cots, and some old machinery of some kind filling up the space leading to the room.

"What is all this crap?" Kerry whispered. "And who builds a basement in a cabin—in Georgia?"

"Rich white folks," Val answered as they stepped through the maze toward the room. "Probably been planning to live down here when the black revolution comes."

Even with fear surging through her, Kerry laughed at the joke.

"You're a mess," she said.

Neither Kerry nor Val would ever remember who stepped into the little back room first. But they'd recall that Kerry was the first to see the bodies. The men with open eyes and mouths on the floor. One with blood pouring out of the back of his head. The other with his stiff hands still clutching his throat. They'd remember it was Kerry who first put this horror-flick scene together in her mind because it was she who'd gripped Val's hand from behind and said softly, yet urgently, and almost as if she'd been accustomed to such images, "Back up! Back up!"

Val was the one who screamed when she took it all in. It was Leaf who was bleeding and some man she didn't recognize who was beside him. She'd remember the gun on the floor.

As if a bomb detonator was ticking over a loudspeaker sounding throughout the cabin, Val and Kerry backed up from the visual like one of the men would wake up and come crawling toward them at any minute and then turned and bolted up the stairs, through the hallway, across the living out the front door.

Hard as she was, Val called out for Jesus and every orisha she could think of the entire way. And though her feet led her to the driver's-side door, every muscle in her body was in shock and she had no idea what to do when she was inside.

Kerry said, "Let's go! Let's go!"

But Val was nearly in a catatonic state with her incantations, so Kerry hopped out of the car and pulled Val out of the driver's seat. "I'll drive," she said, leading Val to the passenger's seat.

Rocks and pebbles popped out from the back of the car after Kerry pressed her foot onto the gas pedal to hustle out of there. Both hands on the steering wheel, she made a big circle in the front yard and sped out the driveway to the road.

"What the hell! What the hell? What the hell!?" Val repeated in different tones of urgency as she came to during the escape. "Was that Leaf? Leaf's dead?"

"Yes. It was him," Kerry said, swerving as she tried to handle the car's speed on the road in their escape from whatever. "Who was the other guy?"

"I have no idea!" Val looked out the back window like someone could be following them. Suddenly, she remembered her clandestine meeting with Leaf that day at the jail and then his last words to her about mentioning the meeting to no one and making sure not a soul followed her to the cabin. "I've never seen him before. And Leaf didn't say anyone would be there."

They passed Delgado's car on the side of the road, but had no reason to really notice it.

Kerry looked over at Val quickly. "You think that man—he killed Leaf?"

"I don't know. I saw a gun on the floor. I don't know. That's what it looked like," Val answered.

"Well, what happened to him?"

Just then, Mama Fee was awakened from a restless nap where she'd seen Delgado fall to his knees and die in a dark room.

"I don't know. And I don't want to know," Val said, not

knowing of her mother's work. She looked out the back window again. "All I know is that we're out of here. Right? We're fine. We're cool," she said. "No one knows we were here. We can get back to Atlanta and just forget about this. Right?" She nervously looked out the window again. "Did you tell anyone you were coming here?"

"No. You told me not to."

Val rubbed her hands along her lap. "Good. Good. And the door was already wide open, so we didn't touch anything in the house. And if there's a—"

"Wait!" Kerry stopped Val. "I touched the light switch. Remember? I turned it on."

Val closed her eyes and told Kerry to stop the car.

"Why?"

"We have to turn around. We have to go back."

"For what?"

Val reached for the steering wheel. "We need to clean the switch."

"What? Are you crazy? I'm not going back to that creepy house. What if the police are on the way? What if—I'm just not going back. No way. What do you think this is? We're not crime-scene cleaners."

Val popped her leg over into the driver's side and pressed the brake, forcing the car to a hard stop.

"If we don't and the place becomes a crime scene, they'll find your prints and then come looking for you," Val explained.

"And I'll explain what happened. We didn't do anything," Kerry said.

"Are you fucking out of your mind?" Val pleaded. "You just got out of jail for murdering your husband and this is the GBI agent who was assigned to his case. They'll put you right back in jail so fast. You want to go back to jail?"

Kerry thought for a second on the quiet road where no

other cars had passed and then started turning the car around. "You're right," she agreed finally. "We have to go back."

In an excruciatingly nerve-racking repeat appearance at the crime scene, Val and Kerry stood at the back of Val's car arguing about why Val didn't have any bleach in her trunk. There was body spray in a suitcase with overnight clothes, rim shiner, and Windex.

"The Windex will work fine," Val said, rushing. "It probably has bleach in it. Just go in there and use it to wipe the light switch."

"With what?" Kerry looked at the overnight bag and jumper cables in the trunk.

"Take these," Val said, handing Kerry a brand-new pair of lime-green lace panties from the overnight bag.

Kerry took the lacey panties and Windex and looked up the driveway to be sure no one was coming.

"Come with me," she said to Val.

"I need to stay out here and keep watch," Val said.

"I am not going in there alone!" Kerry protested. "Just come with me."

"The light switch is right inside the door! Just go in there and spray the Windex on the wall and wipe with the panties. I'll be waiting for you out here."

Kerry accepted her fate to clean up her own mess and tiptoed to the cabin like she was afraid to wake the dead. The entire time she kept looking back at Val, who reassured her by pointing toward the cabin and smiling, though she'd already decided there was no way she'd go into the house again herself.

Inside the house, Kerry sprayed the Windex on the light switch and wiped with one eye on the door and the other toward the hallways leading to the doorway to the basement. Her little bit of intuition visualized a man in all black creeping up from behind and choking her: Something dramatic like that.

Her heart raced as she sprayed and sprayed to make something invisible like a fingerprint disappear.

"Come on!" Val rushed Kerry from outside. She heard what sounded like a helicopter in the distance.

Kerry looked at the switch again like she could see anything and stuffed the wet panties into her pocket. "Okay!" She looked in the path that led to the dead bodies and repeated, "Okay!" before running out.

"I'll drive," Val said, back to her wits.

Kerry was the one who was nearly out of it then, so she agreed without a word and walked toward the passenger's seat. She wasn't in shock with fear as Val had been the first time they left. Kerry was thinking of something, thinking of what could've led to what she was seeing. All of this. This death. What was going on? Her head was spinning with inquiry.

The ticking from the sky was closer. Val heard it more prominently and she looked up at the clouds, expecting to see something before she got into the car.

Val got in and turned the car out of the drive again. She kept looking up toward the sky to find the source of the noise.

"You hear that?" she asked quiet Kerry, who didn't reply. "I think it's coming from the sky. Sounds like a helicopter."

She pulled out of the driveway.

"You okay?" She looked at Kerry.

Kerry blinked. "I'm not sure. Someone killed Leaf."

"I know. I was there," Val said, searching for the source of the sound that was closer still.

"Somebody killed him." Kerry looked at Val. "He was trying to help us and someone killed him." She looked ahead, but not at the road or anything, just ahead. "Oh my God, oh my God, oh my God!" she said as she added things up. "It's true. It's all true. They killed him. They killed him because he was helping me. It's all true. They tried to kill Jamison. They killed

Ras. Charles Brown. They killed Leaf." She paused and said eerily, "And they're probably going to try to kill me too."

"Please don't start with that shit again," Val said, distracted from her helicopter watch.

"It's not shit. It's true," Kerry defended herself. She'd actually been exchanging e-mails with Baba Seti from the Fihankra Center. He'd assured her that Jamison was indeed alive and if she wanted to see him again, all she had to do was come to the center. He, and only he, could connect her to him. "How else can you explain this? How else? Who else could have known that we were coming to meet with Leaf today?"

"You don't know if that's why he was killed. It could've been anything," Val said. "Like maybe that dude in there was his lover or something and something popped off. Who knows."

Kerry waited a second and said, "He had a wedding band on." She could see the gold band on his finger as it was clenching his neck.

"It's not true, anyway. There is no *they*. Just stop that shit! Stop it!" All the anger Val felt toward Kerry for connecting her sudden release from jail to some conspiracy theory she'd read online and not the dark deed Val had done to make it happen, was smashed into her harsh tone. Right then she didn't care if—as Lebowski had pointed out—Kerry was still mourning and most likely just suffering the pain of losing the love of her life.

"There is a *they* and you know it. Just pay attention; you'll see. Stop trying to ignore it," Kerry said. "That's what they want you to do. To pretend they're not there, controlling all of this, and we're just down here killing each other for no reason. How else do you explain it?" Kerry turned back to Val with tears in her eyes. "How else do you explain why anyone would want to kill Jamison?"

Val pulled over and stopped the car.

"Plenty of people wanted Jamison dead, Kerry. Plenty," she opined with no care or regard for Kerry's feelings. She was done with that. She was done. "People like your mother."

"What?"

"You want to know why your mother has been acting so odd? Because she tried to have Jamison murdered."

"No." Kerry kind of snickered. "Stop it. What are you talking about?"

"She did. She hired a hit man to kill Jamison and the GBI was tracking her. Leaf told me."

"No." Kerry smiled faintly. "Not true."

"It is. That's why she wasn't involved when you were in jail. Why she didn't want to be front and center. Why she's been acting so secretive since you've been out. She even admitted it to me. That day I was at the house. She admitted it to me."

"No." Kerry shook her head. "Not true. You don't understand. My mother is crazy for sure, but she's not that crazy." Kerry laughed again. "She didn't come to the jail so much or get involved with my case because it isn't proper. She didn't want to be connected with it in the eyes of her little friends and people she thinks are important. It sucks, but that's her way."

"Wake up, Kerry! Stop protecting that evil woman! There was no excuse in the world for her not to be there for her daughter. Not unless what Leaf told me was true."

Kerry let that new information set in.

"No," she said as new tears found their way to her cheeks. "She wouldn't do that. She knows. She knows how much I love him. She wouldn't do that. She wouldn't have Jamison killed."

"She didn't have him killed. She tried, though," Val clarified with more caution this time. "Leaf told me all about it. You can let her tell you about it."

Kerry wrapped her arms around her waist like she felt pain

coming from her navel area, the clearest connection she had to Thirjane Jackson. Suddenly she could smell Jamison. Hear him laughing. Hear Tyrian laughing.

"If she didn't do it—if the person she hired didn't do it—what happened, then?"

"I don't know. I was hoping maybe Leaf knew. Now he did sound like maybe there was something going on in the inside. At least that's how it came out," Val said.

"The inside?"

"In the GBI. He seemed to think there were some hands in Jamison's files and he was trying to figure out who and why," Val added. "Guess that's what led to this."

Kerry looked down at her lap and said sadly, "You should've told me. Why didn't you just tell me when you found out? Instead of waiting until now?"

"You know how that goes—it's like telling your friend you caught her husband cheating," Val answered. "You'd think the husband would be the one to get the ax—but it's usually the friend. Not the husband. Guess I didn't want to get the ax."

"I would've listened to you, Val."

"Yeah, but would you have believed me?"

Had Kerry and Val been standing outside of the car, they might have felt the wind kick up slightly and seen the shadows of something far off approaching. But instead, the presence of something big flying overhead was only announced when the sound was up close and the helicopter Val had sensed flew right over the top the car.

They looked up at the big blue craft and saw in bright white letters, *GBI.*

"Shit!" Val shrieked.

Both of their hearts went into shock.

Val felt like she was about to faint.

"They're here for us. They're looking for us!" Kerry said. "What are we going to do?"

"Get the fuck out of here!" Val went into action, turning the car on and pulling off, but she kept the car off the road and in the dirt, where it was still partially covered by trees dangling over from the woods. There was popping and the sound of pieces of fallen wood breaking under the car.

Kerry leaned forward and looked out the front window to keep her eyes on the helicopter, which was coming in and out of view and seemed to be getting lower.

"How did they know we're here?" Kerry shouted. "How'd they know how to find us?"

"I'm not trying to find out!" Val pushed her foot down harder on the gas and swerved back into the road.

"Oh, my God! You think they know? They know we were at that house and they're looking for us? They think we killed those people!"

The helicopter crisscrossed the road again, but it had turned and was heading in the opposite direction of them, leading back toward the cabin.

"Maybe we should just stop. Just pull over and stop and let them know what happened? What we saw?" Kerry went on, looking out the back window.

Just then, Val saw the last remaining markings of an old wagon road that was covered with new grass and weeds. She made a sharp right that sent Kerry flying toward her in the front seat. Both women screamed, but Val never let up off the gas.

The forgotten road led deep, deep, deep into the woods, where there was a solid canopy of trees tenting the forest floor. Val and Kerry looked out either side of the car at uninterrupted green. The woods were so dense it was quickly night around them.

"Where does this road lead?" Kerry asked.

"I don't know. Probably to another road and then another road," Val said, slowing down and stopping the car. She turned off the ignition and listened. "You hear the helicopter anymore?"

Kerry had been listening too and she replied, "No."

"This is crazy," Val whispered like the forest had ears. "What's happening? Why are they looking for us?"

Kerry didn't answer, so Val turned to her and saw Kerry's suggestive look.

"Not that again," Val said and shook her head. "Don't go there with that hocus-pocus black Negro spiritual crap again. That had nothing to do with this."

Kerry rested her elbow on the door console and averted her eyes.

"What?" Val pressed. "What? You're thinking it again—aren't you? You really are fucked up in the head."

"Do you have anything better?" Kerry grumbled. "Any other reason why everyone around us keeps getting killed or dying or killing someone else? Do you have a better explanation than the one I've come up with?"

"No, I don't have anything else," Val said, looking out the window on her side of the car. "But that doesn't mean I should just pick up and believe this. It's just a bunch of blogs written by angry black folks who spend all day and night trying to come up with new ways to make us hate this country. They have no proof. It's just lies."

"What if there is proof? What if I can get you proof?" Kerry asked.

"How are you going to do that?"

"This man I've been e-mailing, Baba Seti, he said if I come see him, he can explain everything. He said he can take me to Jamison."

"No, Kerry. That doesn't even sound right."

"Again, do you have anything better?" Kerry turned to Val and held up her hands. "People are dying. Helicopters are flying around. And we don't even know if they're looking for us. Or if they want to kill us too," Kerry said sharply. "We can't exactly just go home. We might as well go there and at least find out. See what he's talking about. Let's just lay low until we can get a little bit of information. Something."

Val made a silent decision about Kerry's plea. She only started the car again and pushed down on the accelerator.

She was right. That one road led to another road and then that road led to the next. Soon, they were out on the highway and headed back to Atlanta. No helicopters in sight.

Chapter 13

Night was new once the Jaguar with the new red country clay caked to its tires and underbelly got off of the Lee Street highway exit in the heart of the West End. The sky was a dusty gray-blue with faint twinkles promising stars dotted just above the tallest buildings.

Kerry and Val barely spoke, expect for Kerry giving an occasional directive about where they were going and what turns Val should make. It wasn't that they were angry with one another. They were just exhausted by the day, the week, the months, all of time that predicted this circumstance. They were thinking about what was next, what was real, what was needed to survive. They both felt like they'd been on a long trip in the cramped seats of one of those countryside crawling buses that always stank of urinal deodorizing pucks mixed with human excrement and urine by the time the trip was over. They just wanted to get out of that car and figure out what the next move was. Val kept her eyes on the road. Kerry looked out the window and listened for another helicopter.

When they'd parked the car and walked to the front of the block-long brick building where Kerry had spotted the address Baba Seti sent in one of his e-mails, Val took a step back and fixated her eyes on the wood carving over the doorway. Every angle of the shape made a demand of her memory. She'd seen it so many times and never really understood what it meant, but knew enough to lock it into her subconscious. It would be back and it would have meaning.

She pointed at it. "Fihankra," she said like a baby who'd learned a new word and image to match it.

"Yes," Kerry confirmed by her side. "That's what this place is called. It's the Fihankra Center."

Kerry felt Val's hesitation, so she stepped ahead and held the door open for her, pointing inside as a breeze of holy oils and incense burning came outside to greet them. It smelled something like an aromatherapy.

Val took one step and then another toward the open doorway. Every time she'd heard *Fihankra* flashed through her brain. There was that time at David Bozeman's office when she'd spoken to him about all of those sizable donations Jamison had been making to the Fihankra Organization. The symbol on the letterhead. The tattoo on Ernest's wrist. Him saying, "It means protection, security. Every time I look at it, it reminds me that I have to take care of my own . . ."

It seemed as if as soon as they stepped on the white tile that complemented the bare white walls in the vestibule beyond the doorway at the Fihankra Center, a short woman with a short Afro dressed in a nursing uniform showed up with a look of familiarity in her eyes.

Kerry tried to introduce herself anyway, but the woman stopped her.

Softly and humbly, she informed Kerry and Val that they'd been awaiting their arrival. They were to follow her.

Val and Kerry exchanged stares behind her back. Kerry took the first step and Val had no choice but to follow.

What looked like an old warehouse that might house a struggling community center or day school from the outside, was actually trimmed with contemporary comforts and the latest technology inside. As Kerry and Val followed behind the woman, who'd mentioned that her name was Mother NuNu, they saw that the walls and floors remained hospital white and hospital clean, but in what looked like maybe it was a waiting area, there were flat screens turned to different news stations, a row of 3-D computer terminals, and one wall filled with nothing but books. In the middle of the floor, there was an information center, where men dressed as security guards watched video coverage of cameras outside the facility.

Sleek black leather chairs comforted people of every anthropological and cultural background. There were white faces in Muslim robes, brown faces donning ascots, yellow babies and mothers, black elders in dashikis. They all turned and looked at Val and Kerry as the women followed Mother NuNu through the facility. Some whispered and pointed. All were silent or fell silent once Val and Kerry crossed their path. Some smiled. One old woman waved and nodded.

Not knowing what else to do, Val waved and returned the nod.

Mother NuNu took Kerry and Val to a fruit-juice bar and handed them prepared juice. She said they looked tired and thirsty and reminded them of the importance of keeping a healthy diet. They had work to do.

At the end of a long hallway, there were two closed oak doors.

Mother NuNu handled both knobs at the same time, pulling them open in some grand reveal.

In an office that was really bigger than the lobby and had even more flat screens turned to news stations and books and cozy chairs, there was a long, conference table–sized wood desk with a man seated behind it. While everything else in the room was big and over the top, this man was actually rather small and frail. Though he was seated, both women could tell he was shorter than them. His colorful kente-patterned kufi was sat back on his head to keep from falling down over his forehead.

He stood before Mother NuNu announced Kerry and Val. He walked out from behind the desk, revealing his long day shirt that matched the kufi.

"You've finally come," he said, approaching Kerry with his arms outstretched. "Welcome, my sister. You are home. I am Baba Seti." He bowed deeply and kissed Kerry's hand, before doing the same to Val.

Mother NuNu took the already emptied juice glasses from Kerry and Val and said she'd come back with refills.

Baba Seti offered Val and Kerry a seat and listened attentively as they shared each detail of their brush with danger that morning in North Georgia. He nodded and added his take on the events throughout the telling. Kerry agreed with everything he said, but Val was just trying to take him in.

On the wall behind his desk was a life-sized painting of some African warrior with jet-black skin. He was all muscles and carrying a shield and spear. Beneath the picture was the name *Shaka Zulu*. Beneath that was plaque that read: THE PEOPLE WILL MAKE THE RULES. THE PEOPLE WILL NOT BE RULED.

Pictures and sayings like that were on all of the walls in the office. One was of an old black woman who looked like a warrior, but she was sitting on a stool and had what looked like jewels or offerings wrapped around her shoulders. Beneath her picture was the name *Yaa Asantewaa*. Beneath that was a quote: WE CAN ALL FIGHT, SO WE WILL ALL FIGHT. BUT ONLY IF WE HAVE TO.

While Baba Seti looked old and frail, his voice and ideas

were as spry as a first-year college professor. He spoke with precision and detail, remembered every word Kerry had said and spoke it back to her with quick interpretation. He seemed to have an understanding and explanation for everything.

"It is a good thing you sisters came here. We can protect you here. What you saw today was no coincidence. It was the dribble of the casualties of war. Of war beginning. Of war continuing," Baba Seti said when Kerry explained how they decided to drive straight to the Fihankra Center from Dahlonega.

Val and Kerry watched, impressed, as he called in a man he called his security director and told him to comb news stations and connect with contacts in the Bureau to see if the agents were really looking for them. He dispatched units to their homes to see if agents had been to the houses.

Val noticed that he kept using the word *agent* for every person outside. Most times she didn't know who he was talking about.

Kerry sighed, sounding relieved by the swift action. "I'm so glad I e-mailed you and that we're here. We didn't know where else to go," Kerry said, taking the new fruit juice from Mother NuNu, who'd entered the room. "I kept telling Val that you could help us, but she doesn't believe—" Kerry stopped and looked at Val like she'd mistakenly let out a secret. "I'm sorry," she said to Val and then turned back to Baba Seti at his desk. "It's just that she's not as convinced as I am. You know?"

Baba Seti looked at Val sympathetically. "No one should need to be convinced of the truth. The truth is reality set before you. But," he continued with his sympathetic look turning to empathy, "there is a structure in place to disguise it. To make it seem like unreality. They even made reality TV to show you what reality is. What it should be. But it's really right in front of you all of the time. Looking at you and begging you to be convinced. Begging you to see past what is placed in front of it." Baba Seti stood and walked out from behind the desk again.

Val and Kerry followed him with their eyes as he spoke and walked to stand in front of the wall of flashing images from news channels.

"Tell me, what exactly do you need help seeing?" he asked.

Kerry tried to speak for Val, but Baba Seti held out his hand to stop her and allow Val to share her concerns.

"Kerry says on your blog you said Jamison isn't dead and that you know where he is."

"Yes. Yes."

"Well, I don't believe that, because I saw Jamison at the morgue. I know he's dead. He was thrown from a roof, so how could he be alive and wherever you claim he is?" Val posed.

"Interesting questions. May I ask one?"

Val nodded.

"What did you see at the hospital?" Baba Seti asked, crossing his arms over his chest to signify that he was interested in what Val was about to say.

"Excuse me?"

"I inquired about what you saw at the hospital. You said you saw him at the morgue and he was dead. Tell me what you saw."

"Well, you know what happened to him, so you know there wasn't much to see."

"What did you see?"

Val knew where Baba Seti was going, so she argued, "They wouldn't let me see his face. The coroner said it would be too difficult to see."

"What did you see?" Baba Seti repeated in the same tone as before. He was allowing Val's points to prove his point.

Val's list hadn't changed: the bloody clothes, his wallet, his hand, his feet. "I know what you think, but I know his hands. I know his feet. It was him."

"No other person in the world has feet like his? Hands like his?" Baba Seti asked. "Look at your own hands. Are they one of a kind? Are you sure? Do you think that if you wanted to, say, make someone believe they were looking at your hands and feet, you could find someone with hands and feet at least similar to your own to make them believe they were looking at your hands and feet?"

Val aborted her point. "Kerry saw him being thrown off of the building." She looked at Kerry, but Kerry turned away to Baba Seti.

"Dear sister, that morning she saw what you saw—what someone wanted her to see," Baba Seti said calmly.

"So no one fell from the roof? People saw it. There were police officers everywhere," Val listed.

"Someone did, but it wasn't Brother Taylor."

Baba Seti told Val about the dead man who took the fall, the affiliations of the people speaking to the media, the coroner's affiliations.

"They were all in on it?" Val said in disbelief. "They were all helping Jamison? They knew it wasn't real?" Val shook her head. "No. That's crazy. How could that many people in this big city be in on the same thing? All agree to the same thing? It would be impossible to pull that off."

"Was it impossible for the police officers to show up on the scene and quickly discern that Kerry was the killer? Lock her up and do all else, except throw away the key?" Baba Seti asked.

"I don't know everything about that."

"Then how do you know everything about this?" Baba Seti walked back to the desk and sat on the edge in front of Val and Kerry. "You don't want to believe, sister, and that's their plan. Brother Taylor is a believer. He supports the Fihankra Center and the movement."

"What movement?" Val asked.

"The movement to reclaim the soil for the people. The movement to have men judge men. There is no justice here and there won't be until men are judged. That is how it's supposed to be. We've gone too long without the men being judged and it's almost time for that to happen. There's this saying: *The people should not fear the government. The government should fear the people.* We are the people and soon they will fear us."

"Again, with all of this *they*—who are *they?*" Val asked. "Do you mean the government—like the U.S. government led by President Barack Obama, who is a black man, might I add?"

"I am not speaking of the government, sister. That's merely a system in place to collect money from you and tell you what else you can and can't do with the little bit of time you have in your life between making them more money or spending the illusion of money they give you and call an 'income,' because the outcome is always an income and after that the rest of the outcome is spent on cable television, wine, and student loans," Baba Seti explained without taking a breath. "So, no, I'm not speaking of the U.S. government led by Barack Hussein Obama. I'm talking about that which governs the government. This government and all others."

By the time the meeting with Baba Seti was over, the lobby in the front of the center was empty and the visitors' parking lot only had two parked cars remaining. The security team had informed them that they had no evidence that police or investigators were looking for Val and Kerry, but they also couldn't find any information about the bodies they'd said they'd seen in the basement at the house in north Georgia.

As Kerry kept saying, Baba Seti promised that he was going to take her to see Jamison in Cuba. He said Jamison was at one of the Fihankra Centers there, working in a community where men, women, and children from around the world had come for refuge, escape, and protection. He'd been handpicked to go there to help the community get stronger, to organize. Soon, all of the centers would connect and they would begin phase three of their plan.

When Kerry asked what that was, Baba Seti put a fist in the air and said, "Revolution."

Val listened to his many proclamations and promises and tried to figure out if Baba Seti was lying or just crazy, but really, after she'd heard everything he had to say, she couldn't confirm either of those things. Of everyone she'd come in contact with who claimed they could help her since Jamison's death, his ideas were the most far-fetched, but also seemed somehow to have the most explanations. Then there was the name of the center—Fihankra—how she'd felt when she saw the sign out front, all of that money Jamison had given the center: five million dollars in insurance money and 20 percent of his dividends from Rake it Up. This couldn't be coincidence. Why would Jamison give them all that money if the things Baba Seti was saying weren't true?

"I want you to come with me," Kerry posed to Val in the car outside of Thirjane's house after the meeting at the Fihankra Center. "Come with me to Cuba to find him."

"I don't think I should go th—"

Kerry cut Val off. "I have to go. I have to find out."

"Fine. Go. Fly to Cuba with Baba Seti and find Jamison. Why do I have to go?" Val asked.

"Because I want you with me. I need you with me," Kerry revealed. In the office she'd told Baba Seti she wanted to go to the Cuban Fihankra Center as soon as possible. She had some money and she'd charter a private jet so they could fly directly and not have to worry about times or being tracked.

"I'm not cut out for this kind of thing, Kerry," Val said.

"So, you don't believe him? You don't believe what Baba Seti was saying?"

"I didn't say that. What I'm saying is that it's been a long few days and there's so much going on right now. I just need to go somewhere and sit down and think." Val looked at Kerry and realized she'd spent the entire day with her. Kerry's eyes were red. She looked so tired. "Maybe you need some time too."

Kerry let out a sad laugh. "Time. I wish I had more of it. Had more time to take time."

"I didn't mean it like that. I meant that you shouldn't just rush into this. If Jamison faked jumping off some roof so he could escape being killed and go help some hippie compound in Cuba, let him stay there. Getting there tomorrow or next week won't change that. Like, why does this Baba Seti want you to go right now? What's that gonna do?"

Kerry looked out the window at the house and got quiet as she had so many times that day. Val could feel her tears.

"I'm not trying to be mean. I didn't mean to make you cry. I'm just—I don't know. I want to make sure you think everything through. Who knows what's in Cuba? Even if what Baba Seti said was true, who knows?" Val said contemplatively.

"I need to tell you something else," Kerry said, struggling to find her voice through her crying. She wiped her cheeks and dried her hands on her lap. "It's about why I was with Jamison the night he died."

"You don't have to tell me," Val said. "I already get it. You two were at the hotel. I know what happens there."

"No. I told you we didn't sleep together. But we did talk. And he told me—" Kerry paused and let out a little sigh before continuing. "Before he left to go up on that roof, he told me that he wanted to marry me again. And I said yes." Kerry giggled softly through more tears. "I'd be his third wife . . . well, once he divorced you."

What should've hurt or sounded like fighting words to a woman who'd been married to the man who'd proposed marriage to another woman just sounded like the truth to Val.

"That's why I have to go see him. I need to ask him why he did that. How he could do that: Ask me to marry him again and it was all a hoax?"

"*If* it was a hoax," Val noted.

"I don't think I can just move on without at least having the opportunity to ask him—face-to-face—how he could hurt me like that. How he could leave me." Kerry crumbled into an ugly cry. One to which Val had to respond with a shoulder to lean on. And a stroke of her new friend's hair.

Val was rocking and stroking, soothing Kerry's broken heart and then she was crying herself. Not because of the comforting Kerry needed. Val cried because of the comfort she was giving. That it felt good. And she wondered why she'd never given it to anyone else.

Val and Kerry separated and began to wipe their tears.

"Uggh! That was ugly," Val said lightly. "Got me crying and such! Like a big old baby."

Kerry laughed as she picked up her purse to get out of the car and go into the house.

"Hey, since we're telling secrets, how about I let one loose on you," Val asked, with her voice turning serious.

"Sure. What's up?"

"Remember that ten thousand dollars I requested?" Val asked.

"Yes. What about it?"

"It was for Coreen. I've been trying to keep up Jamison's payments with her, but I can't afford it and she just won't stop.

I didn't know what else to do. She's been threatening taking her story to the media and I didn't want that to happen. I know that will have a horrible impact on Rake it Up," Val revealed.

Kerry nodded and opened the car door without a peep.

Val looked at her, confused, until she'd gotten completely out of the car.

"What? You're not going to say anything?" Val asked.

"I knew," Kerry admitted simply. "I figured that was what was going on. I knew it wouldn't be long before she came back around. Look, don't worry about Rake it Up. Let her go to the media if she wants. Let her go on a full media tour, telling everyone about how she was extorting money from Jamison and that she intended on extorting money from Rake it Up. We'll see how everyone takes that." Kerry smiled and after stepping from the car, she added, "I don't remember a lot of what my father told me before he died, but one thing I'll always remember, one thing that's always stayed with me. My father said: *The truth will always come out.* Sounds simple, but it's true and easy to forget. You can pay that woman as much money as you want, but one day, the truth is just going to come out anyway. Why not now? I bet she'll change her tune anyway. If she's successful and the company does go under because of it, won't she be losing out too?"

Kerry said good night and started walking toward the house.

"You going to be okay in there?" Val said just loud enough for Kerry to hear her.

Kerry nodded and kept walking, up her mother's front steps and through the front door.

Tyrian sat up in bed and rubbed his eyes sleepily. He'd been pulled from his sleep by a noise and opened his eyes to see the light on in his closet. The door was open. The noise was coming from inside. Being seven years old and half asleep due to the late-evening hour that had the sky outside his window pitch-black, Tyrian's mind went straight to all of those scary movies his mother had told him not to watch. Was there a ghost inside? A demon? A zombie? His little imagination was about to have him hollering.

Just when he was going to scream and wet his bed, the night ghost in the closet emerged. It was his mother. She had his suitcases in her hands.

"Mama?" he called to her.

"Yes, baby. It's just me," Kerry said, dropping the bag on the floor and going toward the dresser to get more of her son's things. "Did I scare you?"

"Yes," Tyrian admitted. "What are you doing?"

"Just getting our things together," Kerry said.

"Why?" Tyrian asked.

"So we can go home."

Tyrian popped out of the bed like it was the middle of the afternoon. "We're going home?" he repeated joyously to be sure it was true.

"Yes." Kerry smiled at his excitement.

"Right now?"

Kerry hadn't decided that, really. She was still trying to figure out what she was going to say to her mother. How she was going to say it. Still, seeing her son look so happy, she decided there was nothing wrong with leaving Thirjane's house that night.

"Sure," she said, throwing a pair of pants and a fall jacket to Tyrian. "Put those on."

"Really?" Tyrian smiled. "Why are we leaving now? Is it because Grandma Janie is getting married to her boyfriend?"

"What?" Kerry asked.

"Her boyfriend. The white man with the black hat from the park," Tyrian explained. With everything happening after Kerry got home, he hadn't told his mother about the park or his investigation. He'd forgotten all about the recordings on his iPad. Until right then.

"Grandma Janie doesn't have a boyfriend," Kerry said.

"Yes, she does. He comes to the park. They talk. She gives him money."

"How do you know that?"

Tyrian had already climbed out of bed and was getting the iPad from the dresser. He handed it to his mother. He told her to press play.

Kerry listened in horror as recording after recording played on. Tyrian had taped three of Thirjane's drunken nighttime breakdowns. Four of her meetings with the man in the park, who sounded like her hit man. She'd given him money even after Kerry had been released from jail.

Once Tyrian was dressed and Kerry had called for a car to come and get them, she took his hand and started leading him out of the house.

With all of the noise in the house, Thirjane showed up in her doorway with her bathrobe on right when the car pulled up outside and Kerry and Tyrian were about to descend the steps to leave the house.

"What's going on out here?" Thirjane asked.

"We're going home, Mama," Kerry said.

"Tonight? You can't take that boy out of this house in the middle of the night. He'll catch cold."

Tyrian hid behind his mother.

"You don't need to worry about that. I'm his mother. It's my decision," Kerry said.

Thirjane noticed that Kerry had been crying. She could see

the trail of old tears on her cheeks and the wetness still in her eyes. "What's going on?" she asked. "You—are you okay? Why do you all have to leave now?"

Thirjane stepped out of the room. She already knew what this was. That the time would come. It wouldn't take long. She'd wanted to tell Kerry herself, but how do you come up with those words?

All she could say was, "I can explain everything."

Kerry was unmoved by this proposal. "Tyrian. Go downstairs and wait by the door."

"No! Wait! Don't send my grandchild away from me. He's all I've got," Thirjane cried.

Kerry pointed downstairs and Tyrian waved his little hand good-bye to his grandmother before following his mother's orders.

"Anything you say will only make this worse," Kerry said when she knew Tyrian was no longer in earshot. "I need to tell you that you have been the biggest problem in my life. The biggest pain. The biggest issue. I don't think you have the capacity to be a mother. You never did. And all I ever did was make excuses for you."

"I tried to—"

"Shut up and listen to me! I made excuses. Do you hear me? I made excuses for why you were so horrible to me. I let you come between me and Jamison. I let you belittle him. I let you ruin my marriage. I let you believe you could kill him and get away with it."

"He was never good enough for you. Can't you see that, Kerry? He wasn't ever good enough for you," Thirjane said.

"No, you weren't good enough for me. That's what I see. That's what I know." Kerry went to go down the steps, but Thirjane grabbed her arm. "You touch me and I'll go straight to the police. I'll turn your ass in and you won't ever see your grandchild again."

"No," Thirjane cried out, pulling her hand back from Kerry's stiff arm. "Please don't."

Kerry walked out of the house without saying good-bye.

It was probably the first fight she'd ever really won against Thirjane. It should've felt good.

It didn't.

Part 3

Chapter 14

Sandwiched between a chatty Baba Seti and fidgeting Tyrian, Kerry was sitting in an uncomfortable upright chair at the DeKalb-Peachtree Airport. It took her a few days to organize the private flight that would require two stops before her party would be allowed entry into Cuba, but through all of the paperwork, she got it done and was sitting there, still wondering if she'd made the right decision. She'd called Val every day, begging her to come along, and though Val kept saying she'd think about it, but didn't sound like she would, she'd purchased Val two tickets and left them at the check-in counter.

Baba Seti must've sensed her hesitation, because he kept calling her "sister" and assured her that she was doing the right thing, but this little action, expensive and bold, was nothing like Kerry. She felt like a fish who'd flopped out of the sea and was lying on the sand. Something wonderful could happen. But her gut was telling her it wouldn't be the case.

She'd only told Tyrian they were going on a vacation. She wasn't sure about what was waiting in Cuba, but she'd promised him she'd never leave him alone again and she intended to keep that promise.

"Is there a beach there?" Tyrian asked, clicking through his apps and games on his iPad between watching planes take off from the gate where they'd been waiting for their pilot to arrive.

"Yes. Lots of beaches," Kerry assured him.

"Will there be other kids?" he followed up with what had to be his hundredth question.

"I'm sure there are. Little kids just like you," Kerry confirmed distractedly.

DeKalb-Peachtree Airport was the smaller airport in the Atlanta area. It hosted private flights and connections for rich and famous residents who lived nearby. Those wanting to avoid the behemoth on the other side of the perimeter of the city that was Hartsfield-Jackson Airport. Still, the gate areas were packed and busy that fall afternoon, just a few days before Halloween. Cobwebs and other festive decorations had been applied to the many check-in stations and service counters at each gate. Women with wrists heavy with diamonds chased toddlers. Old couples sat reading matching bestsellers. Everyone looked at their watches every so often.

Baba Seti was dressed in another kufi and matching long shirt. He arrived at the airport with one shoulder bag that looked like a doctor's old attaché case. "This is all I'll need," he'd said to Kerry after bowing again, like she was royalty. "The community will provide the rest."

Kerry told him not to bring up Jamison in front of Tyrian. She wanted to wait to tell him about his father once they were there and she knew they were to be reunited. This was a boy who believed and was just getting used to the idea that his father was dead.

When the pilot Kerry had hired walked up and waved at them, Kerry told Tyrian to get his things together and stood to look down the long lobby hallway to see if Val was coming.

There was nothing.

An attendant came over to gather their bags and Kerry took Tyrian's hand. While he'd been on several planes before, he'd been much younger and hardly remembered. She reminded him of how long they'd be in the air and that his ears would pop and had some chewing gum stashed in her pocket just in case he complained about it hurting.

"It is time," Baba Seti said like they were about to set off on some valiant mission.

Kerry smiled and remembered Jamison's face in the picture she'd had hanging over her bed at jail. Her heart warmed and she assured herself again that she was doing the right thing.

The party began to walk toward the gate to board the small plane they'd take to hop to several destinations en route to the Cuban airport in Havana.

Just when they got to the door, Kerry heard Val's voice.

"Hold up! Wait for us!"

Kerry felt nerves ease and the tension melt away just with the sound of that voice.

"I'm here! Val Long!"

Kerry let go of Tyrian's hand and turned with tears already welling up.

Val was a few steps away, walking in front of a big brown man with big brown arms that seemed appropriate for all of the bags he was carrying.

Val was waving their tickets and running toward Kerry.

"You came," Kerry said.

"Yes. Change of heart at the last minute. Couldn't let you do this alone." Val hugged Kerry and pinched Tyrian's cheek. She turned to her bag carrier. "And he wouldn't let me do this without him." She pointed to her companion. "Kerry, this is Ernest. Ernest, this is Kerry."

Kerry shook Ernest's hand and hugged Val like she was her sister. "Thank you," she said to Val.

"Of course."

Preparing to land in Havana, Kerry looked out of the window, thinking of how the city looked nothing like she'd expected. From all of the talk about poor people and dilapidated towns in Cuba, she thought it would be some kind of tent city or village of shacks with nothing but mud piles and children running barefoot to be seen from the sky. But this vision was nothing like that. From the little circular window on the jet, this part of Cuba looked like any other metropolis. It was nightfall and the lights from skyscrapers and downtown streets twinkled a happy hello. The city was packed in with concrete buildings and cars on the road. On the outskirts, there were suburban communities with tennis courts and swimming pools. It could remind her of Atlanta if it wasn't for the stunning blue sea rolling up on the shore.

Kerry thought to point some things out to Tyrian, but he'd long tuckered out. And had his heavy head resting in her lap. In fact, everyone on the plane but Kerry and the pilot was asleep. Val had her head resting on her mystery man's shoulder. And Baba Seti must've worn himself out from all of his talk, because he'd nodded off and his kufi had fallen to the floor.

"You ready for this?" Kerry asked herself aloud. It was the thought that got her through the ten-hour hopscotch trip it took to get to Cuba. As her traveling companions had engaged in pedestrian conversation, Kerry sunk inside of herself and considered what it would be like to see Jamison again. What she would say to him. Would she let go of the pain of losing him and finding him again? Would she be angry? Would she be mad? Maybe she'd fight him at first, but in her heart, she knew that wouldn't last long. She had to touch him. To kiss him again. To hear him say he loved her. If she could just have that one more time . . . Just to hear those words . . .

Kerry rubbed at the little band on her left-hand ring finger. It was her first wedding ring. The one Jamison brought her when he was still a poor man with a dream. He'd promised so much. Was filled with so much potential, so much promise. He'd been a contagious infliction of love and light in her life. They were a part of each other.

The steward walked down the aisle and took the announcement receiver from its holder on the wall. "All right. Looks like we're about to land in Havana," he said with his voice still burdened by newly ended sleep.

The party began to move a little to the sound of his voice. Val opened one eye and peeked out of the window. She nudged Ernest and pointed to the romantic Havana night. "We're here," she said.

Baba Seti sat up and looked out of his window too. "We're here," he said. "All praises."

Kerry looked toward the back of the small cabin where Ernest was gathering Val's bags from the tiny overhead compartment. Val was looking forward toward Kerry. Val winked at her.

Kerry winked back.

As the steward moved to open the door, the party was gathered behind him with their eyes focused on seeing the first glimpse of Cuba. It was nearly dawn in Havana, but still the heat was relentless. As soon as the door opened, it seemed to invade the cabin and suck out all the air, drawing every soul out and onto the tarmac.

With Tyrian hiding under her right arm and snuggled into her hip like she was about to leave him at school for his first day, Kerry scanned Havana and thought of it as a possible home. The green in the woods not far away looked neon in the thin light. Leaves were lush and graceful in a slight rush of wind that could hardly be considered a breeze.

While Baba Seti kept insisting everyone come stay at Fihankra Center's community compound, Kerry didn't want to bring Tyrian there until she was sure of how he'd take seeing his father again. She'd already booked rooms at a small family boarding home that featured day care and facilities appropriate for children. If she'd been on her own, she would've demanded to see Jamison immediately after she got off that plane, but being with her child made things a little more complicated and she had to move slower and think like a mother. Val and Ernest decided to stay at the boarding house.

Outside the airport, an old dented van with the Fihankra symbol was waiting for Baba Seti and his little bag. He'd been talking to Kerry about plans of meeting up that afternoon as they walked through the airport. He'd held Kerry's hand, told her he sensed her hesitation, and assured her that this was the perfect plan.

Two men jumped out of the van. While they were much younger than Baba Seti, they were also rather thin and were dressed in simple mud-cloth shirts. One had a short Afro, but his beard was wild and bushy; he looked like he hadn't ever shaved. He was chewing a wooden stick, but his teeth were new white. The other greeter had unkempt dreadlocks with trinkets hanging from the tips. Some were wooden. Some were bronze. Those matched the rings hanging from his ears and nose. Both men were gracious and greeted Baba Seti with a respectful bow that made it clear to all of the people standing outside of the airport how important Baba Seti must be to those young men.

Ernest was actually taken aback by the display. He elbowed Val and whispered, "Interesting" in her ear. When he'd showed up at her house for sleep the night before they left, he found Val in her bathroom staring into the mirror. He asked her what she was looking at and she said she was thinking; she always stood in that bathroom when she was thinking. She then told him about Kerry and her mission to Cuba. She didn't want to go along with it all, but she didn't feel right about letting Kerry go alone. Ernest came up behind her in the mirror and told her what she needed to hear, but already knew: "You're going to Cuba with Kerry." Then he added, "And I'm going with you."

"Greetings, my sisters and brothers," the man with the beard said, nodding to everyone. His American English sounded odd in front of the airport, where white and yellow and a few brown Cubans spoke mostly Spanish. He went to get the bags from Ernest, but Kerry reminded Baba Seti that she was going to the boarding house.

"Oh, sister, I hoped you'd changed your mind. You really must see the compound. It'll open your eyes. Help you to see," Baba Seti said. "Prepare you." He looked at Val and Ernest. "Prepare all of you."

"I think we'll catch up with you all later," Ernest said, imposing his male voice in Kerry's stead. He'd also been following some of the gossip about Jamison being in Cuba. As he'd told Val, he believed it. Well, he didn't exactly have a reason not to believe it. His father was a Black Father and he knew well what the country meant to black militants. It was seen a refuge. A place to sharpen knives. To prepare. Still, as long as he'd known men and women and revolutionaries who'd gone there for just that, he'd never seen any return home. He hadn't told Val, but a part of him was anxious to see what Jamison had in store for this. What was he going to do?

Tyrian quickly adjusted to the Cuban Carribean heat. While his mother, Val, and Ernest had spent the time in their cab to the house wiping sweat and begging the driver of the small van to turn up the half-working air-conditioning, the little boy seemed so happy to be in the tropical sunshine.

It was a short drive to the boarding house. Through the window, Kerry saw that the part of Cuba she was seeing had so many more levels than what she'd peeped from the sky. There were rich and poor pockets. A beautiful young Cuban man in a business suit who looked like he could be worth millions in America would be standing on a street corner, while a man of similar age and build could be hunched over and begging for change. This was interesting to see in a place that claimed equality for all through even income distribution since its revolution. Since then, all eyes had placed Cuba front and center, some in crosshairs, some in rose-colored glasses. Seeing it up-close, Kerry didn't know what to make of the Communist dream.

The boarding house was actually a small and decent hotel on the beach in Playa. From the car, it was clear the place had some decades on it, maybe half a century, but where paint was missing, vines with budding, exotic flowers popped out, making the old beautiful and quaint.

Ernest had sat in the front seat with the driver, picking his brain about everything Cuban. He sounded like he was on vacation and seeking the hottest places to hang out and things he had to see before leaving the embattled paradise.

Val was seated behind him, listening to his voice. How confident he was. Cheerful. He sounded so happy. It was like there was nothing dark inside of him. No secrets. No flaws. Maybe a past, but he was a man who was open and honest. She'd never heard him speak to another person. Not to engage. To have a conversation. It eased something in her. He sounded like a man a woman could love. A solid man.

When the driver opened the van door to let them out at the hotel, Tyrian spotted a few little boys his age playing on a huge, indoor jungle gym in the open-air lobby. He quickly untangled himself from Kerry and begged to join them.

"Okay," Kerry agreed, "but stay where I can see you. And don't wander off anywhere. We'll need to go to our room once we check in." This final message fell on deaf or departed ears. Tyrian was already gone and climbing up the back of a slide behind a boy with blond hair.

Val was standing beside Kerry as Ernest helped the driver and doorman with their bags. She slid her shades down and looked into the lobby behind Tyrian. "Looks like he's about to make some friends," she said to Kerry

"Yeah," Kerry said, surprised. It was the first time Tyrian had voluntarily left her side since she'd gotten home. She'd even kept him home from school a few times to avoid his good-bye tears.

After checking in and being introduced to Anna, one of the home's nannies, who'd been assigned to care for Tyrian, Kerry found herself in her hotel room, staring at bags and bags of her and Tyrian's things. Ernest had volunteered to sit downstairs and watch Tyrian play with his new friends and Val went to their room to shower.

Kerry opened her suitcase and fingered a pair of high-heeled shoes poking out the top. They looked so odd in the bag and she wondered why she'd packed them. What use would they be? This wasn't a party. This wasn't a celebration. When she'd flung the plum-colored peep-toes into the small carrying bag she needed to fill to prepare for the two-night stay—that's as long as she'd thought she'd need to see Jamison and convince him to come home with her and Tyrian—she'd convinced herself that she needed to be ready for anything. Maybe the reunion would be splendid. Something that would require that plum sundress she'd fetched from her bag. Those shoes. The golden earrings. Jamison would show up in a suit with a bow tie. There would be some jazz band or a symphony playing. He'd run toward her, and she toward him. They'd meet. Kiss. He'd dip her low to the ground as if they were ballroom dancing. Then he'd slide a new engagement ring on her finger. Say he loved her and that he'd been a fool.

Standing right there and right then, she knew she could've left those shoes and the earrings at home. There would be no romantic union. She wasn't sure what it would be, but definitely not that. These people Jamison were with—the people from the Fihankra Center, Baba Seti—they were on a mission. One for which Kerry had no shoes, understanding, or identity. She knew that before she got on that plane, but now her head was reeling in worry about it. She was considering that maybe Jamison didn't want her there. If maybe Jamison had no intentions of ever seeing her, his family, his world ever again, and she was scrambling to get to him and bringing it all with her. She'd be rejected, made the fool, turned down and away.

After knocking on the half-open door, Val walked inside in a thin sundress that clung to her still-wet skin. A towel was over her hair. She had her cell phone in her hand.

"You busy?" Val asked.

"Just unpacking. How was your shower?"

"Short, but it'll do." Val held the phone out to Kerry. "I was checking my messages and someone sent me a link to this picture."

Kerry took the phone and looked at the screen. There was a picture of the van parked outside the airport. The one Baba Seti had gotten into to go to the Fihankra Center. Beside it were Kerry, Val, Ernest, and Tyrian. Baba Seti was there too.

The men who'd retrieved them from the airport were bowing to him.

"This is us," Kerry said, interested in the image, but not yet bewildered, as Val expected her to be.

"I know. It's kind of odd. I wasn't sure if I should show you."

"Who took it? Where'd you get this?" Kerry asked.

"It was on some Web site. A news Web site." Val reached over and scrolled the screen on the phone to the next photo. "This next one was on a blog. There's more." She scrolled again and again. The images were taken from various vantage points and at different times. One was taken right outside of the hotel.

Kerry covered her mouth. "This is crazy. Someone's following us?" Kerry looked at the room door.

"Clearly. I read one of the articles," she said, opening the screen to show Kerry. The headline read: TAYLOR'S WIVES ARRIVE IN CUBA TO JOIN THE FIGHT. Val scrolled down to the article itself and explained that the writer claimed they were in the Havana area to lead a rally for the Fihankra Center. There was something about Kerry being an organizer and that she was there to spread Jamison's message of equality for all citizens.

"What rally? I have no idea what they're talking about. I didn't come here to lead any rally. Where'd they get this stuff?" Kerry scanned the article as she spoke.

"Well, there's more." Val showed Kerry the next blog she'd read. It was Baba Seti's blog. Front and center was the picture of them getting into the van at the airport. His headline was more direct than the last: SISTERS JOIN THE FIGHT: THIS REVOLUTION WILL BE TELEVISED.

Kerry took the phone to the bed, where she sat on the edge and tried to make sense of the blog entry that had been posted just minutes before they'd gotten to their hotel. Baba Seti's words and ideas mirrored the content of the last article. Aside from mentioning their marriage and his legacy, there was little mentioned of Jamison being a part of the rally or even in Cuba.

"He just posted this," Kerry said. "But he had to have written it before we left. Like when we were still in Atlanta." She scrolled up to the image and finally her voice was bewildered as she admitted, "He had someone take those pictures of us?" She looked up at Val. "You think he's behind this—these pictures?"

"I think so, but there are so many articles, it's hard to tell," Val revealed.

Kerry looked like she was sick to her stomach. "So many?"

"A lot."

"But, I don't understand. Why would people be interested in why I'm in Cuba? Like, how is that even a topic and why would Baba Seti be writing about it? He had to know I'd see this. He had to know." Kerry looked at the pictures again. She was standing there beside Baba Seti. Tyrian under her arm. The heat of Cuba already had them sweating and glowing. They looked like they were on some great mission. "What do you think I should do?" Kerry asked.

"You need to talk to him about this shit," Val said quickly. "Find out why the hell he's doing this and where the fuck is Jamison. That's why we're here, right?"

"But Tyrian—"

"Ernest can watch Tyrian. You don't even have to worry about the nanny. We got you."

"But I told him I'd take him to the beach."

"Ernest can take him."

"And I told Baba Seti I'd come to the compound later—after lunch."

"Well, you're changing it to now." Val looked at Kerry seriously. "You need to talk to him. Like, you really do. It's not only your image in the pictures—I'm in them too, and so is Ernest. You need to find out what's up with this guy."

"I know."

"I don't know if you really do," Val said.

"What do you mean?"

"I mean, you're in here unpacking your suitcase." Val pointed around the room at various piles of clothing Kerry had arranged to put into the drawers. "You took time to get a nanny to care for Tyrian." Then Val said bluntly, "You brought Tyrian."

"I didn't want to leave him alone. Not after what happened and then us leaving my mother's house. And I couldn't take him back there. I haven't spoken to her since we left," Kerry defended herself.

"Kerry, you're stalling," Val let out. "I think you're stalling. I don't know why. But, look, we're here. All of us. We're here for you. You know? And you don't have to worry about anything. This is what you wanted. To find Jamison. And he's here. So there's no reason to wait. Like you said, you have to find him. So, go. Do it. Don't waste another day, hour, or ten minutes wanting to do it. Just do it."

Kerry rushed to hug Val. It was like she was hearing exactly what she needed to hear and exactly when she needed to hear it. She exhaled in her arms and took a deep breath like a baby who'd just finished crying.

"Okay," she said.

It took a driver Val found in the lobby an hour to get Kerry and Val to the Fihankra Center. They rode in silence in the backseat of an old green Beetle with lots of dents and no air-conditioning. Peering out of either side of the car windows as they sought fresh air, the two actually held hands on the backseat. Kerry had tried, but wasn't able to get in contact with Baba Seti before they left the hotel. At first she thought how rude it would be to just show up there unannounced, but then she remembered what Val had said about her seemingly stalling and remembered that even the idea of pleasantries could have little regard in the circumstance. This was an unusual situation and that required unusual behavior.

When the driver turned onto the road leading to the compound, he turned down his jumping Cubaton retro mix that had somehow matched the bumpy ride they'd endured off-road for the last thirty minutes. The women had discovered when they'd gotten in the car that the youngish Cuban hip-hopper spoke little English. Still, when they got to the road, he turned to them and seemed like he wanted to communicate something.

"*Revolucion,*" he said, pumping his fist. "*Revolucion. Africano. Vienes aqui?*"

Kerry and Val smiled pleasantly and pumped their fists too.

The driver knew they had no clue what he'd asked them about being a part of the revolution, but they'd gotten the gist of his statement, so that was enough. "*Revolucion,*" he repeated, pumping his fist again.

The car made its way through two checkpoints of haggling and questions about who they were and how they'd found the compound. The driver, who Kerry and Val learned was called Yuxnier from his debating with the black men in sand-colored military uniforms each time they encircled the car, was quickly becoming annoyed and seemed understandably unnerved by the guns the guards so freely pointed at him. Still, each time he revealed who his passengers were in the backseat, the muscle quickly backed up, signaling to each other and then bowing to

Kerry and Val quite graciously. One man actually genuflected and opened the back door, begging to kiss Kerry's hand, have her touch his face, and thank her.

"I didn't do anything," Kerry said, confused, but also impressed with the honorable display. She looked over at Val in the car beside her and shrugged.

While the compound was near the coast, a few miles from the port city of Nuevo Mariel, the terrain was hilly and rocky, making the outright paltry land purchase of three million dollars for 100 acres possible. At the third checkpoint, two huge and dramatic boulders that sat so closely together they looked like they might have been connected at one point, marked the final entrance.

Word had already spread throughout the population of people who'd found their way to the compound for various reasons, so there was a small, but growing group of men and women still sporting their modest day work clothes and carrying baskets of food from the gardens and bags of antiquated tools used in the fields and such, gathering behind the entrance to get a look at the visitors. From the backseat of the car, they all looked old or dated. Not age-wise, but more like they'd been transported from some other time period. No one was wearing sunglasses or sunscreen. No one held a cell phone or iPad.

"What is this?" Val thought aloud as the guard explained to the driver that Kerry and Val would need to get out of the car and walk at that point.

Yuxnier turned to them for instruction.

"Wait for us," Kerry said, looking at the crowd and wondering the same things as Val. "Wait out here."

Yuxnier agreed with a nod and one of the women from the crowd broke off and rushed over anxiously to open Kerry's door before a guard or Yuxnier could even get to it.

She was a little older than Kerry. Had two simple plaits with a raw part down the middle in her natural hair. While her face was dusted with dirt from working in the garden, her skin was supple and clear.

Like the guard at the other checkpoint, she genuflected deeply, bowing her neck in exultation as she welcomed Kerry.

This time, though, Kerry was less moved and more embarrassed by the unprompted acknowledgment. She grabbed the woman's shoulder and tried to lift her up, letting on that the action was unnecessary.

"It's okay! It's fine," she found herself saying to the woman. "It's fine. It's fine."

Val's door had been opened in a similar fashion—with women seeking to greet her and thank her for coming to join them at the Fihankra. One wiped her brow. Another offered to carry her bag.

"Baba Seti—do you know where he is?" Kerry asked someone once she and Val were out of the car and being led by hands through the thickening crowd. "I'm looking for Baba Seti."

Val looked around at the land that seemed to stretch out for miles and farther than she could see. In sight were crisscrossing crops, small barns, wooden houses, and storehouses. One structure was a schoolhouse. Children stood on the steps in their simple sheath uniforms, young boys indistinguishable from girls. A woman, maybe their teacher, was standing in the middle of the group supporting a baby on her hip in a mud-cloth sling. All eyes were on Kerry and Val.

"Follow me! I can take you to him!" A woman in a beautiful, deep purple African *gele* that almost looked like a wedding headdress appeared in the middle of the crowd. She was regal, brown, and striking, clearly of different ranking than those around her.

She turned before Kerry and Val could agree and every direction she took led to a pathway that was quickly cleared by the eager onlookers.

Up ahead was an elegant-looking limestone building, newly built and seven stories high. Pillars with African masks carved into each bust encircled the gigantic wooden front doors that couldn't be opened by one or two humans alone. A few yards from the entrance was a limestone obelisk with scarabs and words neither Kerry nor Val could read etched into its base.

Something else Val and Kerry simply couldn't discern was who all of these people were. Of varying shades and shapes, they all seemed to look familiar, but still so foreign, so far from them. The two could hear people speaking in many languages; some sounded like they were straight out of Atlanta or Brooklyn, others sounded West Indian, some Middle Eastern.

Trading quizzical stares with Kerry as they traveled behind the graceful woman in the *gele*, Val thought of Ernest and how mad she was that she'd made him stay at the hotel with Tyrian. There was no way she'd ever be able to describe what she was seeing to him or anyone else and even if she could or tried, no one would believe her.

Once they'd reached the doors of the limestone building, people in the crowd started cheering and singing, some crying out, "Revolution!" Others simply called Kerry's name. A woman with a baby in her arms, propped the little yellow ball with wild black hair up so she could see Kerry and waved her tiny hand toward them. It was the woman, not the baby, who gave Kerry pause, though. There was this look in her eyes. Something hopeful that shot through to a free part of Kerry's heart. It was an immediate connection to something the woman needed or wanted or thought she could get from Kerry, something Kerry didn't even know if she had, but in that moment, if she did, she would've given it right to her.

The woman in the purple head wrap was called, stopped at the wooden doors, and beckoned for Val and Kerry to enter before her. How she walked, her poise and humble gestures transferred directly to women, who seemed to hold their heads up, poke their chests out, and extend their hands from the wrists elegantly when they entered the building.

The woman turned and nodded to the enthusiastic crowd, signaling that they were to remain outside, before the wooden doors closed on some mechanical spring.

The noise of their chanting and singing was quickly dimmed, but not gone. There were a few other people in the lobby. They looked and stared, but no one approached them.

"I am called Nzingha here," the woman said, smiling with bright and perfect teeth. Her voice was soft and calming, but she was clearly American and had a hint of the Midwest in her voice. "I'm so happy you've come to join us here at the Fihankra. This is our sacred building." She directed their eyes to the carefully designed interior lobby that was akin to something someone might find in a cathedral or mosque. "It's a religious building. Just somewhere that we gather and share our ideas."

"We who?" Val asked.

"Us. The people of the Fihankra."

Nzingha's answer was quite definitive, but it still didn't get to what Val was really asking. She was thinking the response would do better at explaining what this was, what the people were doing living on this compound on the coast of Cuba. The Fihankra Center in Atlanta looked more like a community center, but this was an actual community. A real place where people clearly lived. How'd they all get there? Why? Val's questions were in such number she didn't know how to formulate even one.

"I'm here to see Jamison Taylor," Kerry said. "I'm his ex-wife." She pointed to Val and said awkwardly, "This is his wife."

Val smiled at Nzingha.

"I know who you are. I know who both of you are. And I know why you've come, Sister Kerry. I know what you are seeking," Nzingha answered mystically.

"Yeah, but do you know where he is?" Val countered abrasively and with a hand on her now poked-out hip.

Kerry rolled her eyes and snatched Val's hand from her hip. "Do you know if he's here? If Jamison is here?"

Nzingha nodded and said soothingly, "He is with us, my sister. Yes. He is."

Those words were like a winning lottery ticket placed into Kerry's hand. They eliminated her consuming consternation. Made her forget the purpose of this part in the mission altogether. She felt like she'd lost step and was maybe floating.

"Can you take us to him?" Kerry asked.

"It is not for me to do. But I am here to lead you to Brother Krishna," Nzingha said.

"Why does she keep talking like this?" Val whispered to Kerry. "And who the hell is Brother Krishna?"

Nzingha, so sweet, humble, elegant, and spiritual, had a past too and she'd heard what Val had said and in that past, she was the kind of woman who wouldn't've let that slide. Not in the present, either.

"I can hear you," she said, with a slick smile toward Val. "And we do not curse Brother Krishna's name. He is our leader."

Val stepped back, befuddled.

"Leader?" Kerry said. "What about Baba Seti? Where is he?"

"Oh," Nzingha laughed. "He is not our leader. He was simply honored to bring you here to us. Brother Krishna will help you. Brother Krishna will lead the way."

Nzingha turned and gestured for Kerry and Val to follow her.

Val held Kerry back until Nzingha was a few feet ahead and said, "See what I mean—why is she talking like that?" Val asked jokingly, but with a hint of true criticism. "Homegirl is obviously from the Chi. What's up with the airs?"

"Leave her alone," Kerry whispered.

"And what the hell is this place? Do you see this?" Val asked. "Who are those people?"

"I think we're about to find out and stop asking so many questions. You heard her—Jamison is here, so that's all I care about right now. If I can get to him, then we can get out of here," Kerry said lowly, but Nzingha could hear every word in their exchange.

Brother Krishna's office in the building looked less like an office and more like some kind of apartment or lounge. The interior was an eclectic mix of bachelor swank mixed with Afrocentric furnishings—the standard masks and statues. Nothing in the room matched anything outside of it. Nzingha led Kerry and Val inside where three teenage girls were waiting to greet them.

They nearly attacked Val and Kerry with hugs and little tokens meant to pamper them and show respect. They presented them with flower necklaces that looked like Hawaiian leis and fresh fruit.

Nzingha quickly instructed the girls to give the women space and when she snapped her fingers they ran out of the room, giggling.

"Please have a seat," Nzingha instructed. "Brother Krishna will enter."

Val frowning and Kerry nodding, the two sat on the long leather couch set atop a calfskin rug. Immediately, the French door at the opposite side of where they'd entered opened, and out walked a brown man in an immaculate white muslin tunic and matching slacks. Unlike the other men outside, he had little scruff or work on his face. His nails were manicured.

Beard neatly trimmed. He was handsome. In another place and definitely another outfit, he would have been considered fine. Nzingha's near-giddy response to his presence made this clear.

Val looked from him to her and then at Kerry.

"Greetings, my sister," Brother Krishna said, bowing like all the others. He walked into the room and came to sit on the couch beside Kerry and Val. Nzingha sat beside him in a move that said in all contexts that she was making claim to him—or at least trying to.

"Hi," Kerry said.

Val just looked and took him in. The physique in the shirt. The smile. It was to look at a man who was supposed to be so dignified, but who also happened to be handsome without thinking more of the latter than the former. With a name like "Brother Krishna," Val was expecting another Baba Seti with the 1970s throwback kufi and dashiki.

"It is a wonderful day when sisters like yourself join us here at the Fihankra," Brother Krishna said. "I am happy you have come to do the good work. Had we been expecting you, we would've prepared a proper feast and had more of a welcoming tribute. But, no worries. The sistren are steady preparing your feast now."

"I apologize for coming unannounced and it's really not necessary to do all that," Kerry said. "We were just looking for Baba Seti. He invited us here."

"Yes. He is a good man," Brother Krishna said fondly.

"Do you know where he is?" Kerry asked.

"That's not all," Val cut in before Brother Krishna could answer. "We're here looking for my—" She stopped herself and looked at Kerry. "We're looking for *her* husband."

"Jamison Taylor," Kerry said. "Baba Seti said he was here. I want to see him."

"All in time, my sistren. All in time."

"What does that mean?" Val pushed, clearly out of step with the respect Nzingha and Kerry were showing Brother Krishna.

"It means that now is not the time. We are preparing," Krishna said. "This place, here, we don't operate on the clock that moves with wants. We work with needs. And right now we need to prepare for a uniting."

"What exactly is this place?" Val asked.

"We are the light where there is darkness. A refuge for those seeking change and wanting to be free from tyranny, for ultimate rule. Those who want to live in justice and security. Where education and food and health care and love is available to all, and all equally."

"That's how all of these people got here?" Val followed up.

"Yes. Our community reaches far and wide," he said, adding to what Baba Seti had claimed. "Some settlements more advanced than the others, but all growing from generous members and their contributions."

Val remembered the money from Jamison's will and insurance policy. Suddenly, every dollar spent on every item in the room registered in her brain.

"Here in Cuba, we are a self-sustaining facility. We eat what we grow, we provide our own security, medical attention, build our own homes, teach our own children," Brother Krishna added, standing. "Our community all work only for the community to thrive. No more. No less."

"How long have you been here?" Kerry asked.

"The voice has been here as long as time. We have been here a little over a decade."

As Brother Krishna spoke, one of the teenage girls walked into the room and whispered something into Nzingha's ear. Nzingha nodded and the girl quickly left the room again.

When she opened the door, outside, Kerry and Val could hear the chanting getting louder.

Brother Krishna looked at Nzingha, who rose and nodded to him, saying, "It is time."

"Wonderful," Brother Krishna said, walking toward a window of sliding French doors that faced the front of the building. He turned to Kerry and Val. "Ladies, won't you join me in addressing the people," he said.

Nzingha rushed to the window and opened the doors, before waving for Kerry and Val, still seated, to come over.

Kerry and Val looked at her and Brother Krishna and then each other hesitantly.

"Please, sistren. It's really just our evening greeting. We all gather here to give thanks," Nzingha said. "So many people have gathered today just to see you. It would be good for them to know you are here in support."

"Gathered to see us?" Val said.

Remembering the look in the woman's eyes holding the baby downstairs, Kerry rose and began to walk toward the window where loud cheers that neared pandemonium could he heard.

Val saw Kerry almost in a trance and reached for her, but she kept walking.

Brother Krishna nodded and stepped out onto the small Juliet with Kerry, holding her hand.

The sun was setting, and so the heat that had nearly made breathing impossible earlier was now gone in a light breeze.

When the crowd, which stretched impossibly far, almost to the end of the compound walls and included many more people than what Kerry had seen outside, saw her, they began to cheer, "*Torkwase! Torkwase! Torkwase! Torkwase!*"

Kerry looked at Nzingha, who said, "It's what they've named you. It means *queen*."

"Brothers, sisters," Brother Krishna spoke. "You are here to witness the arrival of our *torkwase!*"

The crowd went wild with cheering. Toward the back Kerry saw men holding cameras who were recording and taking pictures.

Brother Krishna went on, "She has come to us to show her support for our revolution. For our community. She is here to let us and the world know that her heart is with the Fihankra. Just like the great Oba."

When he said this, the crowd's chanting changed to "*Oba! Oba! Oba!*" Drums played in the background. Sisters who resembled Auset and her crew at the jail danced before the brothers playing the drums.

Nzingha whispered in Kerry's ear, "That is the name given to Brother Jamison. It means *king.*"

Kerry saw the woman with the baby in the crowd. She waved and this time Kerry waved back. It was almost magical, rather extraordinary to just be there and feel their energy all coming toward her. Brother Krishna was still speaking, but Kerry was busy waving and feeling rather inebriated by the wine of being so exalted.

". . . And she is here to let you all know she has seen Jamison, she has visited with him, and all is well. They are strong. They are ready to unite and help us prepare for our next phase," Kerry heard when she checked back in to listen again to Brother Krishna.

She turned to him. "What?" she asked.

Nzingha whispered in her ear, "Just nod. We will explain."

"No—I—" Kerry started to say, but Brother Krishna cut her off.

"Sister Torkwase will now simply say good night to you. I hope you all understand. She has had a long journey to be here with us."

Brother Krishna turned to Kerry as the crowd began to cheer her given name again. Somehow those distinctive Yoruba syllables put together in a word that was used to identify her, drove Kerry to some purpose that was not her own.

As soon as Kerry looked like she was about to speak, the crowd went fully silent. Even the children did not use one word.

"Greetings all," she said, with her voice suddenly mirroring the dated and rather regal tone Nzingha and Brother Krishna used.

Val was behind her cursing and questioning her tone.

"I am happy to be here to see you. Your home is wonderful. So beautiful. I support you—I mean this. But I have not—"

"That is all we have time for," Brother Krishna said, much louder and overpowering Kerry's speech.

Nzingha expeditiously grabbed her arm and pulled her back from the Juliet.

Brother Krishna quickly closed the doors.

"What the hell was that?" Val snapped as soon as the doors were closed.

"Why did you say that?" Kerry followed up, looking at Brother Krishna. "That I saw Jamison? I haven't seen him. And I don't know anything about what you're preparing for. What was that? Why wouldn't you let me speak?"

"I will explain in time," Brother Krishna said.

"No! We need to know right now, because this is some bullshit," Val said. "What's going on here? You just lied to those people. All of them. Kerry hasn't seen Jamison."

"But they needed to hear that," Nzingha spoke up, but Brother Krishna shot a stare at her that silenced anything further.

"What?" Kerry asked. "What does that mean?"

"What Sister Nzingha means to say is that we had some confusion with our scheduling today and the people were expecting the *Oba* to be here to greet you. So, we merely needed you to say that so they weren't troubled," Brother Krishna tried to say nonchalantly, but he was clearly covering something up.

"That doesn't even sound right. Look, I'm from Memphis and I've known the best liars with the best lies and that didn't even come close. You need to come harder to impress me," Val said, getting up in Brother Krishna's face, but then Nzingha made it clear that whatever Val thought she was going to do to him wasn't going to happen without her stepping in.

"Oh, you want some too?" Val said. Any Buckhead bourgeoisie Val had garnered during her days as the first lady of Atlanta were gone from her then. She was pointing her index fingers at their foreheads and everything.

Luckily, Kerry was there to calm her.

"Wait! Wait!" Kerry tried. "I don't think you understand. I am not here to speak to your people or to help them. I am here to find Jamison Taylor. I was told he was here and that's it. When will I see him?"

"In time, my sister. You must believe," Brother Krishna said, trying to take Kerry's hand.

"I need a definite date and time. I came all this way and I need to see him. Now," Kerry said firmly.

"Let's get out of here, Kerry," Val said. "These people are fucking crazy."

"Excuse your words, sister," Nzingha ordered Val.

"I have something for you to excuse," Val said.

"When?" Kerry posed again loud enough to stop their bickering.

"Tomorrow," Brother Krishna said nervously. "Tomorrow will be the time."

Back at the hotel, Val and Kerry were sitting on the bed in Val and Ernest's room explaining what had happened at the compound in words that sounded like something out of a science-fiction movie. Not one part of it sounded real—well, maybe the part about Val cursing the holy man out. Ernest sat on the small pullout couch, trying to keep up with it all.

"It was just fast. I was standing there and then he said—he claimed I'd seen Jamison," Kerry explained to Ernest.

"Why would he do that?" Ernest asked.

"Because he's fucking nuts. Because they were all nuts," Val said.

"Did you think the same thing, Kerry?" Ernest posed, trying to ignore one of Val's outbursts.

"Not crazy. Different. They were different."

"Different? Please. Dude was up in there talking equality for all, when he was in the big-ass building with air-conditioning and three teenage girls running around behind him."

"So?" Kerry said to Val.

"So, did you see his nails? He ain't building no houses. He ain't working in no fields, and I doubt those girls are just feeding him fruit and putting flowers around his neck. I know Nzingha ain't."

"I doubt that," Kerry said.

"Humphf."

"Anyway," Kerry continued. "The main thing was that they said Jamison was there. So, different or weird or crazy, that's all I care about. That's why I came. Right?" She looked at Val to remind her of the little speech she'd given Kerry before they left for the compound.

"Right, but that still doesn't get to what the deal was there. And where was Baba Seti?" Val added.

"He wasn't there?" Ernest said.

"No. Well, maybe. No one was really talking about him. It

was like he didn't exist. I don't know and I'm too exhausted to worry about it." Kerry rubbed her forehead and got up from the bed. "Let me go to this room and see about this little boy. I know he'll be looking for me soon."

"I doubt it," Ernest said. "He was pretty tired when we got in from the beach. Little buddy went hard in the water. Fun kid."

"Really?" Kerry asked. The whole time she'd been away she'd been worrying about him, wondering if he'd started asking for her or crying.

"Yeah. I took him to the restaurant downstairs to get a little dinner before we came upstairs and he was going on and on about how much he loves it here. He asked me if people live here or if it's just for vacation. That little guy asks some interesting questions. You know he asked me if I knew his father? I told him no, but that I heard he was a great mayor who did a lot for Atlanta. He told me he loved the beach so much because he remembered his father taking him to a beach just like the one here."

Kerry held back tears as she stood there at the door listening to Ernest recounting his time with Tyrian. She remembered that trip Jamison took Tyrian on. Just the two of them went to the Dominican Republic after the divorce. Kerry told Jamison she felt he hadn't been spending enough time with him and Jamison booked the trip. He'd called it the boys' trip. When they got back, every single picture Jamison had taken on Tyrian's iPad was on the beach.

When Kerry got back to her room that night, she opened the blinds at the window and got into bed with Tyrian. She sang a song Thirjane used to sing to her when she was just a girl and longed for the past when things weren't simpler, but just the same.

The next day, after a long breakfast that included strategizing how they'd function when they returned to the compound, Ernest decided to accompany Val and Kerry, so Tyrian did have to stay with Anna at the hotel. While Kerry calmed herself preparing him for her departure, the little boy easily left her side again.

Yuxnier was waiting in the lobby, ready to dispatch the threesome back to the Fihankra.

In the backseat of the car, Val looked through her cell phone, checking the same blogs she'd read the day before and for sure she found images and recordings of her and Kerry arriving at the compound the day before and even more history presenting Kerry standing there on the Juliet with Brother Krishna. Headlines were more shocking: KERRY JACKSON CONFIRMS JAMISON TAYLOR IS ALIVE AND LIVING IN CUBA. One image had made it to the *Atlanta Journal-Constitution*, the largest newspaper in circulation in Georgia. The articles about it on the AP wire were national. Kerry's face was everywhere. In the pictures she was smiling and looked like she supported whatever the headline dictated. Even the video made it seem as if she was in agreement with everything Brother Krishna had said on the balcony. When she'd waved to the woman with the baby in the audience, it was made to look like she was holding out a Black Power fist. Kerry looked like a new revolutionary.

Val passed her the phone.

"What is this?" Kerry asked as she looked through. "Who is doing this?"

The gates at the checkpoints they'd passed just hours ago were now fully decorated and prepared for their return. Yuxnier drove right through with no problem and at the final checkpoint, they allowed the car to pass and continue on to the main building before the obelisk.

The crowd was thicker still. And the plain, working clothing everyone had been wearing was replaced with all kinds of cultural celebratory gear and headdresses.

Yuxnier, who hadn't been allowed inside the day before, and Ernest looked out of the window in awe. Somehow, Ernest thought, everything the women had explained in what sounded like lies was so true. Now he worried about how he could sum this all up to share with someone else.

The people flooded the car and the chanting from the day before continued. Yuxnier had to drive slowly, near a crawl, to ensure that he didn't hit any of the spectators.

"What is that? What are they cheering?" Ernest asked.

"Queen," Kerry said. "It's what they named me."

At the wooden doors, Nzingha was waiting in red with the three girls beside her. When Kerry, Val, and Ernest got out of the green Beetle, the girls ran up to them and placed the new flowers around their necks.

Nzingha nodded to them, but there was some hesitation in her smile. Val noted it, but she couldn't explain it to herself.

Again, they entered the wooden doors. Tables were covered with food and flowers so lovely it was hard not to touch. However, socializing or even eating was not in the mission the threesome had devised over breakfast. They were to go there and demand to see Jamison. That was all. That was it.

"Please eat," Nzingha said, pointing to the tables.

"We ain't hungry," Val said directly, but Ernest had already forgotten the plan and was eating a piece of pineapple that was the sweetest he'd ever had. Val shot a stare at him. "Really? Really?"

"Oh, don't trouble the brother. He is just eating our good food," Nzingha said.

"Mind your business," Val said. "And where is Jamison? That's why we are here. Not to eat. We just came for what we were promised."

Kerry stood beside Val, nodding along.

"In time," Nzingha said, ushering them through the pleas-antries. Again, Val sensed her little hesitation, a slight distance in her voice. Val still couldn't explain it to herself, but she just knew something was wrong.

Nzingha led them to another room, this one just as big as Brother Krishna's office, but less cozy. There were seats in a row that made it look like maybe the room was a classroom or some kind of study room.

"What is this?" Kerry asked. "Is this where Jamison is coming?"

"Have a seat," Nzingha said. She pointed to the chairs in a row and left the room, closing the doors behind her.

"Something isn't right," Val said. "And I know it. I can sense it." She didn't take the seat Nzingha had offered her. In fact, none of them did.

Ernest went over to the bookcases at the back of the room and read titles of what looked like legal manuals and guides.

"Well, she did say Jamison was here," Kerry said, but in her voice it was clear that she'd sensed Nzingha's change. "Let's just see—"

The doors of the room opened again and Baba Seti walked in, wearing the work clothes the others had been in the day before. His kufi was gone.

"Baba Seti," Kerry said when he walked in. "Where have you been?"

"I apologize for my absence, sister," he said. "I have been with my people preparing. And now you're here, so we are ready."

"Bump all that, why don't you try explaining how all of those pictures were taken of us at the airport and yesterday?" Val asked. "And then you put them up on your blog with all of these lies about us and why we're here?"

"It is a part of the preparation," Baba Seti said. "I apologize if you saw it as anything else. You will soon understand. All of you will."

"What is the preparation you keep talking about?" Ernest asked.

"The return," Baba Seti answered.

"Do you mean Jamison? Because he's coming here?" Kerry asked.

"Yes."

Kerry smiled and looked at Val. The smile wasn't returned. Val instead looked at Ernest, concerned for what Kerry wasn't seeing or didn't want to see.

"Where is he?" Kerry asked. "Is he near? Is he close? Is he in this building?"

"He is everywhere," Baba Seti said. "All around us. The *ora*. Yes."

Nzingha stepped into the room and gave Baba Seti a nod.

He smiled and took Kerry's hands. "It is time, my sister. He is here."

"Really? Really?" Kerry said.

"Really?" Val said with less cheer and more surprise. "Really?"

"Yes. Please have a seat." Baba Seti stood there and pointed at the chairs until Kerry and then Ernest and then Val, who held out the longest, would sit.

Outside the crowd was cheering "*Ora!*" so loud it sounded as if the windows would burst. This chorus flooded Kerry's heart with expectation. She was red on the inside. Her heart was aflutter.

Babe Seti left them to go to the door. He opened it and Kerry immediately popped up, ready to see Jamison.

"Jamison!" she screamed ahead of herself before anyone walked in.

Then there were footsteps. The sound of a man's shoes against the floor.

Val stood too, trying to get a look.

And then, in walked Brother Krishna.

Kerry looked past him and repeated, "Jamison?"

"Hello, Sister Torkwase," Brother Krishna said, walking and standing in front of Kerry.

She kept looking over his shoulder and calling for Jamison.

"Where is he?" she said to him finally. "Where?"

Baba Seti closed the door.

"Won't you please have a seat? All of you?" Brother Krishna said. By then Ernest was on his feet too.

"No!" Kerry hollered. "Where is he? You said he was here!"

"Please sit," Baba Seti said.

"I won't sit! You promised me him! Where is he?" Kerry was entering into a rage. The red of love inside of her had turned to fire.

"Where is he?" Val asked. "You said Jamison would be here. That's why we came."

"Sisters. Please sit," Brother Krishna offered again.

"Come on, y'all," Ernest said, pulling an irate Kerry and angry Val to the seats.

"Where is he?" Kerry asked, crying.

"The *ora* is dead. He died," Brother Krishna said.

Baba Seti bowed his head.

"What?" Kerry said. "But you said—" She looked at Baba Seti. "You told me he was alive. You told everyone he was alive. You lied?"

"Oh, no." Val was ready to get up and walk out. Of course, she'd expected this the entire time, but she'd done it all to support Kerry and finally really did hope this wasn't going to be the truth.

"Sister, he is dead," Baba Seti said. "He died that day on the roof. The day you were with him."

"But he was planning to join us here," Brother Krishna added with so much sincerity in his voice, it now was clear that he was from Brooklyn. "He gave us money. He paid for all of this. Even gave us money when he died and we get a check every month."

Val knew then that they were finally telling the truth. She took Kerry into her arms and patted her head.

"He really believed in our movement, you know? He helped bring so many people to us, to the Fihankra, when he died, we thought we were finished," Brother Krishna said. "But then Baba Seti started writing about him and people believed it."

"Believed what?" Ernest asked.

"That he wasn't dead," Baba Seti said.

Kerry's cries and whimpers were heard under the explanation.

"Then we started thinking, maybe he wasn't dead. Like, not his spirit," Brother Krishna said.

"Do you know what Brother Jamison was doing for black men in Atlanta? What his potential was in this world?" Baba Seti asked. "He was going to be the next Malcolm X. He was about to reveal to everyone the truth about the government and tell them what they needed to do to finally get free. Then he was going to lead us all to the Fihankra, then we'd prepare for the war. The fight."

"You think that's why whoever killed him did it?" Ernest asked.

"We don't know. We don't think anyone ever will. Rumors say the FBI. But there's no way of knowing that," Baba Seti explained.

"Why would you lie to me? Lead me here when you knew this was all a hoax?" Kerry asked through her tears.

"When I got your e-mail, I realized it was the final confirmation that what I was doing was right. With you aboard we could convince everyone that he was still alive and here and then we could somehow allow him to die and you could replace him," Baba Seti revealed.

"Me?" Kerry said, lifting her head from Val's shoulder.

"We've been watching you," Baba Seti said. "We all have."

Nzingha stepped into the room.

"We think you may be the one to unite all of the Fihankras around the world. To bring more people to us," Nzingha said.

"We know it is a lot to ask," Brother Krishna added. "Me, Nzingha, and Baba Seti, we are the only ones who know. But we think it will work."

"No," Kerry said, shaking her head. "No. Not this. No. No." She looked at Val. "No. He was alive. He's not dead."

"Please consider helping us," Nzingha said. "It's for our people. We can do great things."

"No," Kerry cried.

"Let's go," Val said, taking her hand.

"Please don't go," Baba Seti begged, chasing behind them as Val walked Kerry to the door.

But Ernest and all of his size jumped between him and the women. "Don't," Ernest said definitively. "You don't want to do that."

❧ • ☙

Back in the Beetle with Yuxnier, there were no I-told-you-so's. Mostly silence and comforting.

It was like the ride in Jamison's funeral car Kerry never got to take because she was in jail. While there was no rain outside, inside, she was in a storm. She leaned her head against the window and poured her soul into the tough work of accepting what she'd already always known. What she didn't want to admit. What had kept her searching and sad. She needed to say good-bye.

Chapter 15

Between night and morning, the sun was busy beginning the complicated work of creating a horizon. Kerry was awake. Maybe she hadn't even gone to sleep. She was standing by the window looking out at the spectrum of color in the sky that was emanating from a sun she couldn't yet see, but knew was there. It was tucked away beneath the darkness that was becoming too weak to keep it below for much longer. It occurred to her then of how particularly peculiar it was that people rose to watch the sun rise. It was never a surprise. It was never a maybe. Just like the night sky, the sun's sky was a sure a thing. There was always light. Even when it seemed impossible, it would come. Even if she was looking away. Even if she had her eyes closed or forget to get up just to see it. The light would be there.

She considered how many times she'd watched the sunrise with Jamison. It was always some romantic feeling they had that they were seeing something special. Together. Her back against his chest. They were naked, standing in a window just like the one in her room in Cuba. Peeking out. Pretending this was a special show. One that no one else in the world would see. They were front row to be witnesses of a new day.

Kerry knew she had to accept that this would be no more. She'd never feel that intimate expectation with that man again. Jamison was gone. And for that, her heart ached in darkness. She felt that. She knew that was real. Just as real as the night. Just as real as the blackness at the top of the sky. But, there somewhere in view, beneath black turned blue turned purple turned lavender turned pink, if she peeked and squinted, maybe she could see just the tip of a bright white yellow on its way up.

She could watch that alone. She could see that alone every day if she chose. She could be in the front row and be a witness all her own.

In the stillness of the morning, Kerry could hear bits of her last conversation with Jamison. They were in the room at the Westin. It was an early morning just like this. The sun was new. They were climbing out of the same bed.

"Marry me," he'd said.

"Marry you?" Kerry rubbed her eyes.

Jamison laughed. "Why do you keep answering me with questions?"

"Because I can't believe what you're asking," she said. "This is crazy. Too fast."

"Then I'll ask it slowly. Would you marry me? That work for you now?"

"I—That's not what I meant. I meant it's happening too quickly for me."

"Quickly? You know I love you. I never stopped."

"What is that supposed to mean?"

"Another question." Jamison cupped her chin with his hand. "Do you love me?"

"I—"

"Don't bullshit me. Don't give me the 'we're divorced and I

have to play from this side of the court' response. Just tell me. Do you love me, Kerry?"

"Yes," she said.

"So would you marry me?"

Kerry listened to the past and decided she didn't want to hear her answer. She wanted to leave that in the past. To stop living in that past. She looked down at her wedding band. She slid it off.

Kerry looked back out of the window and saw that the sun was in full view. Just that fast, it had revealed itself to her. She considered that maybe she was the only one in the world invited to the show.

There were two soft knocks at the door. Kerry slid her old wedding band onto the nightstand beside the window, replaced the sheet over Tyrian's body, and went to open the door.

Val was standing there, holding her bags.

"Hey there," she whispered after seeing Tyrian still in the bed and Kerry in her night clothes. "The car is here to take us to the airport."

"Oh." Kerry sounded like she'd forgotten.

"You okay?" Val asked. She could see the wedding band on the nightstand. "You want me to help you pack? I can have Ernest tell the car to wait. It's still early."

"No. I'm okay. I can do it. We don't have much."

"Okay." Val smiled.

"I see you're carrying your own bags," Kerry pointed out.

"Yeah. I figured I'd give Ernest a break this morning. But this is only until we get to the airport. Then it's all him," Val joked and the women laughed. "Please, this bridge ain't my back."

"I like him for you," Kerry said knowingly. "I think he's—good for you. I see it in his eyes."

"You really think so?" Val scrunched up her face.

"I know so. Don't let him get away."

"Girl, I couldn't get rid of this fool if I tried. Stuck on me like glue," Val said and then she added what was a secret even to her until that very moment, "And I like it."

"You deserve it." Kerry reached over the threshold and touched Val's shoulder lovingly.

"Okay. Well, let me get down to the lobby to tell the driver to wait. Think you'll be ready in, say, ten minutes?" Val peered down at her watch.

Kerry turned and looked into the room at her open bags on the floor, Tyrian sleeping peacefully in the bed, and the window curtain drawn to a sky that was now fully lighted.

She looked back at Val. There was a long pause.

"You're not coming home, are you?" Val asked.

Kerry stepped over the threshold and kissed Val on the cheek.

Tears began to fall from both women's eyes as they looked at one another.

"No," Kerry said. "Not right now."

"But I can't just leave you here."

"You're not leaving me, Val. You've done all you can do. Been a real friend to me—a sister. But now it's time for me to do my own work. To push myself forward."

"And you think you need to do that here? In Cuba?" Val asked. She looked into the room at Tyrian, still dreaming. "And with him?"

"I do." Kerry looked at her son too. "And I think he needs this. To be away from everything. To relax. Build something new." Kerry turned back to Val, her face wet with new tears. "Look, don't worry about us. I'm an Atlanta girl. I'll be back home real soon."

Val hugged her new friend again and allowed her own tears to flow. She stepped back from the threshold and waved with a weak heart as Kerry closed the door.

Don't miss Niobia Bryant's
The Pleasure Trap
Available now at your local bookstore!

The Prelude

*W*hap!

"Wake your ass up, Pleasure."

The sting of the slap delivered to his cheek roused Graham "Pleasure" Walker to consciousness, but just barely. He moaned as he shook his head back and forth to clear it. His tongue felt heavy and dry in his mouth. He could barely lift his eyelids and his eyes burned behind them. He tried to shift his body into a more comfortable position, but grunted in pain at the tight binds around his wrists and around his ankles.

He was tied, but he felt like he was floating aboveground.

Whap!

"Wake your fine motherfucking ass up. We got business to tend to, motherfucker."

Pleasure winced and tried to brace himself to hit the floor, but then remembered he was bound to a chair. One of his leather dining room chairs.

Unable to hold his head up, he let his chin drop to his chest as he blinked and shook his head, slowly waiting for more clarity. When his vision focused a bit more he was looking down at his limp dick lying across his right thigh.

I'm naked?

Pleasure looked up and shifted his eyes to look around at the living room of his Jersey City penthouse apartment as much as he could. The rich black and charcoal-gray décor. The floor-to-ceiling windows that overlooked the Hudson River and displayed the New York skyline across the water. However, it felt almost surreal as he struggled to remember just how he came to be naked and tied to a chair.

Think, man, think.

His thoughts were clouded and varied. He couldn't get a firm grasp on anything.

What's wrong with me?

His eyes drifted closed and his body slackened, but the ties at his wrist and ankles kept him in the chair.

"Do you remember me, Pleasure?"

A firm hand roughly grabbed his chin and jerked his face up. He opened his eyes as a woman stood before him dressed in all black with her face covered by a black ski mask and her hands in leather gloves. He shook his head yet again to clear it.

Whap.

Pleasure winced from the pain. She used the back of her hand that time and her knuckles dug into his cheek with the blow.

"Well, I remember you," she said snidely in his ear from behind him now.

She lightly bit one of his broad shoulders. Slowly, she deepened the bite.

"Shit," Pleasure swore sharply, his tall and muscled frame jerking.

She laughed and smacked the back of his head before coming around his body with her hand trailing across his chest. "Not bad at all for a man-whore," she said, leaving him.

Pleasure eyed her as she moved about his living room and

touched things that apparently caught her eye. *Who is she? What does she want?*

He closed his eyes as he let his head hang back, trying to match her frame or her voice or her movements to one of the many wealthy women who paid to be sexually pleasured by him. He'd put many miles on his dick screwing women and had charged well for his skill. Very well. Over the years, his list of clients was well into the hundreds. Some were regulars; others were one-night stands that he'd easily forgotten as he transitioned from exotic dancer to dick-for-hire.

Woman after woman, trick after trick, he had asked them all the same thing as he would slay them with his dick game and get a rush off the varied looks on their faces as he looked down at them with each stroke.

"Who am I?"

"Pleasure."

"And what am I giving you?"

"Pleasure." But none of them knew him. He was a stranger to them. And that was just the way he liked it.

"You haven't done bad for yourself over the years," she said from across the room.

He slowly turned his head to eye her standing before his fireplace. In between slow blinks, he saw her pick up a picture frame from his mantel.

He blinked again.

She looked at it and laughed bitterly.

He blinked again.

She took a small step back to hold it high in the air.

He blinked again.

She viciously flung it into the unlit fireplace. "Fuck you *and* her," she spat as she flew across the room, like she was rabid, to snatch up his chin again.

He fought hard to muster the strength to snatch his face away from her pinching grip. He tried and failed. He had no strength.

She grabbed him by the neck, pressing her fingers deeply into him until he struggled to breathe. "Just as fine as ever," she whispered into his face, laughing maniacally before she pressed a kiss to his mouth and then freed him with a rough jerk.

"Who are you?" he asked, his throat dry and pained.

That earned him a gut punch that made his body instinctively try to curl into a ball. The restraints kept him locked in place as a deep, throbbing ache in the firm muscle of his thigh finally caused him to wince. The pain brought back the memory of being struck from behind in the hall and painfully pierced with a needle as he unlocked and opened his apartment door.

"Damn," she swore, hating the thought of that. "How dare you forget me? After all these years? After everything I *should* have meant to you, motherfucker?" she stressed.

What?

Over the years, the majority of the women in his thirty years of life were his clients—there were so few women who he would consider more to him than that.

He struggled to open his eyes as he felt her hands on his thighs and then wrapping around his dick. He couldn't lie about the fear that spread through him. What now?

"Don't," he said, his voice as weak as his body.

Moments later he felt her mouth surround his tip, licking it before she took his soft inches into her mouth. He took no pleasure in her work. His already sluggish thoughts were busy trying to figure out who she was and how to get free.

"Don't worry, you're not going to die . . . yet," she said, her threat whispered against the damp flesh of his now-hard dick.

Pleasure's head dropped back, the tips of his long and slender dreads scratched his back as he fought hard to figure out just who the hell she was . . .